P9-EED-575

THE FIVE

THE FIVE

*A Novel of Jewish Life
in Turn-of-the-Century Odessa*

VLADIMIR JABOTINSKY

Translated from the Russian
and annotated by
MICHAEL R. KATZ

Introduction by
MICHAEL STANISLAWSKI

CORNELL UNIVERSITY PRESS
ITHACA AND LONDON

Copyright © 2005 by Cornell University

All rights reserved. Except for brief quotations in a review, this
book, or parts thereof, must not be reproduced in any form without
permission in writing from the publisher. For information, address
Cornell University Press, Sage House, 512 East State Street, Ithaca,
New York 14850.

First published 2005 by Cornell University Press
First printing, Cornell Paperbacks, 2005

Library of Congress Cataloging-in-Publication Data

Jabotinsky, Vladimir, 1880–1940.
    [Piatero. English]
    The five : a novel of Jewish life in turn-of-the-century Odessa /
Vladimir Jabotinsky ; translated from the Russian and annotated by
Michael R. Katz ; introduction by Michael Stanislawski.
        p. cm.
    Includes bibliographical references.

ISBN 978-0-8014-4266-7

I. Katz, Michael R.   II. Title.

PG3470.Z4P513 2005
891.73'3—dc22

                                                    2005002723

Paperback printing   10 9 8 7 6 5 4 3 2

Contents

Translator's Preface   vii

Introduction by Michael Stanislawski   ix

Principal Characters   xv

Instead of a Preface   1

I. Youth   3

II. Serezha   7

III. In the Literary Circle   13

IV. Around Marusya   20

V. The World of Business   26

VI. Lika   32

VII. Marko   38

VIII. My Porter   44

IX. The Alien   49

X. Along Deribasov Street   56

XI. A Many-Sided Soul   62

XII. The Arsenal on Moldavanka   68

XIII. Something Like the Decameron   76

XIV. Inserted Chapter, Not Intended for the Reader   83

XV. Confession on Langeron   89

XVI. Signor and Mademoiselle   97

XVII. The Godseeker   106

xviii. Potemkin Day   115

xix. Potemkin Night   122

xx. The Wrong Way   130

xxi. Broad Jewish Natures   136

xxii. One More Confession   142

xxiii. Visiting Marusya   148

xxiv. Mademoiselle and Signor   157

xxv. Gomorrah   165

xxvi. Something Bad   173

xxvii. The End of Marusya   180

xxviii. The Beginning of Torik   188

xxix. L'envoi   197

Selected Bibliography   203

Translator's Preface

Vladimir (Ze'ev) Jabotinsky (1880–1940) is best known as an orator, politician, and militant Zionist. He was also an extremely gifted linguist as well as a talented and prolific writer whose literary activity began early and continued throughout his life. The annotated collection of his complete work, including letters and speeches, was published in Hebrew and fills eighteen volumes. Born into an acculturated and assimilated middle-class Jewish family in the Black Sea port city of Odessa, he left in 1898 to become a foreign correspondent for a Russian newspaper in Italy and later in Switzerland.

Pyatero (*The Five*) was Jabotinsky's second novel written in Russian.[1] Written in 1935, it has been consistently omitted from the canon of Russian literature (including Western surveys and reference works) most likely because the author was "Jewish," not "Russian."[2] It has also been relatively neglected in the field of Jewish studies, probably because the novel was written in Russian, not Yiddish or Hebrew. And yet *The Five* offers a powerful portrait of Jewish life in Odessa at the turn of the century, as well as a poignant account of the temporary success and ultimate failure of Jewish assimilation in the Russian empire.

Like many other Russianists, I was unaware of the existence of *The Five*. Then I came across a reference to Jabotinsky's "two" novels in Ruth Wisse's survey, *The Modern Jewish Canon*. In the section on Babel, she refers to Jabotinsky as "the author of several Russian novels about assimilating Jews of Odessa and ancient Israel (*The Five, Samson*)."[3]

[1] His first Russian novel, *Samson Nazarit* (*Samson the Nazarite*) was published in 1926 and first translated into English in 1930.

[2] For example, there is no entry on Jabotinsky in the *Handbook of Russian Literature* edited by Victor Terras and published by Yale University Press in 1985.

[3] Ruth Wisse, *The Modern Jewish Canon: A Journey through Literature and Culture* (New York: Free Press, 2000), 102.

A footnote led me to Alice Nakhimovsky's book *Russian-Jewish Literature and Identity*. One sentence in her chapter on Jabotinsky was particularly intriguing: "Unlike *Samson, The Five* is not simply a novel written in Russian, but a Russian novel."[4]

Originally published in Paris in 1936, *Pyatero* was republished in New York in 1947 by the Jabotinsky Foundation. This is the text I have chosen to translate, the first rendition of the novel into any Western language.[5] Three editions of the work in Russian were published in Jerusalem (1990), Odessa (2000), and Moscow (2002). Only after I had begun work on my translation did I discover Michael Stanislawski's book *Zionism and the Fin de Siècle* with its comprehensive section on Jabotinsky and its excellent analysis of *The Five*.[6]

I am grateful to the work of Wisse, Nakhimovsky, and Stanislawski for leading me to and guiding me through this translation; I am especially indebted to Michael Stanislawski for his willingness to write an introduction to this edition.

I wish to acknowledge the assistance of colleagues at other institutions: Otto Boele (IDC Publishers, Amsterdam), Brian Horwitz (University of Nebraska), Judith Kornblatt (University of Wisconsin), and Harriet Murav (University of Illinois); my colleagues at Middlebury College: Alya Baker, Sergei Davydov, Stephen Donadio, David Macey, Judy Olinick, Joy Pile, Ira Schiffer, Robert Schine, Joshua Sherman, and Tanya Smorodinskaya; and two extraordinary colleagues in Odessa: Anna Misyuk and Mark Naidorf, without whose generosity, expertise, and support this project could never have been completed.

Finally, I dedicate this annotated translation to my wife and helpmate, Mary Dodge.

The system of transliteration is that used in the Oxford Slavonic Papers with the following exceptions: hard and soft signs have been omitted, and conventional spellings of names have been retained.

MICHAEL R. KATZ

Cornwall, Vermont

---

[4] Alice Nakhimovsky, *Russian-Jewish Literature and Identity: Jabotinsky, Babel, Grossman, Galich, Roziner, Markish* (Baltimore: Johns Hopkins University Press, 1992), 68.

[5] *The Five* was translated into Hebrew and published in Jerusalem under the title *Hamishtam* in 1946.

[6] Michael Stanislawski, *Zionism and the Fin de Siècle: Cosmopolitanism and Nationalism from Nordau to Jabotinsky* (Berkeley: University of California Press, 2001), 121–236.

Introduction

Michael Stanislawski

This first-ever translation into English of Vladimir Jabotinsky's Russian-language novel *Pyatero* (*The Five*) is a milestone in Jewish literary and political history, for it makes available to readers with no access to the original (or access only to the heavily censored and misleading Hebrew translation), a fascinating and crucial source in the development of modern Jewish literature, modern Jewish politics, and perhaps most broadly, what we might call modern Jewish self-fashioning.

Vladimir Jabotinsky was arguably the most controversial Jewish leader and public personality of the twentieth century. Born into the highly russified Jewish upper-middle class of Odessa, Jabotinsky at first resembled a member of the highly dejudaized upper bourgeoisie of twenty-first-century America more than the stereotypical Eastern European Jew of the nineteenth century: he knew no Yiddish or Hebrew to speak of, except for snippets gleaned from grandmothers' talk or from meaningless bar mitzvah preparations in which "reading" Hebrew was then, as now, a euphemism for its vocalized consonants with no consideration for their meaning. He was schooled at a prestigious, private Russian-language academy that was required by law to dedicate a few hours per week to teaching Judaism to the Jewish pupils, a practice which left no mark on its students' consciousnesses, save a vague feeling of stigma vis-à-vis the Russian-Orthodox student majority. Yet because this was fin-de-siècle Russia—or more precisely, the Russian Empire, for Odessa was and is one of the major cities of Ukraine—Jabotinsky knew in his heart of hearts that he was not a Russian by nationality or religion, but a Jew, even though the latter concept had no precise content or connotation. Rather, his entire linguistic and ideational world was Russian, and his aspiration in life, from his early teens on, was to become a Russian writer and a contributor to Russian literature.

Like so many other European literatures in the 1890s and early 1900s and, not incidentally but unknown to Jabotinsky, Hebrew and Yiddish literatures as well, Russian literature was undergoing a phenomenally rich aesthetic reevaluation and a burst of creative innovation in all genres of artistic creativity: poetry, theater, novels, short stories, and journalism, in addition to music, dance, and the plastic arts. Yet, at the core of this virtually unparalleled creativity was a nagging and an increasingly articulated crisis of meaning, in art and in "real life"—and the connection between the two was at the center of both the creativity and the crisis of the hour. Hence the rise of the so-called malaise of the fin de siècle—a Europe-wide epistemological, ontological, and aesthetic crisis in which thousands of talented creative spirits (and hundreds of thousands, if not millions, of far less talented acolytes and would-be artists) shared, from London to Moscow, from Oslo to Lisbon, and at all stops in between.

Vladimir Jabotinsky partook in this creativity and this malaise, both at home in Odessa and in his youthful stays (like so many other upper-middle-class Russian youths) in Switzerland and Italy, subsidized, in his case, by the liberal Russian-language press of Odessa in which he had begun to publish as a sixteen-year-old and for which he became a daily correspondent both abroad and later at home. In column after column, feuilleton after feuilleton, opera review after opera review, the young Jabotinsky expressed the excitement and the fears of his generation. But unlike many of his contemporaries, Jabotinsky could not find his way out of this ideological and spiritual malaise via its two most popular outlets—socialism and religion. Although he briefly dabbled in the first, he quickly rejected what he recognized as its faux populism and unmitigable utopianism. The second option he never even considered: throughout his life he was totally immune, and one might even say allergic, to religious or spiritual concerns, and thus even the hugely popular route of neo-Romanticism was closed to him. Slowly and painfully, what he came to see as the panacea to the malaise of the world was nationalism—for him, virtually faute de mieux, Jewish nationalism. Without conversion to Russian Orthodoxy he could not truly be a Russian, and Ukrainian nationalism was a phenomenon that he, as a Jew-by-birth and a Russian-by-culture, could be sympathetic to but never a part of. And so, beginning in 1903, at the age of twenty-three, he began exploring Jewish nationalism, especially in its most popular manifestation, Zionism, and here he finally found the stage, and the ideology, that would frame and control the rest of his life. After attending a series of Zionist congresses in Basle, he became an undying admirer of the charismatic but controversial Theodor Herzl, though he also sympathized with the majority of Eastern European Zionists who called for a cultural revolution of the Jews based on the Hebrew language and the revival of a secular Hebrew nation in Palestine. Soon he became one of the most popular and hardworking Zionist propagandists in Russian Jewry, traveling throughout the Pale of Settlement and beyond, preaching its message in what would become a famously dramatic and inspiring panlinguistic speaking style. He began to edit journals, for which he churned out dozens and dozens of polemical articles; to learn Hebrew and Yiddish, becoming an important and influential translator of the former, especially the works of the Zionist "national poet" Hayyim Nakhman Bialik; and to help organize the conferences and colloquies both of the Zionist movement and the Russian-Jewish community as a whole after the 1905 Revolution, in which, in sharp contrast to the West, Jewish political parties were elected to parliaments before the Jews themselves were legally emancipated.

In the years preceding the outbreak of the First World War, although largely still a "cultural Zionist," Jabotinsky emerged as one of the most important proponents of a Jewish fighting force within the Allied armies and one of the most important organizers of the Jewish Legion within the British Army. After the conquest of Palestine by that army, he then helped to found the Haganah, the Jewish fighting force against the British occupation, and was arrested and imprisoned by the British for sedition. During his imprisonment in the Acre prison and especially after his release, he became hugely popular among a certain segment of the Zionist movement, especially those dissatisfied with the pro-British and moderate stance of the leader of the World Zionist movement, Chaim Weizmann. Slowly Jabotinsky began to enunciate a version of Zionism parallel to the integral nationalist stances adopted by so many former socialists and aesthetes from Mussolini to Jósef Pilsudski and beyond: in this case, a commitment to what he called in Hebrew *hadar*—Jewish pride, expressed in the founding of a militarist youth movement called Betar, and a politics centered on the foundation of an independent Jewish state on both sides of the Jordan River; an antisocialist internal politics; and a demand that the Palestinian Arabs' nationalism be subsumed entirely within that of the existing Arab states. "All a Jewish boy needs to learn," he famously quipped, "is how to speak Hebrew and shoot a gun"—resulting inevitably in fury from the moderate majority of the Zionist movement, led by Weizmann, and from the growing socialist Zionist forces centered in Palestine and led by David Ben-Gurion, who responded by dubbing Jabotinsky "Vladimir Hitler." Throughout the 1920s and 1930s this war of words was more than matched by a war of movements and countermovements, as Jabotinsky and his growing number of followers, mostly in Poland, the Baltic states, the United States, Latin America, and Palestine as well, battled for what was now called Revisionist Zionism—an ostensible return to Herzl's principles—periodically leaving the World Zionist movement, rejoining it, negotiating and fighting with Weizmann and Ben-Gurion, then finally quitting it for good and establishing an independent Jabotinskyite movement. The movement itself split, basically between its leader and the other integral nationalists who followed him, and their more radical colleagues who turned, unsurprisingly for the time, to a more Fascist-like worldview that rejected the essentially democratic starting point of Jabotinsky. In Palestine Jabotinsky helped to found the Irgun, a more radical and militaristic alternative to the Haganah, and by the end of the 1930s he was campaigning for a mass emigration of Jews from Eastern Europe to Palestine and vociferously attacking Weizmann and Ben-Gurion, and especially their support for a partition of Palestine, as traitors to Zionism and the Jewish people. Then, suddenly, he died on August 3, 1940, at age sixty, at a Betar camp in upstate New York.

In addition to the political activities that so marked his public life, throughout the 1920s and 1930s Vladimir Jabotinsky continued to write poetry, feuilletons, dramas, and novels in Russian, and to translate into Russian contemporary poetry and prose often of the modernist style. This less famous aspect of Jabotinsky's life has not been studied as much as his political activities, not only because of their more esoteric qualities but also because many of the materials were held in Soviet libraries and archives inaccessible to scholars of Jewish history and Zionism until 1991. Moreover, inasmuch as his belletristic works were read and studied in the earlier decades, they were mostly read in Hebrew translations done by a group of extremely dedicated followers (including Jabotinsky's son Eri), who knew both Russian and Hebrew extremely well but, unsurprisingly, read the works of both the young and the mature Jabotinsky through the eyes of his politics, not his aesthetics, which were so redolent of fin-de-siècle Europe, a world that seemed as distant as ancient Rome. The Hebrew translations of his works, therefore, were heavily censored, both consciously and not, their fin-de-siècle eclecticism, eroticism, self-doubt, and, alas, much of their playfulness elided as well. At the same time, one of Jabotinsky's most creative works of art, his autobiography *Sippur yammai* (*The Story of My Life*) penned intermittently in Russian and Yiddish and then in Hebrew from the late 1920s to the early 1930s, was read—quite naturally—as an accurate presentation of the life and time of its author, despite its many inaccuracies and simple errors on matters both trivial and fundamental. Some of his most responsible biographers recognized the plenitude of errors in this work but dismissed them as mere slips on the part of the all-too-busy Great Man. Now, however, after dozens of works have been written on the nature of autobiographical writing and, more recently, its relationship to the biology of individual memory, we must recognize that *Sippur yammai*, like all autobiographies, was a highly fictionalized and controlling narrative in which facticity necessarily gave way to overarching purposes—a politically useful self-portrait.[1] Perhaps the most intriguing question about this autobiography is the unknowable extent to which Jabotinsky himself "bought" the life story he presented to the public. There are many hints in the work that he did not.

But the most useful and at the same time most enjoyable and fascinating counterpoint to Jabotinsky's supposedly factual autobiography is his autobiographical novel, *Pyatero* (*The Five*), first published in toto in Russian in Paris in 1936. Set in the Odessa of his youth and narrated by a character very much like the one we know as the "real" Vladimir Jabotinsky, this novel recounts the fortunes not so much of its narrator as of a Russified Jewish family he had become familiar with, the Milgroms, through whom we witness the rise and fall of Jewish Odessa from the beginning of the twentieth century to the Russian Revolution. As I have written elsewhere, paradoxically, "for some authors the screen of fictional distortion can be liberating, serv-

---

[1] See my *Autobiographical Jews: Essays in Jewish Self-Fashioning* (University of Washington Press, 2004).

ing to mute or even entirely to remove the terror of truth-telling. The reader is at one and the same time urged to believe and not to believe that what is depicted actually happened . . . that the narrator is the same person as the author."[2] *The Five* may well be a more accurate reflection of Vladimir Jabotinsky's recollection of his past than his autobiography, less trammeled by his need for self-glorification and ideological purity, more redolent of his internal doubts, his fin-de-siècle sensibility, and thus his interior world as a whole.

Michael Katz's translation of Jabotinsky's Russian is more than accurate: it fully conveys the subtleties and the specific Odessan and Jabotinskyite inflections of the original novel. We are fortunate indeed now to have this wonderful rendition into English of *The Five*, so that all readers interested in Vladimir Jabotinsky, in Zionism, in Odessa, in Russian literature, in Jewish literature, or in any combination of the above, can reflect on this fascinating piece of literature.

[2] Michael Stanislawski, *Zionism and the Fin de Siècle: Cosmopolitanism and Nationalism from Nordau to Jabotinsky* (Berkeley: University of California Press, 2001), 227–28. This chapter includes a longer discussion and evaluation of *The Five* than the one I have presented here.

Principal Characters

Mílgroms

Ignáts Albértovich *father*

Anna Mikháilovna *mother*

Their five children:

  Márya (Marúsya)

  Márko

  Lídiya (Líka)

  Sergéi (Serézha)

  Víktor (Tórik)

Abrám Moiséevich *Mílgroms' relative*

Borís Mavrikíevich (Béirish) *Abrám's brother*

Samóilo Kozodói *Anna Mikháilovna's distant relative; pharmacist;*
  Marúsya's suitor

Alekséi Dmítrievich Runítsky (Alésha) *Russian sailor in Volunteer*
  Navy; Marúsya's romantic interest

Nyúta *attractive young woman*

Nyúra *her mother*

Rovénsky *her father*

THE FIVE

Instead of a Preface

The beginning of this tale of bygone days in Odessa dates to the dawn of the twentieth century. At that time we used to refer to the first years of this period as the "springtime," meaning a social and political awakening. For my generation, these years also coincided with our own personal springtime, in the sense that we were all in our youthful twenties. And both of these springtimes, as well as the image of our carefree Black Sea capital with acacias growing along its steep banks, are interwoven in my memory with the story of one family in which there were five children: Marusya, Marko, Lika, Serezha, and Torik. I was an eyewitness to some of their adventures; the rest, if necessary, I will recount from hearsay or surmise. I can't guarantee the accuracy of either the heroes' biographies or the general sequence of events, municipal or national, against which all this played out: memory often fails me, and there's no time to make inquiries. However, one thing is certain: it's no accident that I remember these five children, and it isn't because I loved Marusya and Serezha so much, and even more, their lighthearted, wise, long-suffering mother—but rather it's because with this particular family, like a textbook example, the entire preceding period of Jewish Russification—both good and bad—got even with us. This aspect of the affair, I am sure I will relate accurately, without captious criticism, all the more so since it's now so distant and long ago, became both heartrending and cherished. "I'm a child of my age, I understand both the good and the bad in it, I know its splendor and its decay: I'm its child and I love all its blemishes, all its poison."[1]

[1] Source unknown.

Youth

The first time I saw Madame Milgrom and her elder daughter was at the premiere of the opera *Monna Vanna*[1] in our municipal theater. They were sitting in a box not far from my seat in the stalls; three other people were with them, members of some other family. I noticed them for a reason that was both complimentary and highly uncomplimentary to my own self-esteem. It all began when a young colleague from the newspaper office sitting next to me, a person who wrote about lowlife and the port, remarked over the noise in the auditorium, which was filling up with people, "Look to the right, at that young redheaded Jewess in the third box: she looks like a kitten in a muff!" He occasionally produced splendid similes: the young woman glancing out from under her soft, bright red hair really did resemble a little kitten in a circle of fur on the lid of a candy box. At the same time I noticed that the older woman was pointing me out to the younger one, saying something to her, obviously my pen name at the newspaper; her daughter's eyes grew wide, she shrugged her shoulders in disbelief, and replied (I could read her lips clearly): "Really? Impossible!"

During the second intermission I went up to the gallery to see my student friends. The gallery was an important institution in our mu-

---

[1] Lyric opera (1909) with music by the French composer Henri Février (1875–1957) and libretto by the Belgian poet and dramatist Maurice Maeterlinck (1862–1949).

3

nicipal theater: students reigned there; seats on the sides, it seems, were reserved exclusively for them. Consequently, there was always a police supervisor on duty, some large, handsome fellow, with a forked beard covering his chest like the kind sported by generals, and he always kept a few policemen in reserve. If the students misbehaved (for example, when the old singer Figner would squeak on the high note in *The Huguenots*[2] and, as a result, remind the students of his unbrotherly treatment of his sister, locked away in a fortress at Schlüsselburg),[3] policemen would appear and firmly escort the students away by the elbow, while the supervisor strode behind, repeating deferentially, "Really, Mr. Student, how could you? . . ."

That evening no one misbehaved. For the last two weeks the newspapers had been preparing the public for a performance of *Monna Vanna*; I don't remember how, but undoubtedly some revolutionary meaning had been incorporated into this opera (at the time the phrase was "liberating"; in those years everything was interpreted, both for or against, through a prism of liberation, even the squeaky voice of the tenor, who was referred to as His Excellency's Soloist). The performance exceeded all our expectations. The heroine was played by an actress with whom we were all simply in love at the time: half the young women in town imitated her affectionate, melancholy tone of voice and extended their hands to friends without bending them, palms down, just as she did. The foyer of the gallery, which, during both intermissions usually resembled a grand boulevard where two thick streams of saunterers would stretch parallel to one another, now took on the appearance of a forum: small groups gathered everywhere, and in each, an argument was in progress about one and the same thing—was it conceivable that Prinzivalle sat with the scantily clad Monna Vanna all through the night and never once tried to touch her?

The students in the group where I found my friends were arguing about the same thing; over their extremely excited tones, I heard a heated discussion of that subject in a particularly large group nearby. Suddenly I noticed that in the center of that group stood the very same young redhead. She appeared to be about nineteen years old.

[2] Romantic opera (1836) by the German-Jewish composer Giacomo Meyerbeer (1791–1864) and librettist Eugène Scribe (1791–1861).
[3] Fortress (1323) on Lake Ladoga used as a prison for high-ranking persons and political prisoners.

She was short but well-built according to the sumptuous tastes of that robust time; naturally, she was wearing a tight corset around her waist and sides but, apparently, without a brassiere, which, I was told, was considered to be an indecent innovation among the middle class; her puff sleeves didn't even reach her elbows, and, although the collar of her dress circled her throat in monastic fashion, beneath the collar in front the dress had a low neckline, three inches or so, also considered daring for its time. To complete this external impression, the following fragments of conversation reached me:

"But is it conceivable," a student said with passion, "that Prinzivalle would . . ."

"It's terrible!" exclaimed the young redhead. "If I were in Monna Vanna's shoes, I'd never have permitted that. Such a blockhead!"

Those around her began laughing, while one of them declared aloud:

"You're delightful, Marusya, you always say such things that make me want to kiss you . . ."

"Fancy that, what an honor," Marusya replied indifferently. "Soon there won't be a single student left on Deribasov Street who can brag that he's never kissed me."

I was unable to hear any more, even though I tried hard to eavesdrop.

The performance ended altogether magnificently. After the first and second acts the orchestra and boxes were still waiting to see what the ultimate authority, namely, the gallery, would say; only after receiving a signal from on high did they begin to applaud. But now the boxes and the orchestra began to thunder with applause all on their own. The entire cast came out to take innumerable bows, then Monna Vanna and Prinzivalle, then Monna Vanna alone in her black velvet gown. Suddenly, in the midst of all the applause, the galleries on both sides fell silent. This was a sign that the highest form of praise was being prepared, heretofore reserved exclusively for Italian singers, male and female—namely, students rushing into the orchestra. The rest of the public, still applauding, turned their heads with great expectation; the painted curtain rose once more, but there was still no one on stage—they were also awaiting the sublime jest of our youth. A moment later through all the aisles, blue frock coats and gray double-breasted jackets burst forward; I recall that ahead of them down the middle aisle walked an enormous Georgian with great strides, a business-like expression on his face, serious, threatening, as if racing for the barricades. Reaching the orchestra, he put his cap under his arm and, without haste, perhaps not even very loudly, with great confidence, slowly and distinctly clapped his hands three times ("just like a sultan summoning the beautiful Zyuleika out from behind the screen," it was reported in one of our newspapers the next day). And only then, in reply to the imperious summons of the padishah, did our magnificent Zyuleika emerge from the wings; I saw that her lips were actually trembling, spasms were rising in her throat; an indescribable tempest raged all around; two ushers ran out of the wings to carry away baskets of flowers and to clear the floor for what was then considered even dearer than flowers: onto the stage fluttered crumpled, faded dark blue student caps with their chipped peaks. Behind the students stood policemen and supervisors, each, as if chosen specially, sporting a double beard on his chest; their appearance was benevolent, permissive, majestically festive, a good match for the blazing crystal, gilt, caryatids, red velvet chairs, and partitions, for the fancy clothes of the grain exporters and their dark-eyed ladies, and for all the splendor of our carefree, contented Odessa. I turned to look at Marusya: she was beside herself with joy. She was looking at the students, not at the stage, and she tugged her mama's puffed sleeve and pointed out, apparently, her closest friends among the crowd of blue frock coats and gray double-breasted jackets, uttering each of their names, if I remember correctly—up to twenty of them, maybe more, until the fire curtain started to descend slowly and majestically from the ceiling.

Serezha

Someone told me that the redhead's last name was Milgrom; and, as I was leaving the theater, I recalled that I was already acquainted with one member of that family.

We had met in the summer, not too long before. I was visiting some acquaintances who were spending the last days of August at their dacha near Langeron. One morning, while my hosts were still asleep, I went down to take a swim and then decided to go rowing for a bit. My friends had a flat-bottomed boat with two sets of oars; somehow I managed to maneuver the boat across the coarse-grained gravel (which we simply called "sand") and into the water; only then did I notice that during the night someone had broken off both oarlocks on the right side. There were no spares to be found. Oarlocks on the boats along our banks were really ridiculous—simple wooden sticks to which clumsy, broad-bladed oars were fastened with rope: skill was required just to make sure that the oars didn't twist or smack the water with their flat sides. On the other hand, no skill whatsoever was needed to fashion such an oarlock: one had only to whittle a branch. But that idea never occurred to me. Our generation grew up without fingers, as it were: when a button was torn off, we hung our heads in despair and fantasized about family life, a wife—an astonishing creature undaunted by any challenges, who knows where to buy a needle and thread and how to set about the task. I stood before the boat, hanging my head sadly, as if facing some complicated piece of machinery in which something mysterious had gone wrong and Thomas Edison himself would be needed to salvage the dismal affair.

In the middle of this misfortune a young student from the gymnasium, about seventeen years old, approached me; I learned later that he was barely sixteen but was tall for his age. He glanced at the stubs of the oarlocks with the experienced eye of a worldly-wise man and posed the following question to me in a business-like manner:

"Who's your watchman along this shore?"

"Chubchik," I said. "Avtonom Chubchik, a local fisherman."

He replied with contempt: "That's why there's such disorder. Chubchik! Even the other fishermen say he's a deadbeat."

I looked up with delight. Linguistics had always been the genuine passion of my life; and, living in an enlightened circle where everyone tried to articulate their words in the Great Russian manner, some time had passed since I'd heard the authentic dialect of the Fontany, Langeron, Peresyp, and Dyukov Garden. "Say he's a deadbeat." Superb! "Deadbeat"—there's no point trying to translate it: the word contains a veritable encyclopedia of disapproving judgments. My interlocutor continued in the same style, but the trouble is I've forgotten my native tongue; I'll have to convey his words for the most part in official language, painfully aware that every phrase is inaccurate.

"Wait a bit," he said. "That's easy to fix."

Before me stood a person of a different ilk, a man with all ten fingers! In the first place, it turned out that he had a knife in his pocket, and not just a little penknife but a Finnish knife. In the second place, he immediately procured some wooden material: glancing around to make sure there was no one in his field of vision, he confidently strode over to the nearby bathhouse with steps in front and snapped off the lower baluster from under the handrail. He broke it in two over his knee; he began whittling one half; then he measured to see if it would fit into the hole and whittled some more; he dug out the remains of the old oarlocks and inserted the new ones. The only thing missing was the appropriate verse: "Well, old man, now it's ready . . ." Instead, he proposed a method of payment for his services in the same spontaneous manner, getting right to the point:

"Can I go with you?"

I agreed, of course, but glanced once more at his school uniform and, to have a clear conscience, asked: "The school year's already begun—my friend, shouldn't you be attending your first class?"

"Le cadet de mes soucis [The least of my worries]," he replied with indifference, while lowering the rope rings on the oars over the oar-locks. He actually produced this phrase in French, and it wasn't merely showing off. Later I learned that the younger [Milgrom] children had governesses (but not Marusya or Marko—their father wasn't earning enough money at that time). In general, he wasn't showing off; even more, he didn't concern himself with his interlocutor, or what that interlocutor might be thinking. He was completely consumed by the business at hand: he tied knots in the rope rings, lifted the planking to see if there was any water underneath, opened the box under the bench in the stern to see if there was a scoop, knocked this or that, and wiped something or other. Meanwhile he managed to explain that he'd decided to play hooky, since he'd learned from a fellow student who was renting rooms from a Greek, that is, from a Czech who taught Greek, that this teacher had decided to call him, that is, my new friend, today, out of order, up to the blackboard. Therefore he left a note for his mother (she gets up late): "If the truant officer comes, tell him I had to go to the dentist." He'd stashed his knapsack at the tobacco shop nearby and proceeded to the Langeron.

"Your mama's good-natured," I said with sincere approval. We were already rowing.

"Life's bearable," he confirmed, "tout à fait potable [altogether tolerable]."

"Why then is your knapsack at the tobacco store? Better to leave it at home, if your mama's in agreement."

"I can't because of my papa. He's still not really seasoned. To this day he can't come to terms with the fact that I sign his name on my report card. Never mind, he'll get used to it. Tomorrow I'll write an entire note in his handwriting: 'My son, Sergei Milgrom, in the fifth grade, was absent on such-and-such a date, because he was suffering from a toothache.'"

We set off very well; he rowed splendidly, and knew all the correct boating terms. The wind today would be whipping up a storm around five o'clock; it wasn't simply the wind but "Tramontana," the north wind. "Back water on the right, or else we'll run into that little oak rowboat." "Look—a porpoise has croaked," he said, pointing out a dolphin carcass tossed up by the storm yesterday onto the lower platform of the breakwater not far from the lighthouse.

In the intervals between these nautical observations, he treated me to bits of information about his family. Every morning his father "raced off to the office by horse-drawn tram"—that's why he was so dangerous; when Sergei, known as Serezha, didn't feel like going to school, they'd have to leave the house at the same time. In the evening his house was like a "flea market": "sightseers," mostly students, would come visit his eldest sister. There was an elder brother Marko, a decent fellow, "manageable," but something of a "dimwit" or "scatterbrain." This year Marko was a "Nietzschean." Serezha had composed the following verses about him:

> His pants have a hole in them, but he has fashionable ideas;
> A learned fellow who's been left back in school three times.

"That's my specialty at home," he added. "Marusya insists that I compose verses about each one of her sightseers."

His sister Lika, apparently also older than Serezha, "chewed her fingernails down to the bone and was now bored and angry at all of Odessa." Torik was the youngest but the "foundation of the throne": he understood everything so well that "your ears can fall off just listening to him."

I forgot to say that we made it to the lighthouse in the following manner: after catching sight of a small rowboat that we would have rammed if he hadn't ordered me to back water, Serezha remembered that the Androsov Pier was teeming with small oak boats from Kherson—transporting watermelons from the monastery.

"Would you like to head over there? We can have some lunch: my treat."

I found it very agreeable and amusing to be with him, and no one at the dacha would need the boat until evening; besides, on the return trip he promised to pick up "someone from the eatery" to row while I rested. I agreed and we made for the pier, rounding the lighthouse, spending three hours or so as a result of the wind, the swells, and the need to bail half the Black Sea out from under the planking every half hour or so.

"Your admirals are like infantrymen," Serezha said, insulting my friends who were so remiss about the condition of their boat.

At the pier we had to make our way through the crowd among oak boats, just like at the market on Tolchok: small craft were almost bumping into one another. Serezha knew which was an oak boat, which a launch, which a felucca, as well as another five or ten others. Obviously many people here knew him. From the decks loaded with watermelons people would call out to him affectionately, greeting him thus:

"Oho, Serezha—where're you off to, you scamp? Why aren't you at school, you s.o.b.? How the hell are you?" To which he invariably replied: "Skandibober!"[1] That is, judging by his tone, he was feeling shipshape, thanks. From one felucca a young fellow wearing a red fez, baring his white teeth, shouted something to him in Greek, and Serezha replied to him in the same language; I don't know Greek, but fortunately I caught the end of his phrase—". . . tin mitera sou," the accusative case of the words "your mother." In conversation with me Serezha refrained from that sort of language. However, in stating his views of the young women in various schools of Odessa, he managed to embarrass me by his choice of words: about the fetching student uniforms worn by the girls at the Kurakina-Tekel Gymnasium—he said that their violet clothes fit so snugly that their "boobs" stuck out like jumbo eggs!

At the pier, after strictly forbidding me to contribute my share of our expenses, he ran off and returned with a large pile of comestibles. Right there in the boat, after he thrust his hands into the ice-hole among watermelon rinds for hygienic reasons, we enjoyed the tastiest feast I'd ever eaten. But even better than the food, I delighted in the way Serezha ate. What the English call "table manners" are a great institution—not merely the ability to hold a fork and imbibe one's soup without musical accompaniment, but in general, the entire "ceremony of eating," a complicated ritual fitting each sort of food and every different setting, hallowed and polished by generations of gastronomic tradition. What's a fork? It's no surprise that when there is a fork, it's very pleasant to watch. Here, not only was a fork lacking, but even if we'd had one, it would have been completely inappropriate. A seeded bagel: Serezha didn't break it into pieces but rather slit it open around the outside, into two halves, smeared each with lard, scraped sesame seeds from the shiny side—and then, like an experienced sower in the field, scattered them evenly onto the lard, closed the two halves again, and only then, still without breaking it

[1] A word invented by Serezha.

into pieces, tucked into the bagel with his teeth. The sea-roach: Serezha grabbed it by its tail and struck its flat side a dozen or so times against his left heel, explaining: "This makes it easier to remove the skin." And in fact, his sea-roach let itself be skinned much more easily and completely than mine, even though I was operating on mine with the aid of his knife; I was still cutting away transparent salty layers from the hard spines on its skeleton, while the only thing left of his were the fatty drops on his chin, cheeks, and the tip of his nose. But the culmination of all this ritual was the watermelon. I was about to cut it into pieces when Serezha said hurriedly, "That's not necessary for me." He picked up a quarter of the melon, held it in front of him, delighting in the play of colors—and then, vanished. Serezha disappeared from sight completely: first, there he was, and then he wasn't. Before me sat a school uniform with a mask of green marble instead of a head. I was overcome with envy: I could experience what he was feeling at that very moment. A good melon smells just like fresh water, or, on the other hand, it's indistinguishable; but to drown, as he was, in a watermelon—that's like sailing away at evening into a quiet backwater, lying on one's back, forgetting everything. It's the ideal of nirvana, you and nature, nothing else matters. I was overcome with envy: I grabbed another quarter of the melon and bid fond farewell to earth.

Then "someone from the eatery" arrived and I thought unwittingly, as I had in Berlin: so siehste aus [so that's what you look like]. Serezha introduced him: Motya Banabak. He was about twenty, but in spite of the difference in their ages, they were apparently bosom buddies. On the way home I fell asleep and didn't hear their conversation, but all the rest I recalled later, after the theater, enjoying a cup of Turkish coffee and some Turkish delight in my favorite Greek café on the corner of Krasnyi Lane.

$$\text{---} \sim \text{---} \quad \textbf{III} \quad \text{---} \sim \text{---}$$

In the Literary Circle

On Saturday, after the concert at the literary-artistic circle, as the workers were moving chairs away to allow for dancing in the vineyard hall, Marusya, holding her mother by the sleeve, led her up to me and said:

"This woman wishes to make your acquaintance, but she's too shy: Anna Mikhailovna Milgrom. By the way, I must also introduce myself: I'm her daughter, but she's not in the least to blame."

Anna Mikhailovna extended her hand while Marusya admonished her in a stage whisper: "Behave yourself." Then she went off to choose a dancing partner; the rule according to which the opposite is supposed to happen simply didn't apply to her.

The vineyard hall was so named because its walls were decorated with interwoven reliefs of vines and bunches of grapes. The literary circle occupied an entire private residence; I don't recall to whom it belonged and who'd lived there previously, but obviously it had been some wealthy landowners. The house was in the best part of town, on the boundary between two worlds—the upper section and the port. To the present day, if I squint, I can recall, albeit through a mist that obscures the details, that large square, a monument to the noble architecture of foreign masters of the first third of the nineteenth century, and witness to the serene elegance of the old-fashioned taste of the first builders of our town—Richelieu,[1] de Ribas,[2] Vorontsov,[3] and the entire pioneering generation of merchants and smugglers with their Italian and Greek surnames. Ahead of me—the front staircase to the municipal library and, on the left, against the background of a broad, almost boundless bay, is the peristyle of the Duma:[4] neither would disgrace Corinth or Pisa. To the right, I see the first houses on Italian Street, in my time known as Pushkin Street, since it was there the poet wrote Onegin;[5] turning around, there's the English Club, and farther off in the distance, the left façade of the municipal theater: these were built at different times but all with one and the same love of the foreign spirit of the city (Roman and Hellenistic) with its incomprehensible name, as if borrowed from the legend of a kingdom "to the east of the sun and west of the moon." And here, near the private residence where the literary circle met (also closely resembling the villas I saw once in Sienna), began one of the descents into the abyss of the port; on quiet days you could smell the pitch and hear the echo of grain elevators.

Given the conditions of censorship at that time, our literary circle was an oasis of free speech; none of us ever really understood why the authorities tolerated our circle and didn't close it down. There was never any open sedition; we were all so well trained that words such as "autocracy" and "constitution" had yet to enter our common vocabulary; but whatever we talked about, from the small zemstvo[6] unit to Hauptmann's The Sunken Bell[7]—everywhere was the rumble of sedition. Chekhovian melancholy was perceived as a protest against the existing order and the regime; Gorky's invented tramps,

[1] The Duc de Richelieu (1766–1822) was a French émigré who served as governor of Odessa from 1803–14. He was a progressive administrator who was responsible for much of the city's early growth and wealth.

[2] Joseph de Ribas (1749–1800) was a Spaniard who entered Russian military service, became an admiral, and participated in the Russo-Turkish wars, including the capture of Khadzhi-bei (1789). He then conceived and implemented a plan for the construction of the port of Odessa.

[3] Count Mikhail Vorontsov (1782–1856) was a military and government official and an outstanding administrator who served as governor general of Novorossiya from 1823–44.

[4] Representative assembly in prerevolutionary Russia.

[5] Eugene Onegin is an extraordinary "novel in verse" (1823–31) by the great Russian poet Aleksandr Pushkin (1799–1837).

[6] Elected district council that functioned as an organ of provincial government in Russia from 1864 to 1917.

[7] Romantic play (1897) by the German writer Gerhart Hauptmann (1862–1946).

including even Malva[8]—as a call to the barricades; why this was the case, I couldn't possibly explain now, but that's the way it was. There were no political parties yet, except for underground ones; legal Marxists and populists didn't always know precisely how they differed from one another, and without a word of complaint they were counted along with future Cadets[9] in the general multitude of the "progressive camp"; but at the same time, without having a program, we managed to display programmatic vehement impatience. Someone presented a report about Nadson[10] where it was argued that he was not really a civic poet but a philistine poet, "Kifa Mokievich in verse";[11] for two hours straight, detractors attacked the reactionary nature of his views, and the person presiding, a Greek, an insurance inspector by profession, deprived the speaker of the right to say a last word in his defense, and thus he was forever disgraced; as for the nature of his crime, I don't recall, and it doesn't really matter. But at that time all this was extremely important, and just as that residence stood at the center of town in a geographic sense, so too, were Thursdays at our literary circle the focus of our spiritual ferment.

Looking back at all this some thirty years later, I think that the most curious thing about it was the good-natured fraternization of nationalities. All eight or ten tribes of old Odessa met in that club, and in fact it never occurred to anyone, even in silence, to note who was who. All this changed a few years later, but at the dawn of the last century we genuinely got along. It was strange; in our homes, it seems, we lived apart; the Poles visited and invited other Poles, Russians invited Russians, Jews, other Jews; exceptions were encountered relatively infrequently; but we had yet to wonder why this was so, unconsciously considering it simply an indication of temporary oversight, and the Babylonian diversity of our common forum, as a symbol of a splendid tomorrow. Perhaps one honest and foolish

[8] Strong, willful heroine of an early story "Malva" (1897) by Maksim Gorky (1868–1936).
[9] Nickname for Constitutional Democrats, a political party formed by left-wing liberals in 1905.
[10] Semyon Nadson (1862–87) began his literary career as a civic writer but soon became a poet of the conflict between pain and despair and dreams of ideal beauty.
[11] A peripheral character mentioned in the last chapter of the comic novel *Dead Souls* (1842) by Nikolai Gogol (1809–52): a man of meek character, he was inclined to contemplate absurd philosophical questions, whereas his son, Moky Kifovich, was an equally foolish man of action.

drinking companion of mine, an opera tenor with a Ukrainian surname, best expressed this mood—its conciliatory surface and its concealed threat. One Saturday, after drinking a bit too much, he came
over to embrace me for some speech I had given at dinner:

"Today you grabbed me by the guts," he said, kissing me three
times. "Now we're thick as thieves: we're sworn brothers for life. It's
a pity that people are still going on about religion: one's a Russian,
another's a Jew. What difference does it make? There should be a common soul, just like you and I have. Then again, there's X—now that's
different: he has a Jewish soul, a filthy soul . . ."

—◆◆◆—

On closer examination Anna Mikhailovna turned out to be a
youngish-looking woman with astonishingly kind eyes; she apologized several times for her daughter's ruse. "You don't want to spend
time with an old woman," she said. "You want to dance." I told her
the truth: while still a pupil in the gymnasium, Tsorn, our dancing
teacher, expelled me from class, having determined that I was incapable of ever learning the difference between a quadrille and a three-
step waltz. We sat down in a corner of the room behind a ficus tree
and started to chat; I began in cavalier fashion: "My daughter will
soon turn twenty," she had said. "Who could possibly have allowed
you, madam, to marry while still in kindergarten?" I replied. But she
simply brushed that remark aside and, without standing on ceremony, began talking as a mother:

"Listen, I really did want to meet you. Some time ago while living
on the Dniepr, my husband knew your late father; we speak of you
often, and I've been meaning to ask: why are you, a capable young
man, frittering away your time without any real profession?"

For a first meeting, this was a rather insulting question; but she had
a special talent (later I discovered that Marusya had even more) of
somehow saying the most inappropriate things so nicely as though
she could really do anything she wanted to.

"Without a real profession? But I've been a reporter for several
years."

She looked at me with genuine astonishment, as if I'd said that I'd
been hopping on one foot for the last ten years.

"That's not really a career. You can keep writing for another year,
maybe two; but it's impossible to compose feuilletons one's whole
life. Ignats Albertovich (that's my husband), would gladly find you a

job in his office; or you could consider becoming a lawyer, or something else, but a man mustn't just hang around without a real job."

I was about to argue in favor of the upstanding aspects of my trade, but I felt it wouldn't bolster my defense; in her view, there was simply no rung for it on the social ladder. In olden times, they say, that was how all respectable people regarded actors; perhaps this was Jewish atavism; my occupation seemed to her like that of a melamed,[12] which a person assumes because nothing better has turned up. I abandoned the apologia and took up the offense:

"One candid remark deserves another. I know two of your children: the elder young lady and Serezha. Tell me: how did they take to your wise counsel? They're both charming but not quite in your style, I fear . . ."

"Oh, that's another matter. They're my children: I'd sooner climb onto the roof and take a walk than give them any advice."

"Why so?"

"The last person children ever listen to is their own mother or father, it makes no difference. The tragedy of fathers and sons is repeated in each generation and it's always the same: precisely that which parents preach, one fine day turns out to bore their children to death, and, at the same time, the parents also bore the children. Thanks, I don't want that."

"Clever woman," I thought, and decided that I couldn't spend the evening in a more entertaining way. This family had already begun to intrigue me; I began asking about her children; she replied willingly, at times with such frankness that it would have struck me even from a distance, if it all wasn't said so "very nicely."

Between dances Marusya came running up; she said, pointing to her mother: "Be careful, she's a regular *demi-vierge*—she'll charm the pants off you but won't agree to have an affair." Then she turned to her mother: "I've been dancing all evening with N. N. I'm in love; it's a pity he has a mustache, but I do hope it's soft and won't scratch me," she said and ran off.

"It's all talk," I said comfortingly, thinking that Anna Mikhailovna was upset by the specificity of this prediction; but she wasn't upset at all.

---

[12] Hebrew. Teacher of elementary language to young boys; also used to indicate an incompetent, well-meaning nonentity.

"For girls of this generation, the distinction between words and deeds doesn't frighten them in the least."

"And you?"

"Every mother worries about her children, but I worry least about Marusya. Did you ever play the game of giant steps when you were a child? You climb up almost to the moon and then fall down into an abyss—but it merely seems to be true, when in fact there's a tether and a fixed limit. Marusya has a limit beyond which no mustache will ever scratch her—although, of course, I'd prefer not to know precisely where that limit is. Ah, but here's my husband."

Ignats Albertovich was a much older man, portly, with a shaved chin, wearing glasses; from his appearance even I would have said that he was a grain dealer, and that turned out to be true. Judging from his accent, he hadn't attended a Russian school but had, apparently, worked on his own education; as was often the case with his generation, he read German classics with particular zeal—and subsequently was able to recite from memory whole pages from Börne;[13] among poets, for some reason he loved Chamisso[14] and Lenau[15] most of all. As a result he bore to some extent the vague imprint of that which we convey with the amusing Russian word, *intelligent*, member of the intelligentsia. This word has the same precarious meaning as the English word "gentleman." A true gentleman can have the most unbearably obnoxious manners, while a genuine *intelligent*, can serenely, with as little as a yawn, reveal his ignorance of Maupassant[16] or Hegel: the point is not in the actual signs but in some internal saturation with culture in general. But at the same time Ignats Albertovich first and foremost appeared to be a person from the world of business, knowing the price of things and of people, convinced that this price is, most likely, a measure of their real worth. I learned all this later when I grew close to the family, although even in that first conversation several of his standards were fixed in my memory.

Anna Mikhailovna complained to him immediately about the fact

[13] Ludwig Börne (1786–1837) was a German writer of Jewish origin (named Löb Baruch). He was one of the leaders of the revolutionary Young Germany literary movement.

[14] Adelbert von Chamisso (1781–1838) was a German romantic poet.

[15] Pseudonym of Nikolaus Franz Niembsch von Strehlenau (1802–50), Austrian lyric poet, best known for the melancholy weltschmerz that characterizes his work.

[16] Guy de Maupassant (1850–1893) was a French short story writer and novelist.

that I didn't want to go to work in his office and that I intended to "remain a scribbler for the rest of my days."

"Well?" he said. "This young man, obviously, has his dream in life. Our son Marko gets a new dream every month or so. I keep telling him, God bless. I wish you success. But remember: if you're successful, I'll say, 'Good boy. I always predicted something good would come of you.' But if you fail, I'll say, 'Didn't I know from the day of his birth that Marko was a fool?'"

I thanked him for this lesson but preferred once more to move the conversation away from myself and back to their children; that wasn't hard—Anna Mikhailovna clearly loved that subject, and her husband didn't avoid it either. They described Serezha exactly as I'd encountered him; Ignats Albertovich, while cleaning his glasses, confirmed the description in a somewhat unexpected formulation:

"In general, he's a charlatan: I love charlatans."

On the other hand, about their youngest child Torik (his real name was Viktor), Anna Mikhailovna spoke respectfully: he was a good student, read a great deal, did gymnastics, played the violin fairly well, was polite and very obliging; when his mother had come down with pneumonia and Marusya happened to be abroad at the time, Torik took better care of the patient than any nurse could have.

"There are some people," said Ignats Albertovich, "who like their soup with noodles, and others who prefer it with dumplings. This isn't a trivial distinction—it reflects two separate characters. Noodles are slippery: if you're lucky, you wind up with a bunch of them; but there's also a risk they'll all slip away. But with dumplings, there's no anxiety: you can't take more than one, but to make up for that, you always get some meat, without taking any risks. Our Serezha likes his soup with noodles, while Torik prefers it with dumplings."

I laughed for a good long time, although I'd heard this parable before, in several different versions; but he retold it very skillfully. I said:

"Now I know the entire gallery of family portraits, but Serezha said he had another sister—Lika?"

Anna Mikhailovna looked at her husband, while he looked down at the floor and said somberly:

"Lika. Hmm . . . Lika—that's not a subject to discuss at a dance."

IV

Around Marusya

I soon became a frequent guest in their house; strange to say, even as this was happening, at first I seemed to lose sight of the actual inhabitants of the house—mother, father, and children. They were all submerged into a motley and noisy flock of Marusya's "sightseers." Many weeks passed before, through this throng of people, I was once again able to distinguish Marusya and the rest of her family.

In my whole life, neither before nor after, have I ever seen a more hospitable household. This was not Russian hospitality, actively cordial, warmly welcoming. Rather, it was more fitting to recall a phrase from the ritual of the Jewish Passover: "Let him who is hungry come and eat." Afterward I learned that Ignats Albertovich expressed this same thought in the language of his childhood in Zhitomir, and that it was one of his favorite Yiddish sayings: "*A gast? Mitn kop in vant*"— that is, "When the bell rings, open the door to your guest, and say to him: here's a chair, have some tea and rolls; then, do nothing more; don't try to entertain him, don't worry about him, let him do whatever he wants, even bang his head against the wall." It must be acknowledged that this approach really helped their guests feel at home immediately.

Through the haze of several eternities that have passed since then, I can remember a few of them, the large majority, not as a result of their own distinctness but rather with the help of Serezha's poetic portraits. They were almost all students: there were two or three external students;[1] from among those, a few wore blue student caps in anticipation of future achievements, though that was problematical because of the quotas; some were budding journalists, already well known on Deribasov Street; there were also some, most likely, whose names even Marusya didn't know.

I remember two students in particular, aristocratic reactionaries. One was sedate and well brought up, inserted French words into his conversation, and tried to speak Russian like a Muscovite—but he couldn't pronounce the letter r, which he explained by saying that his governess had "wuined" his accent. He was preparing for an administrative or diplomatic career; he insinuated that his religion would present no obstacle, and he had penned a prize-winning essay on the very promising theme of the desirability of the repeal of the constitution of the grand principality of Finland. He brought flowers whenever he came to visit Marusya; he kissed the hands of all married women but not those of the single women, as was fitting (all the rest of us, the uncouth ones, kissed Marusya's hand, too; someone even tried to extend this treatment to seventeen-year-old Lika, and suffered the consequences). But Serezha saw through him, and the portrait of this "sightseer" went like this:

> He entered like a god, scented with bergamot,
> And once in the room, one smelled an idiot.

The second student was a braggart, rosy-cheeked, always merry, always sporting a big smile showing all thirty-two teeth. "Papa wanted me to become a medical student, in Kharkov," he explained once. "But I persevered: I'll only enroll in one of the dancing faculties—law or philosophy." He adored Odessa and referred with contempt to those who hadn't been born there as "new arrivals." He made Marusya's acquaintance in the following way: one day she was walking along the street all alone; he suddenly came up alongside her, doffed his cap, and, displaying all his teeth, declared:

"Mademoiselle, I am the member on duty from the Society for the Protection of Single Maidens Strolling along Richelieu Street against Insolent Fellows."

[1] A person who takes exams in a particular course of study without being a registered student at the institution.

Serezha's portrait of him was rather mean; I include it here not without some hesitation:

> He burst into the room like a raging storm,
> And once in the room, one smelled chloroform.

Only the most handsome and least thoughtful external students were admitted; as a matter of fact, it was only in this household that I encountered such students at all. In general, external students constituted a very noticeable group of the population in Odessa at that time; they came from places near and far, even from Lithuania ("immigrants from the Pinsk swamp," as Marusya used to say); by day they read Turgenev[2] and Tugan-Baranovsky[3] in the municipal library, and at night they spread either revolution or Zionism around town. They failed their exams in the sixth and eighth grades mercilessly; many had given up in disgust, stopped cramming for exams or even dreaming of entering university, but they continued to be considered "external students," as if this was a social caste. They had a stern, concentrated appearance; I was always afraid of them, reading in their eyes the biblical injunction: "You have been weighed in the balance and found wanting." But only exceptions to this morose type turned up at Marusya's house: "level-headed external students," as she used to say, tame, wearing neckties, even starched collars. She was concerned about their broader education and would try to divert them from conversations on serious topics relating to various branches of philosophy. Nevertheless, other "sightseers" looked at them askance, and Serezha gladly "quoted" their linguistic pearls, supposedly gleaned from compositions submitted at their most recent, unsuccessful examinations:

> "Mankind has long since noted the enlightening significance of science . . ."
> "On the field of battle" (this was a translation from the Greek) "resounded the moans of those who had perished, as well as those who were perishing . . ."
> "The mother was struck seeing her son beating his father . . ."

[2] Ivan Turgenev (1818–83) was a major nineteenth-century Russian writer and author of six novels, including *Fathers and Sons* (1862).
[3] Mikhail Tugan-Baranovsky (1865–1919) was a Russian economist who published a study of industrial crises in England and contributed to investment theory.

Among them there was, by the way, one real external student wearing a Russian shirt, as he should. He came to see Lika, not Marusya, and regarded the rest of us as Lika did, like a wolf. He soon disappeared from the circle altogether. Serezha's critique declared:

> God knows how he was dressed, poorly shaven—
> Better watch him, he'll snitch something.

Of course, I was previously acquainted with the young journalists. One was the same writer about lowlife and the port who'd first described Marusya to me that evening in the theater as a "kitten in a muff." He was a nice fellow and very talented; he knew more about tramps than Gorky, who, I suspect, had never really lived among them, at least, not down here in the south. This fellow spoke their language all the time—he referred to his heart's Dulcinea as a "dame," to his coat as his "threads," (or something like that), to my watch (he didn't have one) as my "ticker," and he asked for a loan in the following way: "Got some dough?" Serezha regarded him as his mentor, generally worshipped him, and stubbornly refused to devote a "portrait" to him. Everyone loved him, especially the simple folk. People who lived on Moldavanka and Peresyp first learned to read, apparently, using his stories; in the Ambarzaki café a young waitress once went up to him, burst into tears, and said, "Monsieur, how amazingly you wrote yesterday for 'Anyutka Oh-my-God.'"

Another student wore painstakingly unkempt curls and sowed decadence in our city; the fact that he didn't know any foreign languages impeded him somewhat; on the other hand, he handled Russian flawlessly, and even titled one of his articles, "I Have Someone Else's Headache." He quoted abundantly from *The Individual and his Property*,[4] but on one occasion he ascribed the book to Nietzsche; he published a poem of about 120 lines but accompanied it with the subtitle "Sonnet." The merciless Serezha immortalized him thus:

> He was inspired in a refined and sublime manner,
> But confused names: Shpielhagen[5] and Beethoven.

[4] This may refer to a late essay by the Hebrew writer Hayyim Bialik (1873–1934), whose poetry Jabotinsky translated into Russian.

[5] Friedrich von Spielhagen (1829–1911) was a popular German writer whose works are considered representative of the social novel.

. . . But I've yet to describe a fifth, even a tenth of the general public.

After getting a close look at them, and, at long last, picking out Marusya at the center like a hedgehog through thick grass, I began to admire how she presided over them all. It was done without effort, without even paying attention, without any attempts to "entertain" them, simply by her inner magnetic charm. She didn't know how to laugh contagiously; it sounded rather husky. In my opinion, she never said all that much—how could she shout down that crowd? But from her presence alone everyone felt comfortable and cheerful, and every word spoken by each person there seemed astonishingly witty. I myself am immune to that sort of magnetism: my beloved could stare at the back of my head for two hours straight, and I wouldn't feel a thing and would never turn around. But I recall the following incident: once I arrived at their house and found no one home. I sat down in the living room and began to read the journal *Niva*; half an hour passed and suddenly I was literally flooded with a sensation of *bien-être*, just as if a stove has been lit on a cold day, or a stinging speck of dust has been removed from one's eye. Marusya had returned, and I, engrossed in my reading, had neither heard the bell nor noticed her footsteps on the carpet; moreover, I was never even in love with her. That was just how it was, something unusually good had merely entered the living room along with her.

I don't know what kind of intimate feelings she had for these "sightseers." To hear her tell it—almost all of them, protractedly or fleetingly, were in turn favored by her magnanimous benevolence up to the "limit," the exact extent of which Anna Mikhailovna preferred not to know. And Marusya, when I once repeated her mother's words, said: "Reassure my mother: my limit is my diaphragm." One time I heard her voice from the next room (she was in the living room, surrounded by five or six baritones): "Oh, papa, don't come in, I'm sitting on someone's lap, and I don't even know whose it is." As she left one evening to hear some music with the red-faced aristocratic reactionary, she turned to her mother and said in my presence: "I'll run up and change my clothes. It's impolite to go to the park with a gentleman if I'm wearing a blouse that fastens only in the back." The student blushed, but the wise Anna Mikhailovna responded critically only in the literary sense:

"Your style is so tedious, Marusya."

Once, after she and I had become friends, I asked her when we were all alone, "Tell me, Marusya, is that only your 'style' or is it really true?"

She cut me off:

"I don't seduce newspapermen, so don't worry about it. And if it were true, so what?"

"There are so many of them . . ."

"Take a good look at me, is my profile any the worse for it?"

In the last analysis, it wasn't any of my business; I've yet to encounter any young woman better than Marusya. I can't forget her; it's already been alleged, between times, that in all my fictional sorties, she always appears in one way or another, her ways, the freethinking rules of her love life, her beautiful red hair. I can't help it. Once, glancing at her from the corner of their living room, I suddenly recalled the words of Enrico Ferri,[6] I don't remember about whom, that I heard during a lecture he gave in Rome: *che bella pianta umana*, "a lovely human flower." At that time I still didn't know how truly splendid she was, how much steel was hidden beneath the velvet, and how bizarre, terrible, monstrous, and sublime the end would be.

---

[6] Enrico Ferri (1856–1929) was the founder of the "positive" school of criminal sociology, a successful trial lawyer, and a distinguished orator who lectured at universities throughout Italy.

V

The World of Business

Of course, in addition to the eldest daughter and her assembled throng, there was another kind of life going on in this household; however, it seemed very much pushed into the background. Ignats Albertovich spoke about himself, his wife, and the guests who came to see them, not Marusya, in the following manner: "We're the second set . . ." Meanwhile, it turned out that in the subsequent course of events in this cheerful and distressing story the more visible roles fell to those formerly in the background; therefore they deserve to be mentioned here.

There were Nyura and Nyuta—mother and daughter; the daughter called her mother by her first name. In fact, the older woman's name was Anna, and the young lady's, Naomi—the father had insisted on a biblical name. They say that he got angry when the mother and daughter, even though unofficially, were said to be namesakes, counter to Jewish tradition; but they didn't take much notice of him. He was a bashful man, reticent, and often traveled on business. Nyura and Nyuta not only devised similar nicknames for themselves, they dressed identically, wore their hair in the same style, and were virtually inseparable. It seems they even wore lipstick—a serious offense in those days. "There's something depraved about Nyura and Nyuta," Marusya affirmed. Serezha, on the other hand, defended them as follows: "Nothing of the sort; they're simply fooling around." Moreover, this exchange of opinions was conducted in the presence of Nyura, Nyuta, me, and some other folks, and no one took offense;

26

the mother and daughter, sitting together, turned to face each other at the same angle and smiled at each other from the same side of the their mouths. The daughter was probably about twenty-five years old; she was officially considered one of Marusya's guests (one of the many young women who gathered there); her mother, of course, was counted as one of Anna Mikhailovna's guests; but the impression was that, wherever Nyura and Nyuta were, at all times they were actually visiting only each other.

Yet another person used to appear there, and it was difficult to say whose guest he was. He was introduced to me about three times before I noticed him. He was Anna Mikhailovna's distant nephew who had come from a small town on the Dniepr River already as a grown man. He was now about twenty-eight years old, no less. He referred to the hosts of the house as "uncle" and "aunt" and used the informal form of address with all the children, but this was the extent of his intimacy. He was a frequent visitor but didn't take part in any of the general amusements, games, and outings; everyone got so accustomed to his passive presence that it no longer bothered anyone, neither the hosts, nor the guests, nor even him. Once I tried to have a conversation with him but was unsuccessful; I merely took away the impression that he despised both me and the entire assembled group; in general, he was a melancholy man and not very kindhearted. He had a strange last name—Kozodoi; within the family circle he was known as Samoilo; he held the position of assistant pharmaceutical chemist and worked in a drugstore, but he pronounced the word "drugstore" in a strange, pretentious manner. Someone spread the rumor that he was in love with Marusya; but they were all in love with her, and it was Samoilo who behaved least like an admirer. He seemed never even to chat with her and replied to the infrequent words addressed to him with indifference and economy, never encouraging the continuation of any conversation. I also recall it being said that he maintained a very lofty opinion of his profession and referred to himself not as a pharmacist but as a pharmacologist. Serezha used to say "pharmaconomist."

Then I recall some other relatives, two brothers, quite old: the elder was called Abram Moiseevich, the younger, Boris Mavrikievich, and this stylistic difference in the use of the same patronymic revealed a great deal about their distinct personalities. The elder one, a wealthy old man, loved to flaunt his primitive lack of refinement. I heard all the common old sayings and witty remarks on this theme from him: "Education?" he would say, fishing out his wallet. "Here's my education." "Convictions? Here they are . . ." Or: "So, Ignats, your Marko was left back in school yet another year? You're the fool, not him. My Syoma's also a sluggard, and what do I do? Just before his exams I meet the director of his school at the club and say to him, 'Mr. Subbotsky, I'll bet you five hundred rubles my son will be left back again.' That's all it takes." Abram Moiseevich couldn't stand his own brother, Boris Mavrikievich, and annoyed him in every way imaginable; behind his back he called him that "shmendrick,"[1] and to his face in front of other people, he used his Yiddish name "Beiresh" instead of the Russian "Boris."

Boris Mavrikievich was only five years younger but was educated, or had educated himself, in a completely different manner. He spoke grammatically correct Russian and, in the presence of Russian speakers, would soften traces of his accent by trying to speak in a bass voice (they say it helps). Many years before, while taking mud baths at the Khadzhi-bei estuary, he had made the acquaintance of Danilevsky;[2] the writer presented him with a copy of his novel *The Ninth Wave;* thereafter Boris Mavrikievich always quoted lines from it related to the subject of any given conversation. Moreover, in the credit union, where he and his brother Abram Moiseevich both served as members of the board, when an obstinate shareholder appeared and created some sort of scandal at the annual meeting I myself heard, with my own ears, what Boris Mavrikievich said about him: "He's a regular Robespierre; he'll also end up being shot by some Charlotte Corday in his bath." He was built like a folk hero and had a well-developed chest; once I met him on Deribasov Street, wearing a loose gray cloak with a cape, like an officer's, and on his head, an authentic nobleman's peaked cap with a red band; the overall effect was completely "Russian Orthodox." He wore sideburns half way down his cheeks, shaved his chin every day, had dark patches on his face, and had a manicure every Friday. At the club he played cards exclusively with our civil servants—and that's when his elder brother loved to walk up and announce to all present: "Beiresh, it's time to go home. Your

[1] Yiddish. An unlucky or unfortunate person; a pipsqueak; a no-account.
[2] Grigory Danilevsky (1829–90) was a Russian writer and journalist of democratic persuasion. His novel *The Ninth Wave* (1874) was one of his more conciliatory works.

wife Fegeleh's worried about you"—although Boris was a bachelor, and no Fegeleh ever existed.

They amused me no end; but I have to confess one thing—these two, together with Ignats Albertovich, were the first to show me something that was confirmed many times afterward in my life: it's much more interesting to converse with merchants than with members of the professional intelligentsia. In my own natural circle I more often encountered men of letters and of law: after talking about books, there's nothing else to chat about, except to tell anecdotes from judicial or editorial life. But when these three "grain dealers," tired after their endless games of cards, planted their elbows on the table, and began to rehash their business affairs, I would unfailingly listen very carefully, and for an hour or so a whole new world would open before my eyes. Along thousands of roads throughout the Ukraine carts creaked and Ukrainians shouted encouragement to their oxen—they were transporting grain from all corners to the piers along our magnanimous Dniepr, and the life of some forty million people depended on how the rates on various grains were set this season by the Odessa brokers in the bulletin. And these rates in turn depended on whether or not the alarming rumors turned out to be justified, namely that the sultan wanted to block passage through the Dardanelles once again; and these rumors were a result of some events in India or Persia, and somehow or other the Emperor Franz Joseph[3] was involved, and the Empress Mariya Fyodorovna,[4] and the French premier Combes,[5] and so on and so forth. They talked about all this not vicariously, not merely as newspaper readers, but passionately, as if about the details of their own vital enterprises. Some tsars they approved of, others they cursed, but about both kinds they seemed to know more than you could ever read anywhere.

My impression was further confirmed by the fact that the youngest member of the household, Torik, became very friendly with Abram Moiseevich. In spite of his great congeniality with all sorts of people, Torik would never waste time engaging in conversation that was not

---

[3] Franz Joseph (1830–1916) was emperor of Austria (1848–1916) and king of Hungary (1867–1916).

[4] Mariya Fyodorovna (1847–1928), daughter of the Danish king Christian IX, married Tsar Alexander III in 1866.

[5] Émile Combes (1835–1921) was a French statesman who served as premier from 1902–5.

instructive in some way. The old man would sit with him for hours: although Marko and Serezha shared one room, Torik, of course, was allotted his own. Once or twice I managed to insert myself into their conversation as a third party; as a matter of fact, the old man could recount in entertaining and enjoyable terms the history of the Sevastopol campaign,[6] Abraham Lincoln's death, the Paris Commune, Skobelev,[7] Zhelyabov's trial,[8] Boulanger,[9] and various affairs pertaining to the Black Sea grain trade. But I recall that I was most impressed not by Abram Moiseevich but by Torik; more precisely, not by Torik himself, who sat still and listened, but by his room. It was crammed full of books reflecting various stages of his spiritual development. *Intimate Word, The Spring, Around the World,* and so on, including the monthly journal *God's World*—everything stashed for safe keeping, in complete sets, with book covers; the Russian classics; an entire shelf of Bibliothéque Rose and all sorts of Morceaux Choisis. Even, to my great surprise, Grätz's *History*,[10] the single book with Jewish content in the entire household. His desk was in good order; school notebooks in blue folders were stacked in a neat column, a colored ribbon hanging from each, fastened by paper seals both to the folder and to the blotter; a class schedule was posted on the wall.

Once, when the boys were not at home and Anna Mikhailovna asked me to bring her Makarov's dictionary from a shelf in Torik's room, I opened the wrong door and ended up in a room that I'd never seen before. I should have left immediately but hesitated because the furnishings and atmosphere so astonished me. It was as if it was from a different house: an iron bedstead, two plain chairs, a chipped washstand with a comb, soap, and toothbrush—nothing more. There were books lying around on the table; I couldn't make out any titles from the threshold, but I recognized them by their format—this type of lit-

---

[6] The site of battles waged during the Crimean War (1853–56) fought between Russia on the one side and England, France, Austria, and Turkey on the other.

[7] Mikhail Skobelev (1843–82) was a military officer who played a prominent role in Russia's conquest of Turkistan and in the Russo-Turkish war of 1877–78.

[8] Andrei Zhelyabov (1851–81) was a Russian revolutionary and leading member of the extremist organization People's Will. As one of the organizers of the plot to assassinate Alexander II, he was arrested, tried, condemned, and executed.

[9] Georges Boulanger (1837–91) was a French general, minister of war, and political figure who led a brief but influential movement that threatened to topple the Third Republic during the 1880s.

[10] Heinrich Grätz (1817–91) was a German-Jewish historian who published a monumental eleven-volume *History of the Jews* (1853–75).

erature was simply referred to then as "brochures";[11] a portrait of La Salle[12] tacked on to the wallpaper testified to the same cast of thought. Surprised to discover all this, I closed the door, found the dictionary in Torik's room, and was about to deliver it to Anna Mikhailovna when I met Lika in the hallway: looking straight ahead of her, she carefully moved her shoulder so I wouldn't brush against the dark-green sleeve of her school uniform, and she entered that very same room.

[11] I.e., revolutionary literature.
[12] Jean Baptiste de La Salle (1651–1719) was a French educational reformer who established schools for the poor and reformatories.

VI

Lika

The Milgroms spent their summers in Srednii Fontan. Their dacha was located near the tenth railway station: it's enough merely to mention this address to an old native of Odessa for it to summon from oblivion before the mind's eye one of the most typical scenes of our way of life at that time.

If I were commissioned to write a monograph about the tenth station, I'd begin from afar, with an extremely poetic subject. Many times before, I'd say, artists have sung the praises of the mysterious captivating power of the nocturnal silver luminary, to which, they say, the tides owe their obedience (on the Black Sea the height of the tides is approximately two inches, but that's not relevant to our topic). On the other hand, as far as I know, the attractive force of the diurnal luminary has not yet been sung; meanwhile, there's one creation of nature whose name and appearance have been borrowed from the sun, and whose worship is actively governed by it from sunrise to sunset, turning its face constantly toward Phoebus' life-giving chariot, etc., etc. From the sunflower itself the monograph would move on to its seeds and would pause to consider in detail the meaning of this custom, not from the botanical point of view, nor even the gastronomical, but rather from the social point of view. A symbol of the common people, the detractors will say with contempt; but it's not that simple. At the tenth station more than once I've seen how the most cultured representatives of humanity, women of fashion, bank directors, police captains, subscribers of "thick journals," having shaken off the fetters of civilization, carry in their left hand a cone of greased paper, and with two fingers of their right hand remove from it a kiss of the sun enclosed in a striped gray holster; their refined conversation is transformed from disorderly urban prose into measured, scanned speech with frequent caesuras, namely, pauses for spitting out the hulls. This ritual unites all classes, mistress and maid, master and servant; and there must be some special secret natural virtue in these places on the earth's surface where this social miracle occurs— where the real human state of affairs is revealed, eternally one and the same, from beneath the variety of class apparel and intellectual finery, and, when provoked by dacha sunshine, one single, common, subcutaneous, petty bourgeois personality responds from all mouths. . . . However, this was observed, primarily, after the setting of the aforementioned luminary, so I could scarcely succeed in consistently maintaining the symbolism of that monograph; but its fundamental meaning, I insist, is accurate. The most characteristic trait of this tenth station was the fact that there everyone shelled "seedies" (no one among us ever used any other word); they loved this pastime and innumerable crowds gathered every evening for the collective performance of this ritual; to its accompaniment, deals were concluded, ideas were debated, love was confessed and implored in return . . .

Once, with permission of the host and hostess, I brought along a painter whom I knew. We had in town an amicable group of southern artists; a mutual friend in those years who was a well-known poet, dramatist, and fiction writer once described this group using the phrase "the twelve cranes." A few times a month they gathered for a merry, drunken supper in a little Greek restaurant near the municipal theater, sparingly allowing a writer or two into their milieu on occasion; I was admitted through the intervention of that dramatist, "for the love of Italy," and on the condition (after an experiment), "never to write anything about paintings in my newspaper." One of them, seeing me in the theater once sitting in Anna Mikhailova's box, had asked: "Introduce me: all the members of that family have such interesting heads." I guessed that the plural was used as a diversionary tactic: he merely wanted to paint Marusya's portrait.

But, sitting there at their table, he suddenly turned to Anna Mikhailovna and declared aloud, with the skilled candor of a specialist talking about his specialty:

"What an unprecedented beauty your younger daughter is!"

We all, some ten people at the table, turned in astonishment to Lika. This idea had never occurred to any one of us; probably, it hadn't occurred to her relatives either. Lika was not only slovenly, her hair was tied up on her crown like a turnip, one that always managed to slip over onto its side; she chewed her nails, her stockings appeared badly stretched and wrinkled like an accordion from underneath her skirt that was not quite long enough. The main thing was—her entire bearing, outlandish and forbidding, took no account of the concept of attractiveness—it was just as unlikely for a person to notice whether a policeman had long eyelashes. Sergei's portrait dedicated to her began thus:

> A great thing indeed—not a tongue, but a lance:
> Well now, jab away, Lika, you shrew.

But now I could see that the artist was right. It's strange: while simple loveliness captures one's attention immediately, one must "discover" great, genuine beauty. Lika's black hair, where it wasn't disheveled, was streaked with dark blue, just like the color of sea water in the shade among rocks on a very bright, sunny day. Her eyes were also blue, at this moment with huge angry pupils, and the shadow of her lashes was cast across half her cheeks. Her forehead and nose comprised one composite feature, a Grecian profile, almost without indentation; the outline of her upper lip recalled a heraldic bow, the lower one protruded slightly in a contemptuous challenge to the offender. As a result of the insult, she hurled a spoon and I noticed her fingers, long, slender, straight, like pencils on the end of her long, narrow hand; even the bitten off ends didn't destroy the oval forms of her fingernails. Before jumping up, she shrugged her shoulders in annoyance; when she lowered them, I noticed for the first time that even though they were still childlike, they'd been designed by God from the statue of Venus in the Capitoline—two sloping sides of a lofty triangle, with no cushion at the start of her forearms. . . . But the spoon she hurled fell in such a way that a spray of borscht with sour cream splattered over the rest of us. Her chair tipped over as she jumped up; without a single word, she left the dining room.

"I gather," said the artist with a sigh, "the young lady will not agree to sit for her portrait."

Anna Mikhailovna was very embarrassed and made endless excuses; the guest, it seems, was not offended, but for some reason it was I who felt highly insulted. If it hadn't been for the fact that I'd never exchanged two words with Lika, I'd have gone to knock at her door that very evening, entered her room without even waiting for her to say, "Come in," and reprimanded her with words that could be allowed only in print. But by chance an opportunity to create such a scene was afforded me several days later.

This is how it happened: one night a large group of us was scrambling over a steep precipice in single file; I was next to last and Lika came after me. It had rained that morning and the path was loose and slippery. A stone suddenly went flying from under Lika's feet; she cried out, lost her footing, and began to slide down slowly. I left the path, bent down, and grabbed her by the arm.

"Let go of me," she said angrily.

I was really annoyed; I dragged her up like a child and just like a stubborn little child, she tried to wrench away her elbows and shoulders but still managed to regain her footing. Then I let go of her; she looked past me, breathing hard, and clearly a struggle was taking place in her soul: should she revile me or thank me? I stepped aside and allowed her to pass; she took one step, cried out a little, and sat down, rubbing her ankle.

"You don't have to wait," she hissed, without looking directly at me.

"The pain will pass and then we'll go on," I replied with genuine rage. "According to my rules of conduct, one doesn't abandon a young, underage girl who's twisted her ankle, even if she has bad manners."

A long pause ensued; we could no longer hear voices ahead of us. Our companions had crossed the edge of the precipice. My irritation lessened; I started to laugh and asked:

"What's the matter, Lika? Or, if you prefer, what's the matter, Lidiya Ignatievna? Why have you taken such a dislike to me?"

She shrugged her shoulders.

"I didn't think I had. As far as I'm concerned, you simply don't exist. Neither you, nor . . ." She was searching for words and launched into a tirade: "Nor the entire horde of worthless people around Marusya, Marko, and Mama."

"From those rejoicing, idly chatting, lead me into the camp of those languishing."[1]

"You may bare your fangs—it makes no difference to me. Moreover, in any case, it's not into the camp of the languishing."

"What then?"

She shrugged again and was silent, rubbing her foot. The half moon was shining right into her face; that artist was absolutely right.

"You know something?" I began. "Once, when you had that same expression on your face, Serezha poked me and said, 'Joan of Arc's hearing voices.'"

She turned to me suddenly and looked me right in the eye for the first time, it seems, and for the last time in all our acquaintance; unintentionally I recalled the words, "When she looks at you, it's as though she's giving you a ruble." The "gift" was not in the sense of affection or kindness; her look was strange and had no relation to me whatsoever; but a small window was opening into an unfamiliar, dark garden. In spite of the darkness, one had to acknowledge that this garden was huge.

"You helped me out," she said in a different tone, calmly and courteously. "I snapped at you unjustly. To make up for it I will answer you seriously this time, although in general, you and I really have nothing to talk about and no reason to converse. Serezha's right, if you like, 'hearing voices.' I hear them all the time from all sides; they whisper or shout one and same thing, one word."

I waited to hear that word, but obviously she found it hard to say it. I tried to help:

"'Bread'? 'Help'?"

She shook her head, without averting her commanding blue eyes.

"Even for a young lady with bad manners it's hard to repeat: 'Scum.'"

Strange to say, I was not jolted by this word (although even now I hesitated before committing these four letters to paper): the crude, vulgar word resounded from the depths of that unfamiliar garden not as a curse, but with some archaic meaning, as if she'd used the

[1] A partial quotation from a popular lyric poem by the civic poet Nikolai Nekrasov (1821–77) titled "Knight for an Hour" (1862). The full stanza reads: "From those rejoicing, idly prattling, / Staining their hands in blood, / Lead me into the camp of those languishing / For the great cause of love!" The knight is a champion of revolution and reform but is plagued by self-recrimination.

language of some Old Testament hermits, or some forgotten, irate chapter of the Bible. Now we looked each other in the eye without mockery on my side and without challenge on hers, seriously and tensely, two sworn enemies for whom the time had come to reach a final understanding.

"Who would that be?"

"Everyone and no one. People in general. The totality. You thought my voices were crying, 'Bread!' or begging, 'Help'? You were doing me a great honor but one I don't deserve: I know about famine, and Siberia, and all the horrors, but I don't pity anyone and won't save anyone, least of all in the camp of those languishing."

"Understood: then into the camp of the destroyers or incendiaries?"

"If I'm up to it, yes."

"Alone, without comrades?"

"I'll seek out comrades when I'm stronger."

"Is that how you find them—judging each person you meet in advance without interrogation?"

"Not true: I interrogate each one immediately, only you can't hear it. I can read a stranger at once."

She thought for a while intensely, and then said:

"It's difficult to define, but perhaps the criteria are these: there are some people with white memory and others with black. The former are those who recall best of all the good things in life and, as a result, are happy. . . . Marusya, for example. While the unforgiving note only the dark things in life: for them 'good' is wiped off the slate after an hour or so, and it was never all that 'good.' In each person I can surmise whether he has a black memory or white; there's no reason to interrogate them. I can walk now; I'll lean on you and up above I'll say 'Thank you,' on one condition—how best to put it?"

I helped her:

"Rest assured, I promise to keep a mile away from you."

VII

Marko

Before the departure for the dacha an important event occurred—
Marko received, at long last, his high school diploma. Among those
who graduated that year were several incorrigible lads who'd been
left back along with him; consequently, their emancipation from the
yoke of the gymnasium was celebrated with extraordinary fanfare.
My colleague Shtrok, king of police reporting in Odessa and the
south of Russia, brought into the newsroom a rapturous description
of this bacchanalia; it was not for publication, of course, but simply
on principle, so that no one at the paper would forget that Shtrok
knew absolutely everything. The entire group of graduating students
had appeared at the Severnaya, the most famous café chantant in
town, where just the day before, still students, they'd been strictly
forbidden to enter; they created such an uproar there that the policeman on duty (even though for these June exploits of graduates, just
as for the riotous conduct of new recruits, the police traditionally
looked the other way) was unable to restrain himself and threatened
to haul them off to the station; at this, the oldest of those students
made, according to Shtrok's account, a reply worthy of recording in
the history books, and since then, well known in all chronicles of
Black Sea Enlightenment:

"Excuse me, Mr. Policeman—such joy comes only once in sixteen
years!"

Moved by this impressive accomplishment, the policeman yielded.

After this I remember Marko wearing the blue cap of a university student on his head; I don't recall whether underneath the cap he was wearing a student's single-breasted summer jacket or simply a jacket, that is, whether he was accepted immediately into the university through a loophole in the quota system. It's curious: my memory has retained the biography of Marko's sisters and brothers, inasmuch as it occurred within my own field of vision or knowledge, as well as their appearance, including even the attractive but peculiar hairstyles and dress of that decade; but Marko himself I have forgotten completely. Neither his height, nor the shape of his nose, nor his slovenliness, sung by Serezha. When I try very hard to summon his image to mind, I see all sorts of other people—sometimes I even know them by name, sometimes not, but I know it's not him. I know that by his eyes, the single detail of his face that I can describe—not their color, but their shape and expression. They were round and open wide, kind and affectionate, and (if one can say it without giving offense) importunate: the hungry look of a man always ready not simply to ask but really to question, and then to believe and to be surprised, even astonished, at every reply he received.

The first time we had a heart-to-heart chat he was still a student at the gymnasium: he sat down next to me somewhere or other, either at their own house or when we were visiting.

"Would it burden you excessively if I asked you to devote an evening to me alone sometime? An entire evening?"

"It's possible," I said. "Allow me to ask what it would be about?"

"I need," he replied, peering at me through his round eyes, "to ask you about something: what is it precisely that Nietzsche wants?" And then he explained at once: "Because, you see, I am a confirmed Nietzschean."

I was unable to refrain from making an ironic observation:

"Something doesn't quite fit. Serezha told me a while ago that you were a Nietzschean; but the first prerequisite would be to know what Nietzsche wants . . ."

He wasn't flustered in the least—quite the contrary; he explained very sincerely and, in his own way, logically:

"I've tried to read him; I have almost everything that's been published in Russian; I'll show you, if you like. In general, you see, I read a great deal; but I was designed in a strange way—if I read something on my own, I can never understand the main point, not only in philosophy, but also in poetry and fiction. I always require a guide who points a finger and says, 'There it is!' Then everything becomes clear to me at once."

He hesitated a little and added:

"My family, you see, and my friends, too, think I'm simply a fool. I don't believe that; but one thing is true—I'm not someone who can use his own mind to think. You see, I'm one of those who's always supposed to listen."

This confession disarmed and even intrigued me; but I asked one more question:

"Then how do you know you're a Nietzschean?"

"Does one have to know the Bible by heart to be devout? I heard the opposite somewhere—in olden days Catholics actually forbade laymen to read the Gospel without the help of a priest—so they didn't fall into error."

I afforded him an evening—it wasn't difficult. The rage for Nietzsche had only just arrived in Russia; three reports about him with ensuing debates had already occurred in our literary circle. I had his books: I can't guarantee that all the pages had been slit, but I had no trouble retelling it in my own words. Marko really did know how to "listen"; even though at first I'd shared the view of him quoted above held by his family and friends, I soon began to doubt that it was entirely true. If he was a fool, then he wasn't a simple one, but sui generis.

As a matter of fact, his family maintained the same qualified view, or at least his father did. Ignats Albertovich once delivered something of a lecture on this theme. It began, I recall, when Marko had made a mess of something somewhere; his father was displeased, while Serezha said to his brother in his older, deeper voice:

"Marko, Marko, what will become of you? Just think—at your age Alexander the Great was already almost twenty years old!"

Afterwards Ignats Albertovich and I were left alone and he suddenly asked:

"Have you ever given any thought to the various categories of fools that exist?"

He then delivered a lecture, warning me in advance that the classification was not his own but borrowed in part from his favorite German-Jewish authors, and in part from folklore of the Volhynia[1] ghetto

---

[1] Located in northwestern Ukraine, Volhynia is one of the oldest Slavic settlements in Europe and was long disputed territory among Poland, Lithuania, and Russia.

where he was born. Fools, for example, come in two varieties, summer or winter. You're sitting at home during the winter, there's a blizzard outside, everything creaks and bangs: you hear someone knocking at your door; you're not sure—maybe it's just the wind. Finally, you say, "Come in." Someone bursts into the entrance hall, so completely wrapped up, you can't tell if it's a man or a woman. The person fusses for a long time, unwraps his hood, extricates himself from his felt boots—and only then, at long last, do you recognize him: before you stands a fool. That's a winter fool. A summer fool, on the other hand, flits in lightly clad and you can tell immediately who it is. Or, one can classify fools according to another characteristic, passive or active. The former sits in a corner and doesn't meddle in other peoples' affairs. This type is usually easy to live with and sometimes even successful in a career; on the other hand, the latter is depressingly disagreeable.

"But that's insufficient," he concluded. "I feel that a third method of classification is necessary; let's say—according to footwear: one category is born with leaden soles on their feet and no force whatsoever will ever move them from the spot. The other kind, on the contrary, wears sandals with wings, in the style of Mercury . . . or Marko, perhaps?"

I observed Marko once again during the New Year's celebration at a student ball in the "morgue." The ball always took place in the splendid palace of the stock exchange (none of my fellow-countrymen would be surprised at my use of the word "palace," and I have no intention of explaining it to foreigners). One of the side rooms was referred to as the "morgue" in such instances; only a select public was allowed, select in the sense of having "progressive" aspirations; they began admitting people only after one o'clock in the morning. They imbibed there rather considerably; by morning some had even come close to consuming a truly lethal dose of alcohol; but the principal form of intoxication there was ideological and rhetorical. Although they allowed civilians in, the great majority of the crowd, of course, consisted of students. There was a table of Marxists and one of populists, tables of Poles, Georgians, Armenians (Zionists and Bundists[2] appeared several years later; I don't recall them from the earliest

---

[2] The Bund was a Jewish socialist political movement founded in Vilnius in 1897. It called for the abolition of discrimination against all Jews.

years). At the center table department and course "elders" presided imposingly, while the majority who'd yet to define themselves and didn't belong to any faction, huddled close by. At each table speeches were delivered and songs were sung; during the first few hours orators spoke from their seats; toward morning they climbed onto tables; even closer to dawn—they preached from one and the same table, both at it and on top of it, while the rest of the room was singing. Around that time the most popular professors tactfully disappeared, but at the start of the evening they, too, took a peripatetic role in the festivities, moving from table to table with short improvisations from the unwritten anthology of table grandiloquence. "Comrade students: this champagne is too expensive for me to toast your health, even more so for you to toast mine. Let's drink to something nobler— to that for which we all wait year after year: this year may it finally come to pass . . ." "Colleagues, among us there is a publicist, a toiler among enslaved words: let's raise our glasses in the hope that words may one day become free . . ."

That evening they let even Marko in—though I don't recall whether he was already a student at the time. He entered indecisively, not knowing which group to join; an acquaintance called him over to their table where a crowd of black-haired students from the Caucasus was standing and sitting—from a distance it was hard to discern their nationalities—and there he remained for the entire evening. When I glanced over at him from time to time, I could see that he felt completely at ease with them: he sang, waved his arms, shouted, encouraged the speakers, even though most of them, it seems, were speaking their native language.

When you yourself drink only a little, it's curious and disheartening to observe how such a raucous evening ends. Gradually the muscles on green and purple faces go wooden, their eyes become glassy, their words, swaying as if on struts, collide in a deadly manner; the tables are drenched, men's collars are crumpled, the ends of their cuffs, soiled; on those wearing tails, their dickeys are crushed; in general, everything has become filthy; the unnoticed cleaning woman stands in the doorway with her bucket and mop. . . . It's astonishing, but in my opinion, one final "Gaudeamus," the most consolatory song on earth, was very appropriate in that morgue.

Marko accompanied me home; he hadn't drunk that much either, but he was intoxicated from spiritual wine, especially from Georgia.

He hummed a refrain and some Georgian words; never once having seen the Caucasus, he described the Georgian Military Highway and Tbilisi for two blocks straight; he muttered something or other about Princess Tamara and the poet Rustavelli. . . . Lermontov[3] writes, "the timid Georgians fled"—what aspersions to cast on such a chivalrous tribe! Marko already knew everything about the Georgian movement, knew the differences between various mountain tribes, and had even mastered their language—he beckoned the homeless dog on the corner, calling "*Modi ak*," then drove it away, crying "*Tsadi!*" (I can't vouch for the accuracy of these phrases; this is how I recall them); and he concluded with a sigh from the depths of his soul:

"It's not fair: why can't anyone simply get up and declare himself to be a Georgian?"

I laughed:

"Marko, there's a Zionist doctor here who has a maid named Gapka; once she served tea to a gathering at his house. Afterwards the doctor's wife asked her, 'How did you like it?' Gapka replied in a reverent tone of submission to fate: 'Well, ma'am, I think we should all go off to Palestine.'"

Marko was offended; he felt it wasn't quite the same thing; besides, Gapka's story was so old he'd already heard it ten times.

"By the way, Marko," I said yawning, "if you're looking for a nation, why not team up with the Zionists?"

He opened his round eyes and stared at me, filled with amazement; it was clear from his glance that even as a joke, at five o'clock in the morning, a normal person couldn't possibly agree to such an immense absurdity.

———

All five children, either directly or in passing, have now been introduced to the reader; I can move on to the story of what actually happened to them.

---

[3] Mikhail Lermontov (1814–41) was a major nineteenth-century Russian poet and novelist.

—✴— VIII —✴—

My Porter

Months passed. I came and went, often losing sight of the Milgrom family for awhile. From time to time someone fired a shot at a governor or assassinated a minister; it's astonishing the amount of unmitigated joy with which this kind of news was received by our entire society: such unanimity in an analogous situation would now be inconceivable—besides, a fully analogous condition simply doesn't exist anywhere else. But, for the purposes of our story, only one aspect of these events is noteworthy: that the "springtime"—from the viewpoint of outside observers such as I was, at first so cheerful, cloudless, and gentle—gradually began to assume a harsher, more brutal character. From the north we received news of punitive raids on entire provinces; it was already clear that the government structure would not succeed in being altered by means of the simple "frame of mind" of progressive society or by individual bullets—that our "springtime" would turn out to be a mass tragedy; however, there was one thing we still didn't understand—this tragedy would be long and drawn out. Consequently, the daily life of our city, recently so easy and carefree, was changing before our very eyes.

I observed this firsthand in the personal evolution of one modest citizen: he was the porter in our building. His name was Khoma and he was a black-bearded peasant from the province of Kherson. I'd lived in that house for a long time and had maintained excellent relations with him. At night, when I rang the bell at the gate, Khoma would emerge from his underground den, "lower the gangplank," that is, open the gate, and, after receiving a ten-kopeck tip, would politely, no matter how sleepy he was, nod his shaggy head and say, "Merci, sir." If, upon entering the kitchen, a member of the household came upon him engaged in some physical contact with our pretty maid Motrya, he would quickly withdraw, grab his cap, and with some embarrassment assure us that his presence could be explained by his concern for our interests—for example, he was checking to see whether the flue was blocked or the damper was broken. In a word, he was a normal member of the working class; he lived his life, let others live theirs, and made no claims for the eminence of his commanding position.

But gradually a change in his psychology became noticeable. Motrya, I recall, was the first one to observe it. One day there wasn't enough firewood: she was told, as usual, to ask the porter to bring up an armful from the cellar. She ran out into the courtyard and came back to report:

"Foma Gavrilych's nowhere to be found: he's gone out."

I didn't even grasp at once about whom she was talking; her use of a past participle instead of the simple past tense particularly struck me. Motrya, who'd worked for a general before she came to us, observed these subtle differences in verb forms and always distinguished between the laundress who "went out" and the mistress who'd "gone out." I had the vague feeling that some process of elevation was occurring in our porter's social standing.

After this episode I myself began to detect alarming signs. At night I had to stand at the gate, stamping my frozen feet, waiting five or even ten minutes. After receiving his usual ten-kopeck tip, Khoma would now examine the coin closely in the dim light of the gateway with an expression clearly indicating that this tradition was not necessarily restrictive. He began to abbreviate his statement of gratitude: from "Merci, sir," simply to Russian—not merely his omission of title but the switch from French to Russian seemed significant. Once, having made me wait almost half an hour in the cold, he even made a nasty comment: "This, sir, is no church. No need to keep ringing the bells!" And the next time, shaking his head, he remarked in an edifying manner. "You're out late. It's bad for your health!"

The result was that, being of a timid nature, I rang only once and then waited obediently; I increased the amount of my tip from ten to fifteen kopecks; and I myself, handing over the coin, would say,

"Thank you," while in reply Khoma would mutter something incomprehensible, sometimes nothing at all. But that's not the crux of the matter: more characteristic of the fever spreading through the empire (the entire empire was reflected in my porter, like the sun in a single drop of water) was the fact that with every passing week Khoma was becoming a more important part of my life. I felt his presence all the time, like a false tooth not properly inserted by a dentist. He'd long since stopped expressing sympathy when I entertained a group of guests: once he rang at eleven thirty at night and asked Motrya if there were some sort of meeting going on, because they hadn't sent him out for beer and he didn't hear any of the usual singing. Another time he collected my mail from the letter carrier and remarked pointedly while handing over my packet:

"You read foreign newspapers?"

I shared this remark with my friends: they all confirmed it. The class of porters was rising swiftly in standing and influence, being transformed into an important instrument of state power. Citizens thought they were storming the bastions of autocracy; in fact, the authorities had given the order to lay siege to fortresses—millions of them, each house, and the vanguard of the advancing army was already sitting in their cellar trenches on this side of the gate.

The nocturnal animation on the streets was also interesting. In spite of all our urban arrogance, we'd grown accustomed to the fact that at two o'clock in the morning, when one was returning home from friendly socializing, there was no one out on the street; and we used to placate our municipal pride by citing the example of Vienna where people also went to bed early. But now, almost every night I'd come upon a silent procession somewhere: the police captain led the way, followed by his entire retinue—accompanied by some other Khoma, or my very own, apprised in advance of a prearranged search; he had waited, trying not to fall asleep, for the commanding bell, and had already enlisted his friend in the role of second witness.

On the other hand, one could see and hear that the besieged were also preparing for an assault. One could hear how throughout the town people whispered that a "demonstration" was imminent. No one knew exactly what a demonstration was—no one had ever seen one, nor had anyone's grandfather; precisely for that reason it seemed that a group of one hundred young men and women marching along Deribasov Street carrying a red banner at their head would constitute a blow of unbelievable force to the enemy, as a result of which both palaces and dungeons would start to shake. Several times popular rumors had even named the exact month and date of the Sunday when a bomb would explode, for the time being, however, inopportunely. But it was already clear who the participants of this menacing march from Cathedral Square to the corner of Richelieu Street would be: they attracted one's attention at every step, both young men and women, as if they'd previously donned some special uniform.

As a matter of fact, it was a uniform: not in the sense of cut and color but in the sense of a general style. I've already spoken about the external students; now, in even greater number, their spiritual female companions began to appear. Serezha was the first to introduce into our milieu a collective name that (he swore) even their own comrades used behind their backs, although for a long time I suspected that he'd come up with the nickname himself: "draglers" from the word "bedraggled," a word that has yet to be included in the latest edition of Dal's *Dictionary*.[1] A man's straw hat shaped like a plate, always badly fastened to their hair and leaning over to one side; moreover, the person wearing the hat would from time to time nudge it back into position with an index finger; a blouse cut in what was then called the English style, with a high turned-down collar and a necktie held by a ring—but often without a tie or a ring; a skirt with buttons on the side, but always missing at least one; shoes with worn out laces, always fastened on the wrong hooks and covered with a week's dust from the Black Sea steppes; and above it all, wire-rimmed glasses and, almost always, the pink sign of a chronic runny nose.

"And don't you laugh," a friend and former classmate said to me; he was subsequently hanged near St. Petersburg at Fox Nose. "You merely change their clothes mentally and you'll see who they really are—daughters of the biblical Judith."[2]

"Judith?" cried Serezha, bursting into laughter, when I repeated this to him. "Look at the way they walk. A person's gait is the main thing: you can't disguise it. Judith walked, whereas these girls run."

"Run"—the word is very much to the point. They themselves al-

---

[1] The four volume *Reasoned Dictionary of the Living Russian Language* (1863–66) compiled by the Russian writer and scholar Vladimir Dal' (1801–72).

[2] In the book of Judith, a work of the Apocrypha, Judith is a Jewish widow of great beauty and devotion who enters the enemy camp, gains the favor of the Assyrian general Holofernes, and then murders him, thus guaranteeing a Jewish victory.

ways had it on the tips of their tongues. It's as if all other speeds and means of transportation had fallen into disuse: "Deliver a note? I'll run and do it." "I ran over to see Osya, but he wasn't home." Even in rare moments of luxury: "Tonight *The Carter Genshel* is playing at the theater; let's run over and see it."

In any case, that friend of mine was wrong about one thing: I wasn't laughing; I was alarmed. One morning in a blind alley of the park, behind the gully that our local lads referred to as the Sea of Azov, I caught a distant glimpse of one of Judith's daughters: she was heading toward me together with a young man wearing a Russian shirt and, as they passed, neither looked at me; they merely lowered their voices. She had neither glasses nor a runny nose, and her gait was different, but all the rest was there: a hat like a plate, worn-out shoelaces, skipped-over hooks on dusty shoes; and I recognized Lika.

—⁓—

Our springtime began to be spoiled in one other sense. In describing the night in the "morgue" at the students' ball where Marko almost turned into a Georgian, I forgot to mention one speech. A second-year student named Ivanov had delivered it; I knew him, having met him on occasion in Jewish households—he was the usual sort of Ivanov, the seventh or the twenty-fifth, relaxed, obliging, inconspicuous, from whom no one could ever expect any spark, least of all, a speech. He delivered his remarks early in the evening, while still sober; I didn't hear the beginning of his speech or what had immediately preceded it, but it contained the following:

"If you please, dear colleagues, it's impossible to accuse us of hostility to a certain nationality; even if this nationality lacks a homeland and, as a result, doesn't perceive the concept of 'homeland'[3] the way we do—that's still not a sin. But it's a different matter altogether if this nationality is the bearer of ideas that . . ."

I recall being surprised that in the "morgue," the age-old kingdom of the unified and enduring *Marseillaise*, such utterances had become acceptable, without approving applause, but also without causing a scandal. At that time I still couldn't foresee that, had this occurred one year later, it would already have been received as a sympathetic response.

[3] An indication of the resurgence of anti-Semitism in Odessa and the emergence of a Zionist movement.

—ᨖ— IX —ᨖ—

The Alien

I was beginning a career in public service: Secretary in the Temporary Administration of the Society of Sanatorium Colonies and Other Hygienic-Dietary Institutions for the Treatment and Education of Students Suffering from Bad Health from the Indigent Jewish Population in the City of Odessa and its Surrounding Areas. It's true: that's really what my position was called; in my youth for a while I was able to say the entire title in one breath. This society also emerged in part with a seditious design: under the guise of "hygienic-dietary institutions" one could organize a program of gymnastics and, under the guise of gymnastics, self-defense. People in the south were beginning to say that this would soon come in handy. Meanwhile, the administration proposed that I find several volunteers to visit the poor—to record who was in need of free coal, or, perhaps, free matzo, I don't recall. I conveyed all this to Anna Mikhailovna's older children. Marko signed up (then he didn't go, forgot all about it, and was very apologetic); Lika, without looking up from her brochure or taking her fingers out of her mouth, shook her head no; Marusya said, "I'll go with you, alright?"

There was nothing unexpected in her offer: I already knew that she had a practical, caring streak in her nature. It was she who, when Samoilo arrived from his village, spent a year and a half helping him prepare for the examination for a career as a pharmacist, and she was still a young girl at the time; even now she was assisting the cook's niece with her studies, very methodically. When one of her "sight-

49

seers" fell ill, someone who had no family members in Odessa, she would visit him three times a day, make sure he took his medicine, change his compresses, even though his time in her good graces (I know this from her) had long since ended. She even knew how to prepare an acceptable breakfast and how to make major alterations to a blouse.

When I called for her on the appointed day, I met Samoilo in the hallway just as he was leaving. He was troubled, biting his lip, even muttering indistinctly. He wanted to ask me something but didn't. I found Marusya and her mother in the living room; they were both silent in the way that people are right after they've had a quarrel. Marusya was obviously pleased that she could now leave; along the way in the carriage she was withdrawn and also bit her lip.

"What's the matter, Marusya? Who offended whom?"

"You have an excellent opportunity to remain silent," she said maliciously. "I urge you to use it."

I obeyed.

———

I recall one house, it might have been Roniker's, it seems, in the district that she and I were supposed to visit. It had a feature I hadn't encountered before: a two-story cellar. The windows of both stories overlooked a trench, of course; but inside behind the windows there was a corridor running the whole length of the façade and the rooms were illuminated only from this corridor. I'm incapable of describing poverty, just as I could never engage in tearing the wings and legs off a fly, or in any slow torture in general. I recall that one banal thought kept nagging me persistently: had a little slip of the good Lord's pen in the book of reckoning occurred when you were about to be born, or had He second thoughts at the last minute and crossed something out and wrote something else beneath—you might be living here today, in this dismal cellar, envying the boys upstairs, and they would be the ones "putting on airs." I was ashamed of my coat, for the fact that before this I'd sat for an hour at a Greek café on Krasnyi Lane drinking coffee and enjoying baklava and spent twenty-five kopecks, their budget for an entire day. And, as always happens when one feels guilty, I passed through these lairs frowning, spoke with the inhabitants in a stern, official voice, and replied dryly to their requests: "We'll try. We'll see. I can't make any promises."

On the other hand, Marusya—there's no other word for it—was instantly exhilarated. In the first room she went up to the cradle fashioned out of a drawer; I followed her. There, under scraps the color of an old sack lay a gray child; two wrinkles, deep as crevices, extended from the ends of his lips to his nostrils, and he had dark circles under his eyes. When Marusya bent over him, all of a sudden his gray face became painfully distorted, crevices stretched to his eyes, crimson gums appeared in his mouth, and his tiny chin became pointed, like a dead man's. His mother was standing right there; she was delighted and said in Yiddish, which I translated for Marusya:

"Just look at those sweet little eyes, Miss: he's laughing."

All the children there laughed with Marusya; they came running, toddling, climbing onto her all at once, as if she were some old friend they'd been waiting for all morning. I left her somewhere on a stool with a crowd around her and finished signing people up by myself, all the while overhearing from the other room the commotion, noise, chirping, and bursts of children's laughter, as if it weren't a cellar at all, as if there really were green meadows on earth, the smell of lilac, and sunshine overhead . . .

"I didn't know," I said, when the visit ended, "that you were such a good governess."

There was not a trace left of her earlier anxiety; she replied cheerfully:

"Children come to me; I always approach them on the street—nannies often get frightened. Only a few days ago mama asked me not to touch any Russian children, or else people might think I'm giving them fruit-drops laced with arsenic: she read in the newspaper that there was such a case somewhere in Bessarabia."

We climbed into the carriage again; according to the custom of the time, I had my arm around her waist. It was twilight; she suddenly pulled the arm that was around her tighter, pressed closer to me, turned her face toward mine, and whispered:

"Would you like to get away from all these Jews? Both rich and poor? Come with me tonight to the Runitskys'; Aleksei Dmitrievich asked me to bring you along—we're the only two he's not afraid of. Are you afraid of him?"

"Hmm . . . a little," I confessed honestly, and suddenly it dawned on me to ask, "Hey, Marusya—was it because of him that the tragedy today ensued with your mother? There was some tragedy, that's clear: all through your apartment it smelled of Aeschylus, Sophocles, and Euripides."

She nodded her head fervently in confirmation:

"Sparks were flying. By the way, Samoilo arrived and Mama even requested his assistance!"

"I never suspected there was such disarray on the upper level of the parents. . . . Oh, Mariya: is there any danger you'll be converted to Christianity and—how can I say it—be recruited into the commanding ranks of the Volunteer Navy?"

She looked at me with the same fervor, her face very close to mine; as she laughed, her teeth shone in the light of the street lamps that had just been lit.

"Oh, no, Mama isn't afraid of that; she's clever and knows everything."

"What's 'everything'? Don't scare me."

"Everything that will happen to me. And she knows, in particular, that I won't be converted and won't marry a sailor in the Volunteer Navy."

"Then what's she afraid of?"

"Mama is, essentially, a very conservative person: she likes it best when there's established order in all things."

"Established order? When we're talking about you, Marusya? My child, muddle's the very name of your existence, not established order."

"That means that there must be some system in the muddle, without unexpected or new elements. Besides, all this is none of your business. But will you come with me to the Runitskys'?"

I'd already seen this Runitsky at the Milgroms' house several times separated by large intervals as a result of his ship's sailings (I don't recall his rank, something below captain, of course—he wasn't even thirty years old—but it was already significant). Even to me he appeared as an unexpected element in their setting. Russian guests were not, of course, an unknown occurrence in our homes, although they were encountered infrequently and acclimatized with difficulty: but they were usually lawyers, doctors, merchants, students—in some sense, recognizable, our own people. No one had ever seen a seaman, except on deck. Marusya had attended the Mariinsky Gymnasium with one of the Runitsky girls; then both families spent a

summer at their dachas not far from each other when Aleksei Dmitrievich was on leave; there, it seems, he would take Marusya on boat
rides together with his sisters; but even this didn't manage to "ground"
him. His sisters rarely visited Marusya, and in general dacha friend-
ships don't produce winter relationships among people of such different, alien circles. He sensed this and was obviously timid among
us; Marusya would try to involve him in conversation, and he honestly tried to adjust to the rhythm, but nothing came of it. All of us
also felt a bit awkward around him, as if he weren't a guest as we were
but an observer. He wasn't a bad piano player and felt as if a great
weight had been lifted from his shoulders whenever Marusya asked
him to play: at least he didn't have to talk; and, at the same time, he
could entertain the group, as he should, according to the rules of
decorum. After seeing him there the first time, I thought, "He'll never
come again." But when he returned from Vladivostok, he came again
and again.

However, Marusya and I spent a wonderful evening at their house.
The father had passed away, but in his lifetime he'd been an active
member of the Duma during the splendid Novoselsky period.[1] Before then it seems, he'd been a member of the zemstvo; this was felt
in the climate of the family (back then, of course, they didn't use the
word "climate," but it's appropriate.) Back further still, there was a
country estate, a garden with a pond, old paths lined with trees, lin-
den or whatever they were supposed to be; God knows how many
generations of peace, respect, comfort, and gracious hospitality;
guests came from afar and stayed overnight, and there was plenty of
room for everyone. . . . Culture? I wouldn't have chosen that word at
the time—in my own life it was too closely tied to education or,
maybe, erudition. The mother, a graduate of Smolnyi Institute,[2] had
never heard of Anatole France, and her daughters referred to the baritone Giraldoni[3] as "sweetie." Aleksei Dmitrievich was a little weak
in spelling, even though (he said it was "because") he had studied in
St. Petersburg at an impressive lycée, at the insistence of some high-

---

[1] Nikolai Novoselsky (1825–1902) served as chairman of the Odessa municipal
Duma from 1867–78.
[2] A prestigious private school in St. Petersburg established in 1806 to educate
young women of the nobility.
[3] Leone Giraldoni (1824–97) was an Italian-French operatic baritone who taught
at the Moscow Conservatory.

ranking uncle. It was only while sitting in their house that I could appreciate how much exhilarating brilliance there was in our own everyday conversation at Marusya's house—and I suddenly felt how very nice and cozy it was when this brilliance was lacking. They drank tea—and talked about tea; they played the piano—and talked about the sweetie Giraldoni, but the younger sister much preferred Sammarco;[4] Aleksei Dmitrievich talked about Singapore, how they rode around in rickshaws, and the mother talked about her time at the Institute some thirty years ago; everything lacked brilliance; they used everyday, commonplace words, not long, not short, not witty, not moving—simply nice words; unadorned, ancestral thoughts, a sweet infusion of the soul, Galakhov's anthology[5] . . . we spent a wonderful evening.

"Did you enjoy yourself?" Marusya inquired craftily as I escorted her home.

A few days later Anna Mikhailovna began a conversation with me about Runitsky; we'd become good friends by then; she started it, and with great agitation.

"He's not like one of your gang. With them everything's like water off a duck's back. But he takes things seriously. Didn't you notice it yourself after spending a whole evening there with him and Marusya?"

"I really didn't notice, or else I'm not very observant or my pince-nez isn't very discerning."

"I'm telling you: he's starting to fall in love with her, for real, as in a Turgenev novel."

"The main thing is Marusya; you once told me yourself that you have no fears on her account."

"I may have said that, but then she was surrounded by her own kind. I don't know how to reckon with such a naval bushman. What if he's not the sort to go only so far and no farther, and then to be told 'bye-bye,' that's that? I'm afraid: I smell not fireworks but dynamite."

"Well, do you think as a result of this onslaught that she'll give in unexpectedly and marry him?"

"She'll get married, but not to him. You're talking nonsense. But

---

[4] Mario Sammarco (1873–1930) was an Italian operatic baritone who performed in Russia.

[5] Aleksei Galakhov (1807–92) was the editor of several popular anthologies of Russian literature and history.

she's also excited in an unusual way. . . . I'm scared; I wish he'd go away to his island of Sakhalin and stay there forever."

"May I ask you something?"

"Yes."

"Are you afraid that Marusya . . . will forget her limits?"

We'd already become very close; she spoke with me often and at length about her children, sharing her anxiety about Lika and the hopeless Marko. My question couldn't shock her. She thought a bit.

"That? That never occurred to me. No, I don't think so. It doesn't look like that. I don't know what trouble will befall us, but something will happen. . . . In a word, let's leave this topic; besides, it can't help."

She stood up and went over to straighten the pillows on the sofa; then she stopped suddenly and turned to face me.

"Marry him? You're talking nonsense. I've known for a long time who Marusya will marry, and so does she. And you'd know, too, if God had given you a better pince-nez."

X

Along Deribasov Street

This episode occurred on Deribasov Street, about two years after the beginning of our story.

At that time our editorial office was located at the upper end of the street, in the passageway next to Cathedral Square. Every day on my way to work would I walk the entire length of the street, the queen of streets in the whole world. It's impossible to prove by argument why it was the queen of streets: almost all the houses along both sides, as I recall, had two stories; the architecture was, for the most part, unexceptional, without any important monuments. But such things are not proven by argument; every honorific is a mirage—once it's attached and holds without coming unstuck, the bearer is considered worthy of it, and that's that. At least in those years, I, for one, could never simply pass along Deribasov Street as if it were the most natural thing in the world, without failing to realize where I was: as soon as my foot touched that sacred ground, I was immediately overcome with an awareness, as if some special event had transpired or some privilege had been bestowed on me. I straightened up involuntarily and checked to see if my necktie had come loose; I'm sure I wasn't the only one who did so.

The queen's maids of honor, the intersecting streets along the path of my pilgrimage, each had their own faces. I usually began my walk from the lower end, the corner of Pushkin Street, an important street, majestically sleepy, with no shops on that block; for some reason even the large hotel on the corner didn't stick out, didn't create a commotion; once, having lied and told others that I was going out of town, I spent a whole month in that hotel, dining on the terrace, and not one acquaintance ever walked by. I don't know who inhabited the splendid houses nearby, but it seemed that grand, classical antiquity was living out its last days on this section of Pushkin Street, where grain traders were still called merchants and mixed both Greek and Italian phrases into their conversations.

The next corner was Richelieu Street; the first thing that announced its special face were the tables of the moneychangers, right there on the sidewalks under the acacias. One could marvel at all the gold under glass on these tables and at the banknotes from all planets in the solar system; the street-side banker with his black mustache, sitting on a wicker chair, wearing a bowler hat or a felt hat perched on the back of his head, would tear himself away from his foreign newspaper and serve you or cheat you swiftly, speaking any language imaginable. Thus have you made the acquaintance of the upper thoroughfare of Black Sea trade. As I crossed it, I'd always cast an envious glance to the left, where from both sides glittered gilded signs of banking offices, unattainable stores, and Olympian barbershops where they could shave a man's face to an azure tint.

It was here, one wintry day at about four o'clock in the afternoon, that I witnessed a strange scene: the policeman on duty, directing carriage traffic at this crucial intersection, had gone off somewhere for a minute or so; his place was suddenly taken by two young men, one wearing a student's overcoat, the other, a skillfully sewn sheepskin jacket and a tall Caucasian fur cap. Staggering and clumsily leaning against each other, before the eyes of the astonished population, they headed for the middle of the intersection; conscientiously and thoughtfully, with keen eyes, they determined the exact midpoint, moved a little to the right, then a little back, until they wound up in the geometrical center; they bowed to each other politely and with great dignity, turned away from each other, leaned their backs up against each other for support, and each, placing two fingers in his mouth, filled the surroundings with a whistle of indescribable purity and power. Hearing the familiar signal, all carriages and cabs from the north, south, east, and west automatically slowed their pace, cursing audibly, and searching for the policeman who'd issued such a peremptory sound. Seeing in his place this inexplicable dyad, they were all taken aback and stopped completely. The young man in the fur cap, although somewhat unsteady in his articulation, roared in an awesome bass voice with a great range, "Come on, you bums, why'd you stop?" And, in fact, they began moving again according to his command; both friends, gesticulating with their white gloves, started directing traffic any which way they liked. The bass voice coming from under the fur cap seemed somewhat familiar; but by now the policeman came rushing toward them from wherever he'd been, his fierce eyes bulging, obviously prepared to drag them both away and punish them—when suddenly, some five paces away from these usurpers, the expression on his face became benevolent, even sympathetic: he realized they were soused, and, obviously, it touched a fraternal string in his Russian heart. It was impossible to make out what he said to them, but undoubtedly it was something tender like: "Don't worry, my dear sirs, I'll take over from here." And the two of them, bowing imposingly to him, staggered away arm in arm in my direction. When they drew near, the one in the fur cap—now I definitely recognized Serezha—leaned up against my shoulder and, in the same voice, murmured to me confidentially:

"Take us somewhere outside the gates: the second bell's just rung and I have to heave . . ."

Then came Catherine Street: a mishmash, neither one thing nor the other; it had pretensions of wealth, flaunted tall, dandified houses in yesterday's styles, and for some reason "hereabouts" in the evening the main flow of pedestrians would pour into Deribasov Street and a boulevard nearby. A little farther along on the right, noisy as the sea at a massif, filled to overflowing with seated customers, surrounded by those waiting to get in, one could see the trading terraces of the cafés Robin and Fankoni. But at the same time "hereabouts" nannies also brought their charges to the nursery tucked away under the precipice of the boulevard itself; shop assistants and messengers, both with packages and without, scurried between the town and the port; and port folk themselves, wearing peaked caps pushed to one side, ladies in white kerchiefs who often, rather than dragging themselves through the plebian "gullies" and "slopes" assigned to this social class, preferred to ascend the heights proudly right from the harbor, climbing all one hundred and ninety-eight granite steps of the famous flight of stairs[1] (one of the eight wonders of the world)—

---

[1] The Odessa steps made famous in Sergei Eisenstein's film *The Battleship Potemkin* (1925).

and from above, past the statue of the duke[2] in a Roman toga, to encroach immediately on civilization and to scatter the sidewalks of Catherine Street with a stream of sunflower seed husks. This wasn't merely the intersection of two streets but a microcosm and symbol of democracy—of bourgeois efficiency and aimless loitering, of rags and high fashion, of the staid middle class and the down-and-outs. . . . There was only one person I never expected to meet on this corner—but did: my porter Khoma.

For the past several weeks, every Sunday, I encountered Khoma on Deribasov Street: very prim and proper, wearing a dark blue shirt and white apron just laundered and pressed, his beard neatly groomed. The first time our eyes met there, I was surprised: what was he doing here, at the other end of the world, far from his own courtyard? He wasn't carrying a folder—that means, he wasn't heading to the police station to register new residents, and he wasn't returning from there; besides, this corner wasn't even on the way to or from the station. Was he out for a stroll, like everyone else? That couldn't possibly be, according to the very nature of things; besides, he wasn't moving at all, just standing in the entryway of a house with the look of a citizen who knew his place, and it was precisely there, where he stood. It was only the following Sunday that I noticed he wasn't alone: behind him, in the shadow of the entryway, I caught sight of a few more white aprons. This time, as it happens, Shtrok, our police reporter, was with me, a man who knew everything: he explained it all.

"You really don't know? It's all because of the expected demonstration; they've summoned brawny porters from all over town to lend the police a hand."

I would travel the block between Catherine Street and Harbor Street with a sense of gastronomic enthusiasm (even though I'd just had dinner), most often crossing over to the sidewalk on the right side of the street. There in the huge and squat Wagner house, in the depths of its deserted courtyard, sat the old Bruns Tavern, where at midnight, after the theater, heavenly angels using a magical recipe from paradise, created in the kitchen ambrosia in the form of sausages and potato salad, while Ganymede and Hebe themselves (I confuse demonological cycles, but such appreciative enthusiasm doesn't follow any rules), drew some March beer from the keg behind the partition. Here, at Bruns Tavern, on one such night, for a reason that will be ex-

2 The Duc de Richelieu. See chap. 3, n. 1.

plained at another time, Marko suddenly pushed away a plate of sausages he'd been served, and announced to me that from then on he would adopt a strictly kosher diet.

... The hand itches to render similar praise to remaining corners: Krasnyi Lane, with its tiny houses only ten feet wide, the last bastion of semi-Turkish Aegean Hellenism in the city which at one time was called Khadzhi-bei; quiet Harbor Street, where it was quite useless for cabbies to turn in; Cathedral Square, where Deribasov Street ended and another world began, with a different character to the streets and the indistinct flavor of the poorer districts nearby—Moldavanka, Slobodka-Romanovka, Peresyp—just as if two different cities met here and, without merging, merely abutted each other outwardly. But it's impossible to yield to these temptations endlessly: the main thing's been achieved—we've arrived at the corner of Deribasov Street and Cathedral Square, where it all began and where, a minute later, it all ended.

I didn't even see it, but suddenly my colleague Shtrok ran into the editorial office, called everyone over, and communicated the news in a half-whisper: a "demonstration" had just taken place. There were almost a hundred of them, all young people, mostly Jews, about a third, young women; one red banner, and a police officer we knew swore that it had the slogan "Down with Autocracy" (in the genitive case) embroidered on it. They'd proceeded only some twenty paces when from all sides a horde of policemen and porters fell upon them; women's cries could be heard; there was a scuffle and some panic; Cossacks appeared and began to disperse the crowd, clearing the sidewalks with their horses' hoofs and whips. Then they chased the demonstrators to the neighboring police station; the gates were closed and soldiers stood guard so no one could even pass by; people throughout the city were frightened, their faces downcast, and everyone whispered: "They're beating them to death, one after another . . ."

At about three o'clock the editorial assistant called me into his office; he was the single Russian Orthodox in the entire establishment, except for the typesetters, but his name was Abram:

"A lady's come to see you."

This lady turned out to be Anna Mikhailovna Milgrom. It was the first time I ever witnessed genuine human grief up close; it was worse than grief—you grieve about something that's already happened and has passed. But she looked as if a rusty nail had been driven into her head; it was still embedded and there was nothing she could do about it. It hadn't "passed," but was occurring then, taking place at that very moment, just around the corner, almost before her very eyes; she was sitting there on a leather armchair, and although it wouldn't help, it would've been embarrassing for her to scream.

"Lika was there!"

I said nothing; I asked Abram not to admit anyone; I closed the door, and stood next to her. She sat there, both of us silent and thinking; all of a sudden I, too, felt the same rusty nail being driven into my head. Whatever I tried to think, every half minute I kept coming back to that rusty nail. That must be why they say, "to pound a nail in." One thought kept hammering away: how that summer at the dacha I'd held Lika by the arm, merely to help her climb back onto the steep path up the cliff, and how she pulled away; and how, passing someone in the hallway, she always kept to one side, so that, God forbid, her puff sleeve might not touch someone. She was a sensitive person in all the nerves of her skin, down to the threads of her clothes. And now, these descendants of our gorilla forebears were beating her with their hairy paws. Anna Mikhailovna sat there in that office for about an hour without saying anything at all and then she got up and left.

I heard a few details at home later that evening from our maid Motrya; she'd been told by Khoma, an eyewitness and participant. When the gates were closed, he'd done some work on the contingent of male demonstrators; the bones of both his fists were still aching as a result; they chased them into the fire brigade stable, brought them out one at a time, and then carried them away. It was different with the young women: you couldn't treat them the same way; the police station's not a tavern. They dealt with the young women delicately, said Khoma, paternally, without offending their modesty—in the sense that no one else was present at the time, except for the officials. He, that is, Khoma, offered his services, but the superintendent wouldn't allow it; the door to that room was closed tight, and only city police were allowed inside to do that work.

—ᴠᴠ— XI —ᴠᴠ—

A Many-Sided Soul

There was a picture postcard and a letter from Vologda waiting for me in the editorial office. While tearing open the letter's envelope, I also examined the postcard. The postmark was from town; the colored picture depicted a gaunt, nasty lady beating her husband with a large wooden spoon. Underneath was printed in ink, without signature, in block letters, "This is what will happen to you, too, because of your article about cardsharps." In fact, one week earlier I'd written that several young people had appeared in town who were cheating at cards, some even wearing students' double-breasted jackets, and that this was a very bad thing: at a time of such heavy censorship, a despondent publicist had to get rid of deposits of civic indignation, and in less philistine outlets. This was the first anonymous letter of my career, and the first threat I had received: I was very flattered and decided to show the document to my colleague Shtrok.

The letter in the envelope was from Marusya; she wrote approximately as follows:

"... Every morning I test myself: do I remember the name of this town? I'm afraid of confusing it with either Suzdal or Kostroma: I never imagined that I'd get here, and by railway at that. I thought it only existed in Yanchin's textbook.[1] It's a very nice little town, with nice people, only they speak Russian in a terribly amusing way, just

---

[1] I. Yanchin was the author of several geography textbooks used widely in Russian schools during the early twentieth century.

like in the theater. But they turn around to look at a young redheaded woman in the street, just like in our city. Yes: just imagine, only after my arrival did I realize that I don't have an internal passport: Papa said something about it, but I was in such a rush to reassure Mama (who was worried about how Lika would manage all on her own in this vast Arctic Ocean)—I muttered that it was all taken care of, and the very day I got here, I was summoned to the police station. There was no time to convert to Christianity; therefore, in my conversation with the superintendent, I lowered my maidenly head and looked at him from under my brows. That trick—looking from under my brows—is my most effective weapon, a well-worn instrument, et me voilá, I became a genuine native of Perm, or whatever they call the local residents.

". . . I settled Lika easily; there are lots of exiles here, even women; it's an unusually nice group of people—don't forget to remind me when I return to join some political party or other, just as long as there are no Jews in it. Lika's living with a young woman from the same factory; imagine—at a priest's house. His wife and three daughters adore her. I feel, however, that soon she'll begin to growl at them, too.

". . . Go see Mama: yell at her and stamp your feet. She thinks that everyone here's in shackles, and that they'll still be ice-skating in July; she doesn't believe anything I say. Explain that I'm telling the truth. I asked Samoilo to do this, too: he's a solid man and my parents trust him. You, on the other hand, have a journalistic nature, but Mama loves you, and love is blind and trusting.

". . . I think I'll come home in about two weeks. Meanwhile, I embrace you to my loving bosom (don't worry—in a purely maternal way). Yours always, M.

". . . (I'd add that Lika sends you her greetings, but she never sends anyone greetings.)"

Of course I decided to talk to Anna Mikhailovna again, but I'd already spoken with her on this subject many times; and they'd already begun to calm down at their house. Lika had been expelled from eighth grade but kept in jail for only a short time, and exiled for only two years. I didn't see her, of course, and for some reason I didn't want to ask about her mood; I knew only that she was in good health. Anna Mikhailovna managed to say in passing that Lika, after learning her sentence, rejoiced at the prospect of Vologda. Ignats Albertovich turned out to be a big help: he accepted the misfortune like a sober man of the time; he didn't grumble or whine; he found many quotations in Heine[2] and Börne to prove that it's more shameful to be an oppressor than a victim. Once, even when I was there, he brought out a red leather-bound volume of Lenau from his study and read us some verse about three gypsies; I don't remember exactly what happened to those gypsies, but they really had some bad luck; then one of them starting playing a fiddle, the second one lit a pipe, and the third lay down to sleep. I remember the ending in Serezha's translation:

> And their threefold lesson was engraved on my heart:
> If you're destined to endure torment—
> Drown it in song, in smoke, and in sleep,
> And in threefold bottomless scorn.

The children also helped. Even the good-for-nothing Marko, though in his twisted mind he could never find even one appropriate word to say to his downcast mother, followed her around everywhere like a clumsy, shaggy mutt, and looked at her with his big warm eyes, as if asking how he could help. One need hardly mention Marusya: she took control of her mother, forced her to eat, and didn't let her lose herself in thought. Torik did what he could—brought home high grades from school and in June brought home highest honors along with a promotion to the sixth grade. But the best and most useful of all was Serezha—as soon as the initial pain had subsided, he began to heal Anna Mikhailovna with the most reliable medicine: laughter.

Long ago I'd developed great affection for Serezha, and during these months it increased all the more. One can make beauty and artistry out of any character trait, if one yields to it entirely: in him this trait was lightheartedness. Those three gypsies hadn't grown as high as his waist: when he had bad luck, he didn't need a fiddle, a smoke, or even scorn—he simply didn't notice, like a millionaire who loses a few rubles. Serezha was woven entirely of unlimited sincerity, even when making up tales. He'd begin by saying, "You can't imagine what happened to me today! Watch out—I'm going to lie,

---

[2] Heinrich Heine (1797–1856) was a major German romantic poet of Jewish origin who became a leading figure in the literary movement Young Germany.

but don't try and stop me." And he related what had "happened" to him better than any true story; every figure encountered even in passing, came to life right there in the living room from the top of his head to the ends of his toes. To this very day I can still recall figures I would have forgotten completely but for their voice and gestures from Serezha's skits. His generosity was never-ending and he was a great spendthrift: a "charlatan," as Ignats Albertovich had expressed it in his southern manner, who'd several times refused to provide him with pocket money because of his excesses; but Serezha always seemed to have money, and then again, he always seemed to be broke. He danced the mazurka better than anyone at the student ball, even though there were some Polish experts present; once at the dacha he hurled a steel ball high up into the sky, and when the ball began to fall, he tossed up another ball to hit it; once he swam all the way from Isakovich's bathhouse to the lighthouse and back again, without a rest. He knew how to do electric wiring, juggle plates, draw a cartoon of Nyura and Nyuta in a moment of tenderness, or one of Abram Moiseevich and Boris Mavrikievich engaged in a squabble; he could build a house of cards with as many floors as you like. Without being able to read music, he could play Chopin and Strauss waltzes on the flute, the piano, and the cello; he assured us that for one hundred rubles he'd play all three instruments simultaneously, and I believed him. And in everything he said and did, up front was the sparkling, good-natured, amusing order of things, manners, and situations; and in those weeks he launched all of them in a full assault on Anna Mikhailovna's grief. At first, she tried not to surrender, but it didn't last long; as soon as it became clear that nothing more terrible would happen to Lika, their apartment once again gradually filled with merriment and, after having been scared away by a period of mourning, at that time still uncommon in our circle, the "sightseers" began reappearing. The house became like a house again, and Marusya worried in vain from such a distance. It would do no harm, of course, to show the letter I'd received to Anna Mikhailovna and to "yell" at her.

I put the letter away and remembered the postcard; by the way, my colleague Shtrok's agitated voice could already be heard from the reporters' room. His voice was always agitated. He didn't merely "head up" the police chronicle at the paper—he experienced every robbery vicariously along with the thief, every accident at the Razdelnaya Station along with the victims; a roaring conflagration or a premeditated homicide constituted a real event for him. At that time, he was probably the only toiler in the press in all of Russia who had the right to brag: "I'm satisfied—I write about exactly what I want to write about." The censor didn't interfere with him, though he would "cut" whole columns from the rest of us, even from lead articles about the municipal economy and the sewage-farm. Shtrok had only one active encumbrance: our colleague who edited the municipal chronicle, a determined, composed, and precise man. He never infringed on Shtrok's content, but he wreaked havoc on his style. Shtrok's manuscript would depict an uxoricide on Kuznechny Street in the following way: "Then Agamemnon Popandopulo, feeling the torment of Othello in his bosom, brandished a shining kitchen knife above his wife's head, and, with a wild scream, hurled himself on the defenseless woman. What occurred between the unfortunate spouses afterwards is obscured by the murkiness of oblivion." But in print the following would appear: "The owner of a grocery shop, a certain Greek national, yesterday stabbed his wife Evlaniya, aged 34, with a kitchen knife; the circumstances of this affair have not yet been explained by the police inquest."

Shtrok knew everyone in town and everyone knew him, beginning from the very top. He began his literary activity during the time of Zelenyi, seaman and town governor, known for his ability to curse both at sea and on land (just recall that nice young man in Goncharov's *Frigate Pallas*,[3] where, still known as "midshipman Z.," he sings constantly, chuckles, and eats grapes with their skins on, "so they'd seem like more"). Some foreigner, Professor Rudolf Falb,[4] was predicting the imminent end of the world; Shtrok replied with a scientific brochure in which he tried to prove that there was nothing to worry about: it didn't matter which of the two occurred—one day the earth would either cool down or else it would crash into the sun. On this occasion he became personally acquainted with the town governor: Zelenyi dispatched a policeman to fetch him, and may the scene that ensued in the palace really be obscured by the murkiness of

[3] A travel account (1855–57) written by the Russian novelist Ivan Goncharov (1812–91) describing his adventures on a government-sponsored trip to Japan.
[4] Rudolf Falb (1838–1903) was an Austrian scientist who wrote about volcanoes and earthquakes. In 1895 a booklet titled "Don't Be Afraid of the End of the World," setting out some of Falb's theories, was published in Yiddish in Odessa.

oblivion. However, he befriended the policeman on the way to the palace and back to the station; some time ago that policeman became the superintendent, and now Shtrok is considered one of their own among the police and the bard of their investigative exploits. The simple townsfolk knew him, too, from the reputation of his leaflets, although published without assignation, of course. The "lower classes" knew him, as well: it would happen that three days after the publication of a sensational issue, an entire delegation from Peresyp would turn up at the office: "Be so kind, young lady, we want the paper where Mr. Shtrok wrote about the robbery on Sobachya Square." We used to tease him and say that he borrowed "his crimes" from cheap popular novels circulating among the simple folk after the Dreyfus affair, but he'd reply proudly:

"You think I'd steal my crimes from other people's novels? Why, they compose their novels according to my crimes!"

"Shtrok," I said, handing him the postcard depicting the mean wife and the long-suffering husband. "Soon you'll be listing in your chronicle an attempt on the life of a promising young journalist."

He looked at it, turned it over, and suddenly said to me:

"Come here. I've been meaning to talk to you about this matter for some time."

We went into an empty room.

"It was a mistake to get involved," he began. "It would've been better not to meddle in this gang of cardsharps."

"Shtrok!" I replied, sticking out my chest. "Whom do you take me for? 'I'm brave, and fear neither knife nor fire.'"[5]

"Rubbish! No one will touch you, but that's not the point. Simply— there's no reason to meddle with one's own friends."

"Friends? What rubbish are you talking, dear colleague?"

"Shtrok doesn't talk rubbish, but he knows. When were you last at Fankoni's?"

"In general, I don't frequent such splendid places."

"Get an advance from the office and drop by. Around ten in the evening. You'll see the entire gang seated at a separate table. And, in the place of honor, the soul of this society, you'll find your friend Serezha Milgrom presiding."

---

[5] This famous line is uttered by Zemfira, the heroine in "Gypsies" (1823–24), a romantic poem by Alexander Pushkin (1799–1837).

The Arsenal on Moldavanka

I enticed Serezha to come to my place and without any further ado subjected him to the most brutal interrogation. At first he feigned ignorance and asked:

"What's the problem? Why shouldn't one fleece that wealthy guy? And what does it matter how one fleeces him?"

"Drop the metaphysics. I'm asking you: are you or are you not working with this gang?"

"Do I have to tell the truth?"

"The whole truth!"

"Well then, at the present time I'm just trying to get a better look at them. Three times or so I've played quite a game of faro in one such house, but I was so lucky, there was no reason to summon the red-headed fellow to my aid."

"What do you want to get a better look at?"

"These guys and their technique. The guys are fascinating; Marusya would take on any one of them as a "sightseer" in a minute—here's your gift certificate. But I won't let them anywhere near Marusya. Their technique, on the other hand, is Paleolithic. They're like fourth graders in elementary school! I'm much more skillful. Watch!"

He reached inside my breast pocket and with two skillful fingers pulled out a queen of hearts, holding it by one corner; I didn't even have a deck of cards in my house.

"Serezha," I said, restraining my anger and agitation, "give me your word of honor immediately that you'll swear off this gang and this whole business. You've already been targeted by some reporters. What do you want? To embarrass your father and mother before all Odessa? Don't they have enough heartache already without your creating more?"

He stared at me intently.

"Hey, you're really upset," he said in sincere astonishment; it was clear that he himself saw no reason for me to get so excited. "Alright, I'll avoid them. It's a pity to offend a good man, even though you're acting against my freedom of personality, and therefore, behaving in a reactionary manner. It's settled; I'll avoid them. I swear by Allah's beard and so on and so forth. And, as for my ancestors, you're right: let them get some rest from familial pleasures."

I believed him; in such circumstances, having made a promise, it seems that he didn't lie. Subsequently my colleague Shtrok also confirmed that Serezha had "avoided" them. For another two months I continued to suffer a gnawing pain inside; but I loved him dearly, and soon everything faded.

—✺—

As for Marko, in fact, after the incident with the sausages at Bruns, he did switch to a kosher diet.

It began obliquely: I was invited to a secret meeting to discuss an organization for self-defense. It was before Easter; if I still recall the sequence of events accurately—I can't swear to it—it was about half a year after the unfortunate incident with Lika. I was provided with an unfamiliar address, on Moldavanka Street or somewhere nearby. It turned out to be something like an office but without a nameplate on the door. We were received by a young man, about twenty-eight, of pleasing appearance, with a black beard. Samoilo Kozodoi, whom I met there, referred to him as "Heinrich," but the others didn't use any name—apparently they weren't personally acquainted with him. Around half a dozen young people had gathered there, mostly students. "Heinrich" brought in a teapot, glasses, and biscuits, and said: "If you need anything, I'm at your service." He went into the other room and no one tried to stop him.

There we decided to declare ourselves a committee, to collect a large sum of money, and to arm a lot of people. Two of the students did most of the talking: one—obviously a great philosopher, peppered every sentence with many foreign terms; the other, on the contrary, was of a more realistic nature, even a little cynical, with obvious Jewish intonations, somehow astonishingly appropriate to his way of thinking.

"I can't," declared the philosopher. "I can't rid myself of a certain skepticism in the face of this concept: our Jewish masses as the subject of protection."

"Are you afraid they'll run away? Well, and if they do, what of it? They'll get beaten up? Let them: it'll teach them and they'll be braver the next time."

"But wouldn't it be more rational," insisted the first, "to make use of the more revolutionary elements: to assign this function, for example, to the politically conscious proletariat?"

"Really?" replied the second. "We'd have to pay three rubles and sixty kopecks for each 'bulldog,'[1] and I still don't see where we'd go to get the money; besides, if we turn this all over to your conscious proletariat, a big question will arise: whom will they shoot?"

"That's a completely unfounded and offensive insinuation!"

"Perhaps; but to let my money be used to shoot my own people—excuse me, go find yourself some other madman."

Samoilo, who'd been silent the whole time, suddenly spoke out (that was almost the first time I heard his voice):

"In addition to us, they invited two others who are 'party members,' but they didn't come."

"They don't like the apartment," someone explained, lowering his voice and glancing over at the closed door to the other room.

"Aha!" the cynic cried. "It's clear: the quarters are more important to them than Jewish bellies; but we need the sort of people for whom bellies are more important than these quarters."

Because of my pride I felt uncomfortable asking what was wrong with the quarters; the rest, apparently, knew, so I also assumed a knowing look. The majority declared itself in favor of the cynic's point of view; we made some decisions, summoned Heinrich to bid him farewell, and then parted. Samoilo lived in my part of town, so we walked together through the empty midnight streets.

"Who's that Heinrich fellow?" I asked.

He was even a bit surprised that I didn't know. It turns out that he was the local representative of the shrewd gendarme from the

___

[1] A pistol or revolver of large caliber and with a short barrel.

capital, Zubatov, who, at the time, was organizing (even I'd heard about it, of course) legal workers' unions supposedly without politics, with precise instructions: go on strike against proprietors—if you please—but as for the state system, don't interfere, that's the sovereign's business.

"Hmm," I said. "As a matter of fact, the staff quarters are inconvenient."

"Try to find another place where everyone can attend and a storehouse can be established; Heinrich guarantees there won't be a search."

"And he won't turn us in?"

"No, I know him; he's from the same town as I am. He's a fool and has gotten mixed up in a hopeless cause, but he won't inform on us."

"Is it only 'hopeless'? People say it's a nasty business."

"Why?"

"Well, just think: in the first place, there are the gendarmes; but the main thing is—it's in defense of autocracy."

We could speak freely: there was no one around, and we had intentionally chosen to walk in the roadway; we spoke quietly, of course. I was no longer surprised that Samoilo was being so talkative; recently even Marusya had confessed that she could "chat with him for hours and that was more amusing than talking with you."

He didn't respond to my words but after a moment said:

"Autocracy isn't really going to come crashing down because people throw bombs or organize rebellions. In my opinion, if you want to guarantee some sort of incident, you don't have to do anything at all; you don't even have to talk. You simply have to want it and want it and want it."

"How's that? In silence?"

"Yes. Where there's a person, even one out of a whole crowd, who wants something, I mean who really wants it, no matter what—there's no reason for him to try to do anything. It's enough for him just to want it all the time. And the longer he remains silent, the stronger it is. It will end as he wants it to end."

"So how will it happen—by some black magic or some new kind of hypnotism?"

"Hypnotism or animal magnetism, the doctors will figure it out; I'm merely the pharmacist. I know what a pharmacist knows: excuse me, but if one person in the room smells of carbolic acid, ultimately the whole room and all the guests will start to smell of carbolic acid. And why do you say 'new kind of hypnotism'? That was always the case, both in large matters and small, even in a person's own life."

It occurred to me vaguely that he was talking about himself, about his own intentions; in fact, after a short pause, he added:

"Take me, for instance; I was moping in Serogozy, dreaming of coming to Odessa and becoming a pharmacologist, but I didn't have any money. What do you think I did? Did I flounder, bending over backwards? Nothing of the sort. I simply wanted it, with all my might. Suddenly Uncle Ignats came to visit; he took one look at me and said, 'Pack your bags. We're leaving.' And that's the way it will be with everything. Here's where I turn to the right; good-bye, Monsieur so-and-so, and thanks for your company."

He still hadn't gotten used to calling people by their first name and patronymic, obviously considering that too familiar. We parted; I walked on alone, and, because of my youth, marveled at the fact that even such an ordinary foot soldier in life turns out to have his own ideas and his own view of things.

Soon all the drawers in the tables at Heinrich's filled up with "bull-dogs" and cartridges. Later I heard complaints that the cartridges weren't the right caliber, and someone referred to our six-shooters as "six mis-shooters," but they were going fast; from morning to night university students, butchers, external students, porters, and apprentices kept arriving, showed notes from members of the committee, and left with a bulging pocket.

Serezha also showed up, with a gloomy young man wearing a peaked cap; he was a strange-looking fellow, although vaguely familiar. For a worker he was too neat and foppish; but shop assistants don't dress like that either—a colored scarf around his neck and trousers with a large checkered pattern; my coworker at the newspaper, the one who writes about our port and its surroundings, had described something like this before. Even his face was a little familiar to me.

"This is the Jew Motya Banabak," Serezha introduced him. "You and he met some time ago on the boat; you remember, when I was teaching you how to eat watermelons? Give him six firearms for himself and his gang: I can vouch for them."

I wouldn't have relied on Serezha's guarantee, but Motya Banabak produced an authentic note from the cynical student, with the notation "Important."

"Who's that character?" I asked Serezha after he'd left with a package. "Don't get angry—but by any chance does he smuggle young girls to Buenos Aires?"

"You, *caballero*, are a lout and an ignoramus: those fellows wear bowler hats, not peaked caps. You'd be better off asking the fire chief Miroshnichenko about the fire in the Stavrid house on Slobodka: who rescued Hanna Brashevan and her baby? Motya. The firemen chickened out, but Motya and his gang ran up to the third floor and carried them out!"

"What did they carry out?"

"What do you mean 'what'? Hanna and her infant. Isn't that enough?"

"Anything else? Not in their arms, but in their pockets?"

He burst into broad laughter.

"I don't deny you pose the question correctly. But what kind of people do you need now: honest contenders for lowly elected positions—or cutthroats with five fingers on each fist?"

All was lost: that fellow was already gone, and there was no point in continuing the argument. Moreover, the cynical student, who'd showed up meanwhile, supported Serezha's opinion:

"Although," he said, "we're a musical nation and so forth, we aren't militant; that's the sort of rogue we need now—how did he say it, that poseur?—'as the subject of protection.'"

Marko spent his days and nights with us, and it was here that he "learned to shoot." Someone told him it was alright to do it even indoors: you had to stand in front of a mirror and aim until the muzzle disappears and only the reflection of the bore remains. He managed to destroy Heinrich's mirror practicing this maneuver, but he ran right out and bought two more—one to keep in reserve. I doubt whether his training was successful because he was frequently distracted from his "shooting" as soon as some new client arrived: he got involved in conversation with everyone, gawking at them and greedily drinking in their every word. I still can't recall Marko's face, but it seems to me now that he must have had huge ears protruding in the direction of his interlocutor, and from each ear wide pipes leading directly to his heart.

Samoilo had to be summoned once again: he was the only member of the committee who knew how to translate a proclamation into their "jargon" and to write block letters using aniline ink. After examining the hectograph, he shook his head: it won't make thirty copies. I'll crank out two hundred. He left, brought back some gelatin, a bottle of glycerin, I don't remember what else, and spent a whole hour fussing; the next day, as a matter of fact, he managed to print a whole pile of purple leaflets. While he was developing them, pressing and straightening them, I asked impatiently:

"How much time does each page take?"

"There's no other way," he replied, instructing me. "There are two rules for every undertaking: don't rush, and the death grip."

(Marko took on the distribution of the leaflet packets to ten addresses, but along the way got distracted and a month later I found half of this literature under a table at his place; but I'm not to blame—he was entrusted with this task when I wasn't there.)

Samoilo also turned out to be a useful strategic ally. While he brewed the liquid for the hectograph on the kerosene stove, we discussed which brigade to locate where on the eve of Easter. We decided to place one near the boatman at the lower end of Quarantine gully—the boatman was Persian and a sympathizer. Samoilo intervened.

"When there's a gully, it's foolish to station people beneath it. Put them at the upper end: it's easier to shoot from above."

So that's what we did: meanwhile, all this proved unnecessary. The pogrom did take place that Sunday; it was bloody, and it hasn't been forgotten to this day, but that time it didn't take place in Odessa. We organized a last liquidation meeting, informed the owner of the gun shop, Rauchverger, that we had no way to repay the five hundred rubles we owed him, and said goodbye to Heinrich. He shook my hand for a long time and said:

"Don't thank me: I'm so glad to assist in a matter where there are no arguments as to whether the business is clean or dirty . . ."

As he said this his eyes had a particular expression that I recalled for a long time to come: my eyes would look just as miserable if fate—or my faith—had forced me to make my way through the streets with the stigma of a renegade on my forehead, and everywhere people moved aside or turned away. Who knows, perhaps he was really a good man.

But Marko, who rejected the sausages in Braun's tavern, went home, woke Anna Mikhailovna, and demanded: first, that they buy all their meat from that day forward in a Jewish shop; second, that they keep separate sets of dishes for meat and dairy products, just like at Abram Moiseevich's; and they should begin tomorrow. She sent him off to bed; then, using his own money, he brought home two dishes, washed them separately, and refused to eat any homemade meat cutlets; instead he bought a supply of Warsaw sausage with garlic. He stored the sausage on a nail in his room, although he shared a room with Serezha; I don't even know how to relate the number of outbursts that took place in the house as a result of all this. It lasted three weeks until Marko declared to his mother that he'd resolved to become a vegetarian altogether; I also don't recall in what connection he decided to begin a study of Persian literature in the original, and for that purpose was intending to move to St. Petersburg in the autumn and to enroll in the faculty of Oriental languages.

━━ XIII ━━

Something Like the Decameron

In the course of events determining Marusya's fate, I particularly re-call one summer night, initially at sea and then on the Langeron. It will be difficult to describe it so that not one word will be painful: for the sake of Marusya's memory I don't want to say anything clumsy or awkward. She had a way of making everything turn out "nicely" (as I've said before), even—for its time—the most eccentric reckless-ness, but it won't be easy to preserve this aspect in my account; I'm very much afraid of these next two chapters, but I have to proceed.

There were seven of us in a large flat-bottomed fishing boat: the look-alike mother and daughter, Nyura and Nyuta; two students with reactionary views described above (or two others, it's not im-portant); Marusya, Samoilo, and me. After the events at Heinrich's apartment, Samoilo didn't avoid me as much, although he'd gone silent once again. With two sets of oars, we got quite a way out; we had consumed all the meat pastries and pears before sunset.

Marusya seemed restless, first laughing and boisterous, then thoughtful. I knew why. As she and I were descending toward the shore and had fallen behind, just the two of us, she suddenly turned to me and whispered, bubbling inside with excitement and joy:

"Alesha's returning in a month."

At first I didn't know whom she was talking about; then I real-ized—Runitsky. When we'd been there to visit a year ago, she'd called him Aleksei Dmitrievich. I didn't know how many times since then he'd departed "for Sakhalin," how many times he'd returned, and whether or not they'd met; apparently, they had.

Now, in the boat, she seemed to be acting crazy at times; she jumped over the crosspieces, climbing on the rowers' shoulders, and rocking the boat so much that Nyura and Nyuta shrieked in unison; spying the small steamship *Turgenev* off in the distance returning from Ochakov before evening, she ordered that we "cut off its prow," insisting on doing it herself immediately. She seized the helm from Samoilo and executed the undertaking so successfully that a chorus of curses burst forth from the deckhouse, which, thank heavens, was partly drowned out by their horns sounding an alarm; but Samoilo sat next to her in the stern and watched, screwing up his eyes; it was clear that if necessary he would have replaced her and come to our aid. After this heroic exploit, she went to the prow, curled up like a ringlet of hair, and fell silent for a long time, staring at the sunset. Then she took a smoking lesson from one of the students—at that time our women still didn't smoke; there was much merriment as a result of the fact that on the inside lid of the student's cigarette case, etched in silver so that everyone to whom he offered a cigarette would have to read it, was the well-known inscription in Slavic ornamental script: "Smoke your own, you son of a bitch."

At the same time his colleague was teasing Nyura and Nyuta, assuring them that they were both secretly in love with Serezha: "in equal parts, of course." Their love notes to him all began as follows: "Our dear . . ." and the mother would write one line, her daughter, the next.

"That's not necessary," Nyura and Nyuta replied in jest, "we have the same handwriting."

But I noticed with some surprise that both of them blushed slightly—"in equal parts." However, it might simply have been the reflection of the sunset: that evening it unfolded with unprecedented beauty. We stopped rowing; the boat didn't even rock. Someone sighed: the Lord has fine decorators.

Afterwards we played *Überbrettl*[1]—Nyura and Nyuta, both educated women, had seen it recently in Vienna.

---

[1] A song or humorous skit modeled after the famous cabaret in Berlin; presumably a similar establishment was opened in Vienna.

The student with the cigarette case sang some harbor songs very sweetly. The majority of them were ordinary, but one of them I'd never heard before, nor since: it contained an entire novel. At first he and she are young children: "playing" somewhere on Kosarka and teasing a snail: "Little snail, little snail, stick out your horns, I'll boil up some potatoes for you." Then the girl, growing up and getting pretty, starts teasing him; later—he begins to get jealous: "Who bought you those earrings?" In the end she leaves him; he's a stevedore in the port, while she's taken up with a wealthy Greek; she meets her former beloved and turns away from him.

> Little snail, little snail, stick out your horns,
> Our paths have diverged.

Nyura and Nyuta related a story from a French collection of legends. A clever tale: it was only many years later, and based on other experiences, that I realized how clever it was. Once upon a time there lived a knight who was born without a heart, but a watchmaker he knew fashioned a complicated mainspring for him, placed it inside his chest, and wound it up once and for all. This knight with a mainspring instead of a heart rode out along the highways and byways and defended widows and orphans; during a crusade he saved Baldwin[2] himself, and was the first one to scale the walls of the Holy City. From a tower guarded by a dragon he rescued the beautiful maiden Veronique and married her in the cathedral; it was a splendid mainspring. After all this, decked out with honors and wounds, he went in search of that watchmaker and beseeched him in Christ's name: "I love neither widows nor orphans, nor the holy grave, nor Veronique; it's all because of your mainspring. I'm fed up with it: take it out!" Nyura and Nyuta managed to relate the story "jointly," that is, one spoke while the other nodded her head, but the impression was that they were telling it together.

The other student with reactionary views, obviously a persistent fellow, made up a story about a shipwreck. Only three people survived on an uninhabited island: a midshipman and two female pas-

---

[2] Baldwin the Leper (1161–85), king of Jerusalem (1174–85), who defeated Saladin in 1177; but in 1183 Saladin captured Aleppo and completed the encirclement of Jerusalem.

sengers (from the "second class," he added maliciously), a mother and a daughter. On the island both women fell in love with the midshipman ("in equal parts"), but, being "diabolically well brought up," they couldn't conceive of taking any liberties. And miraculous things occurred: first, it turned out that on that uninhabited island the law permitted polygamy; and second—once, when the mother prayed very fervently to God, He took pity on them: her daughter ceased being her daughter and became her niece, and so on and so forth.

He narrated this nonsense in a very amusing way. One couldn't even see whether Nyura and Nyuta blushed again: night was falling swiftly and the moon had yet to rise. Only the stars shone so brightly that it was possible to tell the time, and the smooth water, brimming with phosphorus, seemed strewn with nails of crystal beads at every light splash.

In my opinion, I told the best story of all, and it wasn't nonsense, like all the others, but true: about the republic of Lukaniya. When we were in third grade, two lines from the ode "The Immature Mind"[3] made an enormous impression on my friends and me:

> After belching thrice, the rubicund Luka declares:
> 'Learning destroys concord among people.'

We formed the secret Society of Rubicund Luka—there's no point in setting forth its program, it's all too clear—we occupied one small valley, there on the Langeron, and in honor of our cheerful patron christened it the Republic of Lukaniya. In view of the fact that half the audience was composed of women, it was impossible to relate the whole history of our state, but the part I could tell was well received: how we built a fortress of stolen bricks; how the mailbox functioned—a two-pound tin can that used to hold Vysotsky tea, buried deep in our native soil (when I had to communicate urgently with one of our members, during the break between classes in our gymnasium, I would whisper into his ear: "Check out the mailman." After class he'd rush to the Langeron, dig up the tin can, read the message, compose his reply, bury it, run to my house, summon me to the door, and

---

[3] Satire by the eighteenth-century Russian writer Antiokh Kantemir (1708–44), actually titled "To My Mind: On the Detractors of Learning" (1729).

whisper, "Check it out . . ." Then I'd go running over there . . .); and about our newspaper *Shmarovoz* where a mandate from the Ministry of Education had been published concerning the reform of classical education: "to replace Greek with Latin, and Latin with Greek"; how we implemented a bold and completely unparalleled governmental scheme—having elected Lelka Raklo as president, and then, so that his opponent Lelka Pomidor wouldn't be offended, we chose him to be king of our republic. In my opinion, it was an excellent story; the only thing that grieved me was that my audience didn't believe its authenticity: offended, I pointed to where the night had concealed the shore of the Langeron and swore that even now I could still locate that valley and even uncover the remaining traces of our fortress . . .

All of a sudden Marusya called out:

"Will you show me? Tonight, even, on our way back? I'll walk home with you."

After this it was Samoilo's turn. I expected him to mutter some refusal, but instead, he accepted his obligation, and began thus:

"Once upon a time there lived a young woman who constantly loved to play with fire; in the end she got very badly burned. The end."

Even by the light of the stars I could see that Marusya stuck out her tongue at him. But . . . is it only now it seems that I felt a sudden chill in my heart as a result of these words, or was that really the case? Probably, it only seems so: I don't believe in premonitions. But Marusya jumped up, stood on the prow of the rocking boat, and declared:

"Now it's my turn. Once upon a time there lived a young woman who loved to play with water; once there was a miraculous night at sea and she decided to take a swim right from the boat. Boys, don't you dare turn around! Samoilo, get to the stern and sit there facing the other way."

"Won't you . . . catch cold?" Nyura (Nyuta's mother) asked timidly. Nobody else said a thing; Samoilo changed seats in silence and lit up a cigarette. I don't know what the others were thinking, but I had a strange feeling—as if even this idea of hers was in the normal order of things, that the night had to end this way, and that Marusya could do anything she wanted. I was sitting on the forward crosspiece, closest to the prow of our boat; her clothes, made of cambric, were rustling right above me; there's nothing embarrassing about confessing that I had to bite my lip and hold my knees together with my hands to suppress the feverish tremor I felt deep inside. They say that not one young man of the new generation would be excited by this nowadays; he'd merely sit facing away from the young woman and calmly dispense useful advice about how best to jump into the water; but back then, times were different. It never occurred to any of the four of us to speak to her at that moment—it would have involved turning around, and that was ungentlemanly. The reactionary student sitting next to me, suddenly burst into song again; I realized that he unconsciously wanted to muffle the rustling of her dress, and at that moment his worth rose considerably in my estimation. Nyura and Nyuta also fell silent; I couldn't see their faces, but I noticed that for defense they clung more tightly to each other, as if Marusya's audacity had also torn some invisible veils off both of them.

"Adios forever!" Marusya cried, and I was doused by a splash, while alongside the boat on both sides ran sparkling crests of waves.

One could tell that she was swimming like a man, with powerful strokes: she was clearly a good swimmer, almost noiseless; by the even strokes of her arms I could count how far she had gone. Ten paces . . . fifteen . . . twenty-five.

"Marusya," Nyura or Nyuta called out to her nervously. "Why so far?"

From out there her elated voice came back:

"Nyura, Nyuta, look—I'm swimming all in fire; pearls, silver, emeralds—Lord, how wonderful! Boys, now you can look: the final number in the program—dances in Bengal light!"

Something vaguely white swept over mounds of diamond fountains; and deep beneath the water a pearly bonfire shimmered; sparkling rings ran right up to the boat and spread out even further.

A little bolder, Nyura asked: "Isn't it cold?"

"It's splendid, cozy, impossible to describe . . ." She laughed with genuine, playful bliss. "Now turn away: I'll lie on my back—like this—and fall asleep. Don't you dare wake me!" After a moment of silence she added, in a really sleepy, somnolent voice: "I'd tell you what I'm dreaming, but it wouldn't be proper . . ."

When she'd swum back to the prow of the boat and grabbed hold of the side, she didn't have enough strength to lift herself up, and she drawled plaintively: "What a catastrophe!"

"We'll pull you out," Nyura and Nyuta hastened to say, getting up. But Marusya was even faster to speak and declared:

"Oh, no, there's no way you could do it. You don't have the strength. Not you . . ."

She didn't say who did; but Samoilo stood up silently, tossed his cigarette into the water, and went toward her, stepping over the seats and our knees. He said abruptly: "Grab hold of my neck." The boat listed forwards sharply, the prow rose up high; he returned and took his previous seat in the bottom of the boat.

"One moment more, don't get angry," Marusya said behind us. "I have to dry off." Her voice seemed to be asking, but underneath, one could sense that she was still laughing in some kind of private delight.

A minute passed (the student began singing again), then there was another rustling sound. In a moment she jumped noisily to the bottom of the boat, exclaiming: "Ready—you have the patience of angels!" She grabbed my neighbor by the head, pushed it back, and kissed him on the forehead, adding: "That's for everyone."

But that still wasn't the end of that night.

Inserted Chapter,
Not Intended for the Reader

Honestly, I'm writing this chapter out of pure cowardice. Three times I've begun to narrate the continuation of that night, but I've found it very difficult; I'm too timid. I just tore up three pages of paper. For a break, I'll write about something different. One critic, leafing through one of my works, reproached me for a major deficiency: there's no description of nature. That was about ten years ago, but my pride was hurt: so I must make an attempt. Such a chapter, of course, is not intended for the reader: without doubt, the reader doesn't read descriptions of nature; I, at least, always skip over them mercilessly. I could, for the sake of my above-mentioned pride, scatter in various places a dozen or so recollections of the landscape, but this would be a trap; the most principled approach would be to collect them all into a separate chapter (all the more so, since I feel so timid and want to take a break), and to title the chapter honestly, something like, "If you don't like it, don't listen."

In summer our shore . . . (In summer; as for winter, I don't even want to know about it. In general, I love life a great deal, particularly my own life, and I love to recall it, but only from April to September. I don't know why God created winter; poor thing, in general He made several mistakes and created a number of unnecessary things. The majority of my friends assure me that they really like snow: not only decorative snow, the summit of Mont Blanc, simply white paint on a picture, something you can admire and then turn away from—but supposedly they even like snow on the streets: in my opinion, today's snow is simply tomorrow's slush. I remember only summers.)

In summer our shore, as seen from the sea, presents a combination of only two colors, yellow and green; to be more precise—bright yellow and gray-green. Our shore was high, one large precipice for dozens of miles; from a distance one couldn't make out whether or not it stood higher than two hundred feet, but it's high. The yellow sandstone of its backbone was rarely interrupted from the outside; the cliffs were covered with the same reddish clay, and on them, in the indentations or crevices, grew groves of trees and bushes. I don't know what species predominated, but as a result, the general appearance was grayish; perhaps it was wild olive. Good Lord, what miracles of the palette one can create with only two shades of color! Once I became engrossed looking at it from a boat—at that time the sun was shining on the cliffs from a very special angle—and suddenly it seemed that everything I saw was made not of clay and leaves but of metal. A giant lay stretched out asleep along the Black Sea, and this was his bronze cuirass. He'd been sleeping a long time, rains had washed over him for a hundred years, and thick clumps of green spring wheat had taken root in the cavities of the bronze. Once, many years after leaving Odessa, I saw this same rainbow of two colors in Provence and almost sang out in my excitement, but there were other people in the railway car.

I recall actual stone cliffs only below, at the water's edge or actually standing in the water. There were also granite cliffs where we gathered shrimp (we called them "little crayfish") and "musuls," that is, in proper speech, "mussels." But most of the cliffs were made of porous sandstone; the tallest was called the Monk, near Malyi Fontan, and every year the sea would wash away another piece of it; there's probably nothing left of it by now. And there were also some "cliffs" of some greenish clay; we used to call it "soap," and in fact one could break off a handful and use it to lather up, even in salty water.

Of course, there was also a third color—the sea; but what color was it? I scarcely remember it as blue; I certainly recall dark green, with a golden lining where stripes of shoals showed through. Someone once expressed surprise in my presence and asked why the Black Sea was so named: with my own eyes I have seen it black, right beneath my oars and for a mile around, not merely in a storm or on a gloomy day, but even in sunlight. But in my opinion, one had to behold our sea when it was white. You have to get up an hour before sunrise, sit down right near the water on sharp stones, and watch how the dawn is born; you have to choose a perfectly still morning. Then there's a quarter of an hour when the sea is white, and all along the milky background there stretch changing, wavering stripes, also absolutely white, but of a different whiteness: some with a shade of steel gray, others slightly lilac, and very infrequently a little bit of blue suddenly appears. Gradually the east begins to hang decorative curtains on the proscenium to receive the sun—rose, orange, and emerald—Good Lord, I don't know all the right words in Russian. And reflecting, this entire chorus of colors begins, still muted, slightly tinged by echoes, to be woven into the principle white melody of the sea—suddenly everything begins to light up and sparkle, and then, of course, the sea looks like any sea. I saw all this best of all when the fisherman Avtonom Chubchik took Marusya and me back to the dacha after our night in Lukaniya; but I'm getting ahead of myself.

In descriptions of nature it's customary to refer to various plants by name; I used to be able to do that, but all those names, it seems, were not genuine. There was, for example, a plebian red flower on a tall stalk, with a collar of thorns around the blossom: we called it a "Turk"—you walked along the path and lopped off these Turkish heads with a stick. Once I smote three with one stroke, just like Pan Longinus Podbipenta, of the Zervi-kaptur coat-of-arms, in Henryk Sienkiewicz.[1] Or there was a particular bush we called a "Chumak or ox-cart driver": if you rubbed the leaves on your hand, it would smell like tasty buckwheat kasha. However, it's best not to rack your brain over the names: if you simply lie down on your back and screw up your eyes, a symphony of aromas would envelop you forever more powerfully with divine horticulture than committing the whole dictionary to memory.

From divine husbandry the most splendid animal we had was the lizard. Whether it was because in Europe there was a different species or because I'm getting older, nevertheless, through all these years and in all the countries I've visited, elsewhere lizards seem to come in

---

[1] Henryk Sienkiewicz (1846–1916) was a Polish writer whose war trilogy, *With Fire and Sword, The Deluge,* and *Pan Michael,* glorified the struggle for Polish national existence in the seventeenth century.

only gray. But near the Black Sea ours were multicolored: semi-precious emerald scales, tail, and snout, while the throat and belly would range in tints from rose to golden. One evening, while we were still second graders in Lukaniya, we intentionally caught about a dozen or so, confined them to our fortress, and for a solid hour lit red and green fireworks, thick Bengal lights; the frightened lizards darted first from wall to wall, then froze in one place, and it was such an intoxicating display of color, that I've never seen anything like it since, even in theater productions in big cities where the directors are revered as masters of "color schemes" and the whole enterprise costs thousands of rubles.

There was one other nice entertaining creature, but completely different—the crab; he lived in underwater crevices below the massifs. The massifs are huge stone cubes which for many miles in length provided the facing for the shores, piers, and breakwaters of our port; under them hid flounder and Gobius, even mackerel or palamida ("or," because when palamida were present, there were no mackerel—the palamida ate them). But most of all there were crabs. We caught them with the help of stones, string, and psychology . . . but I've written about this elsewhere in an old story: I repeat myself too often. I'd love to sit on the massifs for half an hour now—I wouldn't even disturb the crabs: I'd merely sit there, dangling my bare feet, like Antaeus,[2] to touch the ground of my childhood.

There was another Black Sea, even with its own Sea of Azov nearby, with a strait, just as it is supposed to be, but without any water: two large trenches in the Aleksandrovsky Park, intentionally devoid of trees and grass. Gangs of us played ball there. . . . Lord, how lifeless that sounds in Russian: "played ball." We didn't just play, we were absorbed in it; not just ball, but ballgames; not merely absorbed in play, but having the time of our lives in all sorts of wonderful children's games; but I've also described these elsewhere. When you spend your whole life writing, you wind up in the end ashamed to say anything. It's terribly foolish. Life's a foolish thing . . . but marvelous: if you suggest that I repeat it—I'll do so, exactly as it was, with all the sorrows and squalor, if I can start all over again with Odessa.

—⁓—

[2] In Greek mythology, Antaeus was the son of Poseidon who became stronger whenever he touched the earth, his mother Gaea.

By the way, since this is an interruption: that song about the "little snails" has been spinning around for so long on the threshold of my memory, it's been asking to be put down on paper ever since I first mentioned it in passing, and now I can't resist: I sat down for one night and more or less reconstructed it. On the other hand, now I can consider it my own work: in my opinion, it's the best of all my poetic plagiarisms. True, a foreign reader will need an entire dictionary to understand it—who among them, for example, has ever heard of an *alvichka*, delivering sticky sweets in a round glass case? But, in the last analysis, I'm really not writing this story for new arrivals: it's all right with me if they don't understand. Here's the song:

> Nyuta and I lived not far from
> Doctor Valtukha's hospital.
> Her eyelashes were long, arched like an umbrella,
> She could touch her mouth and her forehead with them.
> I would go diving off the stone jetties
> And bring her back handfuls of mussels in my pockets.
> I would pick her lilacs near the Three Fountains,
> And collect snails for her in the park.
>> Little snail, little snail, stick out your horns,
>> I'll boil up some potatoes for you.
>
> When she grew up,
> Nyuta turned capricious:
> She would tell me to get lost,
> Call me back, and then send me to hell.
> First angry, then overjoyed,
> Now soaked, then dried out—all because of Nyuta.
> But once she went skinny-dipping
> With me under the pier.
>> Little snail, little snail, stick out your horns,
>> The mouse is sad to be caught in the cat's paws.
>
> Odessa stands on a hill,
> The Androsov pier lies below,
> Like a princess, Nyuta parades
> Before her stevedore.
> Once a year she meets me at the Duke's tavern,

I treat her to sweets from Alvi's . . .
But then—lift your oars, the outing's over:
Off she goes to the redheaded student.
  Little snail, little snail, stick out your horns,
  Who bought you those earrings?

Year in, year out, schlepping up and down,
Tramping between harbor and tavern, always alone . . .
Once on my way from Greek Square
Down to Quarantine Bay—
I caught sight of Nyuta sitting in the Café Fankoni
Wearing a fancy hat, some Greek at her side.
She wouldn't even look at me, as if
A tramp isn't a real person.
  Little snail, little snail, stick out your horns,
  Our paths have diverged.

—◆— XV —◆—

Confession on Langeron

The moon rose late over the republic of Lukaniya, a gibbous moon, but unusually bright.

It was hard to make our way through the thick bushes, wild pear and olive trees, acacia, elder, and bird cherry. The acacia had already faded; only a hint of its former dominion remained in the bluish moonlit silence. It was so deserted, as if the whole world had forgotten all about Lukaniya; even during the day no one came here. In fact, now the tall, silky grasses filled the bottom of the shallow gully, while during my time there it was always trampled down. From all sides bushy hills crowded around—you couldn't see or hear the sea, or any dachas, or the town; as we made our way, we could still hear music coming from some outdoor activity somewhere in the distance. But now, after midnight, the members of the orchestra had already dispersed to their own homes.

"Are you pouting?" asked Marusya, her voice still suppressing inner joy.

On the way home she'd demanded that we row not to their dacha which lay farther to the south, but here; she jumped out onto the shore, extended her hand toward me, and ordered the others to go off wherever they wanted. "He'll escort me home later this week; if someone sees my mother tomorrow—tell her not to worry: there won't be any baby." They all obeyed and rowed away, saluting *sans rancune*—the way she'd trained them all some time ago; but I was not quite myself.

"Don't complain," she begged, holding me by the arm, and pressing up against me. "They won't be worried at home." (This was true: in that carefree family, not only Marusya but even the younger ones would often spend a night out in the boat with a group.)

"Am I complaining?"

"Sort of. You're ... giving me the silent treatment. Today you mustn't; today you must give me a pat on the head. I know what the problem is. You're afraid of what the others will think: now, at long last, Marusya's recruited him as one of her 'sightseers'—even he couldn't escape! Right?"

I confessed that she was right; but my annoyance quickly dissipated as a result of the closeness of her face, the moonlight, the beauty, and the quiet all around.

"Sit down," she ordered, "and I'll lay my tempestuous head in your lap. That's not taking too great a liberty, is it?"

I spread my jacket on the grass and sat down on a tussock; she lay down, taking some time to position her head in my lap, all the while chuckling softly to herself. She finally got settled, sighed with relief, reached out, took both my hands, and asked, "Are you comfy?"

"Very. And you?"

"Oh, extremely comfortable. Just like when I was swimming in the water but even better. Did you get angry at me for taking a swim off the boat?"

I freed one hand and made a gesture, as if tweaking her by the ear: "That's all, now you're forgiven." She laughed softly and demanded: "Give me back your hand: that's part of my coziness." Then we both fell silent and became absorbed in looking around. It's a writer's habit to seize upon every opportunity, and I was about to mock myself by saying that everything around us was just as it is in books—a summer night, a valley, the light fragrance of fading blossoms, even the moon, and not a soul anywhere for miles around—but no sarcasm emerged; I suddenly felt that the age-old colors of God's palette were very fine indeed, better than anything else on earth; there was no irony in my soul—only a liturgy. And I had one other thought for the first time in my life: that youth is not merely a number of years, but a particular, genuine, essential quality—that there would come a time when it would cease to be; on the other hand, today it resided in me and Marusya; the whole valley and the sky above were serving us and bowing down before us.

Marusya raised her eyes to me and asked in a whisper, very naturally, as if it were a perfectly reasonable request:

"Am I allowed to cry?"

"You are."

She covered her eyes with my hands; her cheeks were cool and her eyelashes tickled my palms affectionately. I don't know if she wept; her shoulders sometimes shuddered slightly, but that was no proof. We were silent for a long time; suddenly she took my hands away, raised her eyes to mine again—they really were moist—and whispered:

"My dear . . . rebuke me with all your might."

I asked, also in an undertone:

"For what?"

"Come closer, or else the bugs will overhear. . . . For all that you think of me, or would think of me, if you weren't so foolish, and kind, and . . . such a stranger."

"I'm not a stranger!"

"I know better; but we're not talking about you now, but about me. Rebuke me."

"Why do you want me to?"

"Just so. It's necessary. Or else I'll start banging my head against a tree trunk."

I didn't understand what was happening to her, but it was clear that this was not some game or trick: for some reason or other she had a genuine craving—it was necessary to help her, to respond. But the response was coming by itself, apart from my intention—all the magic of the moment, the surroundings, and her proximity had grabbed hold of me. I asked obediently:

"Prompt me: what should I rebuke you for?"

She opened her eyes:

"For the escapade on the boat; for the fact that I always tease and taunt everyone and intentionally make things murky. For the fact that all of me is . . . soiled by handling. It's true, isn't it?"

I was silent.

"Repeat it," she begged, squeezing my hands with all her might. "Murky." "Soiled."

I kept silent.

"And one more thing: 'Cheap.' Repeat it!"

"Marusya," I replied sharply. "Open your eyes and look who's here with you. It's me; I'm not a nobleman from Chernigov, a member of an established gentry family or whatever dumb thing it's called, named Alesha."

"He's not a dumb thing," she whispered. "Don't you dare. He's right."

I was silent; I was really angry.

"Isn't he right? Isn't all this—about me—the real truth?"

"Even if it's 'true,'" I said, "it still doesn't mean he's 'right.'"

This often occurs: you touch a person—and you strike precisely the nerve center of pain. Most likely, these words of mine hit upon just what was tormenting her. Up to this time, if I strain my memory, I can still hear her long, passionate confession and her defense; I remember it all by heart. Her face, eyes closed as she spoke, was terribly serious: neither I nor even "Alesha" stood before her then and accused her, but something different, something I'd never seen in her before.

"With God as my witness: I don't tease or taunt anyone intentionally. I live and I laugh and . . . I make friends just as it turns out. If it turns out badly, that means that I myself am essentially bad and that God has cursed me from my birth. But I don't do anything for a specific purpose.

"I haven't hurt anyone. Here they all are now before my mind's eye, every single one of them, the whole . . . lot; which of them is any worse off because I behaved as I did? We had a month's fling, then grieved for a month, and now we're grateful both for the good time and for the ending. I'm not profound, I don't poison a person's whole life; I'm a glass of wine mixed with water; you take a swallow, shake it off, and forget it. Is there really no right or place for such people on earth?

"'Soiled by handling': all right, so be it. I sometimes think: if I were a famous singer, and a friend came to me, simply a casual acquaintance, and said: 'Sing something for me, Marusya'—what then? Should I sing or not? Is it permitted to give another person some part of my being? Everyone will say, 'Yes, it is.' But isn't talent a form of affection? Perhaps it's even much more sacred and secret than affection. For me affection is simply one aspect of friendship; I may be bad, but it's the truth."

I knew that she was smart, but up to this time she'd never talked to me with such concentrated conviction; I never suspected that she had such original thoughts. I asked:

"Is that sophistry or do you really think that?"

"I swear I do."

She suddenly opened her eyes, let go of my hands, pressed her little fists to her chest, and said aloud:

"I will confess something else to you; I haven't said this to anyone. I don't begrudge affection; it's a trifle—like a kind word, a smile, or sugar candy. But, if I really had any talent, something unique, unrepeatable, chosen—then I would be really stingy! In that case, I might not only refuse to sing for a guest, but I might even be hesitant to perform at a concert, to reveal my real, genuine secret to others. I might hide away from the whole world in some dark corner; I might wait for a holiday, wait for that slave owner appointed by God, the kind described in novels. He alone would hear how I sing, and I'd kiss his feet for one word of praise: oh, Marusya also knows the worth of holy things, but let them be very sacred objects!"

Several times she clenched and released her fingers, as if grasping something in her full, undivided power, and her triumphant gaze was directed at me. I carefully raised one of her hands, brought it up to my lips, and kissed it.

"Am I absolved?" asked Marusya, making herself comfortable again. Once more everything within her rejoiced, and again, the moon, all the stars, the verdure all around, and I—we feasted our eyes on Marusya alone.

"Give me back your hands," she whispered, "or else I'll be lonely . . ." And again she laughed softly, pressing the heel of my palms to her cheeks, now hot; only her eyes were visible, somehow inexpressibly happy.

"Marusya?"

"What?"

"May I ask more?"

"You may ask anything."

"This Alesha—does that mean a 'slave owner' has arrived?"

She shook her head slowly.

"N . . . no. After all, I'm not a profound person: 'I have a mainspring instead of a heart.'"

"But it seems to me that the mainspring's already wound up very tightly . . ."

"Yes, but I know myself well, and I won't be able to keep it up for long. But to make such a big mess of things for the sake of one year of pleasant evenings: baptism, surrounded by strangers one's whole life, half-breed children who are mine, yet not really mine. . . . I'm not cut out for such heroic deeds."

She thought for a while and then added, almost to herself:

"One should marry simply, imperceptibly, and without upheaval."

I said quietly and seriously:

"May God keep you, Marusya, just as you are. If I were able to remake you, I would refuse. Perhaps each real person prays in his own way. There was *Le Jongleur de Notre-Dame*.[1] Perhaps you're like that: in your own way you diffuse warmth or grace—that's your way of praying; you don't know any other way and you don't have to. Today I'm glad that I never touched you and never will: on the other hand, my judgment is stronger; there's no young woman on earth better than you are, Marusya."

She impetuously removed my hands, revealing her whole face: it was filled with avid gratitude, and a pale rainbow of tears covered her eyelashes.

"My dear, my dear . . . I don't know whether it's true or false, but you are a dear."

Suddenly she laughed at one of her own thoughts and explained it to me thus:

"The Christians have come up with a good idea: confession. But (I'm trying to continue your comparisons), to cast everything off—as I did on the boat—can't that sometimes be a confession, too?"

"That may be," I replied confidently. Just a day earlier I wouldn't have understood how this could be a "confession," but now, whatever she proposed seemed clear to me. Someone had judged her, told her that her behavior was impure; she was calling upon God, the night, and the sea as her judges, and demanding vindication: am I really impure? Most likely it was at this point that I remembered Phryne;[2] I must have told her about the judgment of Phryne; in any case, I understood and replied confidently: "That may be!"

"Since morning," she whispered (she'd received a letter this morning), "since morning I've been restless and dreaming about a confession; that's why I threw myself into the water, why I dragged you here . . . but I'm still not satisfied."

[1] Opera in three acts (1902) by Jules Massenet (1842–1912) in which the juggler offers to the Blessed Virgin the only gifts he possesses—his songs and dances.

[2] A Greek courtesan charged with impiety and defended by one of her lovers, who secured her acquittal by exhibiting her in the nude.

Gradually her expression changed, she withdrew into herself, and something tense and concentrated appeared in her eyes, as if she would experience pain caused by happiness.

"Come closer."

She whispered into my ear:

"I've never given you anything. May I? Not as I do for others, but different?"

"You may."

"Close your eyes."

Through my pounding temples I heard once again the same rustling as on the boat—I felt that she was moving and turning near my knees; for some sweet reason I didn't want this moment to end and for her to say, "Open your eyes." Or else, I did, but later, not right then. She didn't call me; she was no longer stirring, and the rustling went quiet, but she still didn't call me, and then she said softly at first:

"Judgment Day for Marusya. I won't want to go on living if you think I'm teasing; that's not it at all. . . . Now, open your eyes."

I obeyed. I was struck by her expression—frowning, agitated, almost suffering. As before on the boat, it seemed to me once again that all the nerves in my head and my chest were vibrating like musical strings. I wasn't a child; in Rome, in Babuino, on one moonlit night, a crazy artist allowed me in his studio, when a Ciociara[3] named Lola, il più bel torso a piazza di Spagna,[4] was posing for him as a Shakespearean beggar-woman at the feet of the legendary king; but even Lola, dressed only in moonlight to the waist, was no more beautiful than Marusya. Once more I brought her hand up to my lips; that's just what the king was doing in the painting.

"I had to," Marusya whispered. "You're not angry?"

From my face she could see that I was "not angry," and she was laughing again. Suddenly I also felt lighthearted, as if all this had to happen. I felt that I could be with her again, converse, and joke simply and freely: the blood was still pounding in my temples, but that didn't hamper me.

"Give me back your hands; both of them!"

"Here, Marusya; but—mind."

"Why?" She laughed happily. "I'm not trying to get you. But why do you say, 'Mind?'"

[3] A person from Ciociaria, a region south of Rome.
[4] The loveliest body on the piazza.

"Each person likes to pray in his own way, not as those have done before him."

"Alright. I promise. But can I say anything?'

"Yes."

"Do you like me?"

"You know the answer to that."

"And you're not afraid that I'll maim you for life?"

"Your reach is too short," I laughed.

She made a face:

"Or you have bouillon in your veins instead of blood. No, no, I'm just chattering; don't get angry. Will you always be my friend? When I take refuge in some dark corner, will you come visit me?"

"Have you already chosen your dark corner?"

"As if you don't know whom I'm going to marry, and very soon."

"I didn't know it would be soon. As for whom, I guessed that to-day on the boat."

"Do you give your blessing?'

"To everything that Marusya wants, I give my blessing."

Suddenly I wanted to ask her one more question, and she understood:

"Say it. You're mine today, all thoughts are mine."

"I want to ask you about Alesha again—because you said what you did about bouillon. That must be true: we're like that in our circle. Our race has grown old, perhaps. But an outsider's another matter altogether. Who knows them, those Pechenegs?[5] Maybe they have a heart inside their chest instead of a mainspring? You might get hurt—and not be able to repair it?"

She screwed up her eyes, her face fell, and she bit her lip—something wolf-like or squirrel-like, very primitive, showed in her face at that moment.

"It doesn't matter," she whispered. "What will be, will be. I'll have to pay . . ."

. . . At dawn I dragged my old friend, the fisherman Avtonom Chubchik, out of his hut on the bank; he gave us each a piece of yesterday's bread with some sheep's milk cheese and took us back to Marusya's dacha; she sat quietly all the way home smiling to herself.

[5] Turkic people who occupied the steppes north of the Black Sea. They gradually moved west and attacked Russian territory.

—⁓— XVI —⁓—

Signor and Mademoiselle

In the autumn of that year I found myself in Bern; I arrived there from Italy, where I had spent a very amusing month.

During September Nicholas II was expected to pay a state visit to the Italian king; when the solemn announcement of this event was made at the parliament, someone on the extreme left cried out: "Forewarn St. Petersburg that we will heckle him!" The entire right-thinking half of the Palazzo Montecitorio[1] replied with guffaws at such boasting. Afterwards it was said that it was precisely this outburst of merriment that played the decisive role: this one deputy's shout was impromptu and ad-libbing, everyone was prepared to forget it, but in reply to the guffaws—sedition decided to win out. Meetings took place throughout the country and resolutions were enacted: to heckle him indeed. The radical press maintained that supposedly thousands of whistles and noisemakers were being purchased in shops; the government was rumored to be about to forbid the free sale of such goods, but for the intervention of the minister of justice. The moderate press, on the other hand, hinted that many vacant cells in Roman prisons were being readied, and that on the eve of the visit there would be an enormous roundup. Not only in the Café Aragno, but also in every tavern, an uproar arose as a result of all the arguments between hecklers and defenders. It was a very amusing month.

Once, I remember, I went to the Palazzo Montecitorio to delight in

---

[1] The building where the Italian parliament meets.

its usual parliamentary pandemonium. The spectacle turned out wonderfully: the president rang the bell with both his hands, but the sound was inaudible as a result of the choral efforts from all sections of the hall. In the gallery policemen moved among the public and kept close watch so that we, the spectators, wouldn't somehow interfere in the legislative process; but, as a matter of fact, if my neighbor on the right had suddenly begun singing "Carmagnole" or "God Save the Tsar" at the top of his lungs, the policeman would have been able to surmise such a violation of the serenity and grandeur only by the movement of his lips. This neighbor on the right, by the way, turned out to be a dear, old friend of mine (at least, that's what he thought); he almost hugged me when I sat down next to him, squeezed both my hands, and said something in animated fashion; but what he said, and even in which language he said it, remained a secret between him and the all-hearing heavenly Ear. In appearance, however, he was undoubtedly Italian, and his face was vaguely familiar.

Suddenly, at the height of the commotion, he jabbed me and pointed to the extreme left, and, by reading his lips, I could make out the name: Ferri.[2] I glanced over: the tall, thin acrobatic figure of the famous criminologist stood not on a bench but on top of a desk—he seemed to be restraining his closest neighbors with both hands, while they pushed and shoved excitedly and appeared to be shouting at each other: "It will all happen soon." Ferri had been my professor at one time; I knew his stentorian voice, but here it was incredible— even the siren of an ocean liner would have been drowned out. But I was mistaken: he opened his mouth—and not from where he stood but from somewhere in the middle of the ceiling there of different material or emanating from the fourth dimension—a sound that simply had no relationship to other human sounds; they wouldn't hamper it, it would pass through them without delay, like a ray of light through the air or a knife through butter:

"We-will-heckle-him!"

My neighbor waved his arm for some reason, took both my hands to bid me fond farewell, and then ran off.

Around that time in the newspapers there appeared the information that Signor M.-M. had arrived in Rome: he had a double sur-

<hr />

[2] See chapter 4, n. 6.

name, Russian, and even then was fairly well known both in Russia and in Italy. I knew this M.-M. personally, although I had ceased being proud of our friendship. Much earlier, during my student days, I was introduced to him by a visiting Russian writer, who, just like me, was innocent and ill informed about the composition of the Russian secret police abroad. I recall how astonished we both were at Signor M.-M.'s odd official post: on his calling card was printed something like "Representative to the Holy See"—even though, of course, he was not the ambassador to the Vatican. His occupation supposedly consisted of managing an ancient townhouse inherited from the kingdom of Poland and the grand duchy of Lithuania on the via dei Polacchi—which, in reality, he didn't manage at all. But then there are all sorts of miracles in the world of diplomacy; yet the man was genial and polite. Only afterwards, in Russia, we learned about his actual role. . . . To this day I don't know on whom he was carrying out his surveillance at "the Holy See" at that time when there were so few Russians; but now, in anticipation of the tsar's visit, it was clear why he made another appearance: to determine on site, whether the tsar would be heckled or not.

Apparently, he fulfilled his assignment conscientiously. He himself had many acquaintances in Rome; there was also a special native informant whom I had met at some point at his hotel, a certain Doctor Vernicci. Together they investigated everything accurately and reported honestly: the tsar would indeed be heckled. One cheerless day it was announced that the state visit would not take place after all: the amusing month came to an end, and I left for Bern on personal business.

I had also spent one semester here during my youth, when the university, for some reason, was still located in the same building as the police. I looked for many of my old friends among the political emigrants; but, just as my alma mater had already moved to a new location, far from the police station, I was also unable to recognize the student members of the "colony." My first impression was that they were all dolled up. The "dregs" of both sexes were in the minority. The young ladies, who in my time had all adopted the "simple life," now all sported fancy hairstyles; they wore blouses with ornamented insertions and skirts with flounces even to lectures, and showed up at evening parties in one-piece dresses; already appearing on the horizon, although I had no idea about it, was the future décolleté dress. As for the men, I thought there was something missing, but I didn't immediately guess what it was: they were missing the yellowish cardboard collars made by the Leipzig firm of Mey and Edlich, which, in my day, we all, to a man, considered to be the universal arbiter of fashion—now everyone had collars obviously made of fabric, even if it was difficult to vouch for the date of the last laundering. I walked into the student union dining room after dinner, when it was empty, and found a pile of books on the windowsill, obviously left there until supper by someone hurrying to a lecture: the selection of literature also indicated the new tunes. There was, in fact, Seignobos[3] and Zheleznov;[4] but there was also a worn copy of the *Northern Messenger*[5] from the age of Volynsky[6] and Gippius[7] (in my day we never picked up such heretical texts); there was also a copy of *Les Fleurs du mal*[8] in the original; there were even some works of a purely erotic nature—and, that's putting it politely—with very explicit full-page illustrations.

"Yes," the dean of the colony said to me in a melancholy tone of voice, a distinguished Menshevik, "obviously something's changing back there in Russia. They come here filled with all that decadent stuff, at meetings they jabber about some sexual problem . . . of course, it's still not dangerous; and, after talking, they all disperse and spend their night alone—at least, that's what I suppose . . ."

Nevertheless, the political pulse was quivering feverishly. But it also took a novel form: in my day everyone cursed autocracy in concert; now for the most part, people abused each other. It was during the first years following the rupture in the Social Democratic Party: it was here that I first heard the use of the words Bolshevik and Menshevik, terms that were still little known in Russia outside the underground. "Your Lenin—is an exasperated imbecile," one of them declared; another replied: "On the other hand, he's not a fop like your

---

[3] Charles Seignobos (1854–1942) is best known in Russia for his *History of Russia in the XIX–XX Centuries: A Survey of the Emancipation Movement* (1906).

[4] Vladimir Zheleznov (1869–1933) is the author of *Studies in Political Economy* (1901).

[5] An important, so-called thick (i.e., serious) journal published in St. Petersburg from 1885 to 1899.

[6] A. Volynsky was the pseudonym of A. L. Flekser (1863–1926), a literary critic and art historian.

[7] Zinaida Gippius (1869–1945) was a symbolist poet, novelist, critic, and playwright, and the founder of a famous St. Petersburg literary salon.

[8] The single volume of poetry published in 1857 by the first "modern" French poet, Charles Baudelaire (1821–67).

Plekhanov!"[9] As much as I understood the difference, one group was demanding that the upheaval should take place in Russia on an appointed day according to a precisely prearranged plan, and all the party committees "to the last man" were supposed to be appointed from above, that is, from abroad; the other group stood for the elective principle and the "organic development" of revolution. After looking closely, one could clearly discern in the midst of all this diversity a rigid hierarchy in degrees of revolutionary orthodoxy; no one, of course, would admit that he considered his opponent more orthodox than he himself was—but it was immediately obvious who was attacking and who was defending, swearing: "If you please, I, too . . ." The Plekhanovites apologized to the Leninists, the Social Revolutionaries to the Marxists, the Bundists to all the rest, the Social Zionists of various stripes to the Bundists; simple Zionists were generally considered to be out of bounds and didn't even attempt to beg forgiveness.

Sitting in Russia, we thought we were enjoying our "springtime," and that things were "simmering"; but from here, Russia on the eve of 1905 seemed like a shallow backwater, not even just deep, still water—as opposed to this rumbling torrent of words, where there was no need for any hints, where anything could be uttered in extreme language and printed in bold letters—and nothing could be actively undertaken. For the first time during that autumn month in Bern I understood the venomous curse of the emigrant's existence, and for the first time I appreciated the old comparisons: a wheel with enormous force turning through empty space, the force—a result of the absence of a transmission and the fact that there was no way to steer it; "and the soul's juice was being used up in this torment, just like a mother's milk dries up during separation from her suckling infant." But the soul's juice is not reabsorbed; it accumulates, hardens, and burns the consciousness forever; and if fate ever wills it thus and the exiles en masse suddenly return to their homeland and become its sovereigns, they will pervert all paths and all measures. I recalled this often afterwards when I saw in Istanbul how the returning Young Turks[10] managed to destroy liberated Turkey; and subsequently, in

[9] Georgy Plekhanov (1857–1918) was a revolutionary writer, social thinker, and one of the chief exponents of Marxism in Russia.

[10] A nationalist and reformist group in the Ottoman Empire that forced the restoration of the constitution in 1908 and eventually succeeded in deposing the sultan.

connection with Russian events—but this chapter isn't about that; this chapter, as a matter of fact, is about Lika.

Once when I returned from Lugano, I found a telegram at home and a letter, both from Odessa. The telegram was already three days old: "Lika, Bern, Matenhoffstrasse. Find her. I wired two hundred to such-and-such a bank in your name. Anna Milgrom." The letter was from Serezha, sent at the same time as the telegram: he wrote that Lika had escaped from Vologda and made it to Switzerland. I remember the main points almost word for word: "Imagine, she didn't even hide along the way: she simply washed—and not only the gendarmes, but even her own beloved brother couldn't recognize her. . . . Who got some money to her? Guess! You take me for scum, but I got it for her and delivered it where needed (through a friend in Motya Banabak's gang); I said not a word to my dear parents, so as not to raise their expectations. . . . You ask, how did Serezha lay his hands on such a large sum of money? Read on and feel ashamed: there are fifty-two weeks in a year and the same number of cards in a deck; a genius remains a genius, in spite of the iron shackles with which you manacled the free rein of my tactics. . . . If the rendezvous with the indomitable Katherina ends when an azure imprint remains on Petruchio's cheek,[11] then I can affirm on the basis of personal experience, that the plant arnica helps cure black eyes . . ." He also wrote that Anna Mikhailovna had the flu but that she would make a trip to Bern, as soon as she recovered. At another time Marusya would have come, but "now she's gone off her head—her sailor has moored: there's a deep freeze in our castle and a military siege, but they'll tell you all about it when you set foot beneath our gothic vaults."

I hastened to Matenhoff and knocked at the designated door in the attic; from there I heard the word, "Entrez": it was so distinct and splendidly guttural that I wondered if I was mistaken, but then I recalled that Lika and her younger brothers had had a governess for a long time. I entered and almost cried out. Serezha had excessively oversimplified her transformation: "she washed." Before me stood a creature from another planet, elegant and refined from the lofty hairstyle to the narrow high-heeled shoes. Her figure made such an impression on my memory that even today, if I knew how, I could recreate on paper the fashions of that day: a high collar reaching her

---

[11] The hero and heroine of Shakespeare's early comedy, *The Taming of the Shrew*.

ears, a blouse with a mass of little buttons down the front, close-fitting shoulders, a wide, "overflowing" waist—and sleeves, tight on top, but wide at the wrists. An artist's vision was no longer needed to notice Lika's absolutely dazzling beauty. It was only on her hand that she extended to me and then quickly withdrew, that I noticed her bitten off fingernails: it was really the only trait I could recognize. As a matter of fact, in that guise she could be incognito not only in Vologda but even at home in her own living room.

On the way to the bank, she chatted politely, but not much, and looked straight ahead; she didn't mention her escape, didn't inquire after her family, and asked only one thing about me: how soon did I intend to leave? She did say, however, that she planned to enroll in the university.

Complications ensued at the bank. The money had been received in my name—Lika, of course, had no documents; but I had completely forgotten that I myself had left Russia—I don't even remember for what reason—with my colleague Shtrok's passport (I recall that the border guard at Volochinsk shook his head for a long time because I looked so young for a thirty-year-old). In those happy years it was still possible to wander around Europe without documents, but in the bank it was necessary to produce something more respectable than a calling card. I was very embarrassed. Of course, I could have gone to fetch one of my acquaintances, a longtime inhabitant of the city, to vouch for my identity; but it was already nearing four o'clock, which would mean postponing it all until the next day, whereas I clearly felt that one meeting with me was more than enough for Lika, and that she was standing there, despising me for my indolence.

All of a sudden an elegant man in a bowler hat walked over to me—more accurately, ran over to me; he grabbed both my hands and merrily started speaking Italian. Once again I recognized that neighbor on the right from the Palazzo Montecitorio, and once more I realized that I'd met him somewhere before. He shook my hands and inquired how I was, but I noticed that he was looking at Lika, not at me; he was actually staring at her.

"Excuse me, I accidentally overheard: you're having some kind of problem? If you'd like me to testify that you really are who you say you are, I'd be glad to assist: I'm well known here. Or, is it necessary for the signorina? Please."

And, removing his bowler hat, he introduced himself to Lika, saying in reasonably correct Russian:

"I'm very glad to be of service. I love your compatriots; my name is Vernicci."

Even before he'd said his name, from the moment he began speaking Russian, I suddenly remembered who he was: Doctor Vernicci, comrade-in-arms of Signor M.-M., Italian collaborator for the secret police in Rome. I almost burst out laughing: fate had selected quite the person for me to introduce to Lika!

But Lika was destined to keep astonishing me that day. In the first place, she extended her hand to him, not merely politely but even affectionately; in the second, she replied to him in French, with such an authentic accent, that one would have thought she was a native-born Parisian—in any case, a Parisian would have taken her, let's say, for a native of Lyon:

"I don't understand Russian, but I do speak a little Italian; I'm very grateful to you; the remittance is really for me."

In one moment he arranged the whole matter. Lika put the money away and said, "Merci" to him and to me at the same time. He proposed that we have a cup of coffee together; I, of course, left that decision to Lika, with the absolute certainty that she would decline, but she accepted, nodding her head with entirely patrician indulgence. I bit my lip to keep from laughing and annoyance but tagged along with them; I have to confess that they made an attractive couple— tourists we met along the way turned to look (the Swiss themselves don't pay any attention to visitors, except for business reasons). Vernicci switched to French, which he spoke rather well; Lika replied cordially—and the main thing is, she actually spoke! Once it even seemed to me that she smiled. I remained silent, trying to understand what was happening. Perhaps the embittered loathing she bestowed on us did not extend to a man from another world—just as an unsociable person can still love horses or cats. Or else, perhaps the three daughters of the Vologda priest had managed to soften her? Or simply—*menschliches, allzumenschliches*[12]—had she taken a liking to this chivalrous, southern gentleman? He was very proper: though he learned she was staying in Bern, he didn't inquire for what purpose;

[12] German. This phrase, "human, all too human," was adopted as the title of a work published in 1878 by the German philosopher Friedrich Nietzsche.

nor did he ask her address or even her name; on the other hand, he asked for my address (I said that I was leaving the next day), gave me his, and explained that he would stay in Switzerland for about three months "on personal business."

He took his leave on the street. I didn't know what to do next: observe decorum, that is, escort her home, or else, relieve her by bidding farewell right there? But she resolved all my doubts: she neither paused at the exit nor asked meaningfully: "Which way are you headed?" She merely set out along the road and I followed behind; almost immediately she inquired, without looking at me:

"Who is that man?"

I replied truthfully and even apologized that she had to shake his hand; but it really wasn't my fault.

Suddenly she laughed and said:

"I have nothing against making such acquaintances. It may even come in handy."

I accompanied her to her house; as we said goodbye, she didn't invite me to return, nor did she send her regards to her family; however, she did thank me again, took her arm from mine, and withdrew with a regal gait.

The Godseeker

I left Switzerland but spent a long time abroad and wound up in St. Petersburg just before the outbreak of the Russo-Japanese War.

Marko was now studying Sanskrit, not Persian, and living in student rooms. I don't remember if he was still a vegetarian, but his soul was filled with a new passion—he attended meetings of a religious-philosophical society. He was dropping the names of bishops, monks, and priests as if I was supposed to know who they all were. Piles of exotic books were stacked in his room and he entertained me with conversations about monastic structure, autocephaly, and the role of laymen in the church; he informed me that there was not one but two catholicos in the Armenian-Gregorian church, and in addition, three patriarchs, and with them, "ecclesiastical orders" of the sixth and seventh degree; but, as for the Armenian congregation in Vienna and Venice—that was a different matter, they were Catholic monks (he despised Catholics). He was indirectly interested even in Judaism and told me enthusiastically about "bald Borukh." It turned out that at meetings of his religious-philosophical society, a certain bearded Jew nicknamed bald Borukh was very popular; he was actually a Marxist and considered to be an enemy of the Bund, but from his youth, in concert with an invincible Litvak[1] agent, he had retained an enormous supply of quotations from the Talmud and even from the Kabbalah; and, as regards casuistic resourcefulness, he "slew" (in

---

[1] A Jew from Lithuania, usually implying a shrewd, clever man.

Marko's words) all Russian Orthodox academics. As a result of my own utter ignorance, it was hard for me to understand precisely what it was that he "slew" them about; but Marko now knew all the subtle distinctions between Judaism and Christianity in the perception of the divinity; he compared its feminine emanation with the idea of triunity and in general was unbearably profound.

I didn't listen to him very much but examined his surroundings. It was strange: was there really a meticulous maid who brought order to these student rooms? It was odd: in the corridor, at two o'clock in the afternoon, I made my way through several generations of unswept trash. And it wasn't only the neatness that struck me but also a small mirror decorated with bows, and the picture gallery on the walls—all postcards, and each one in provincial taste: a lad, a lass, the moon, Grandfather Frost in shimmering mica, and a supreme council of naked infants in an efficient and physiological pose; meanwhile, a little farther along, a portrait of a plump young lady wearing a large hat, sporting a tropical forest on the brim. I assumed the expression of Sherlock Holmes and asked without formality: "Your neighbor?"

"My neighbor," he replied and suddenly began to rearrange the books on his table. "She's a student; that is, she's not taking any courses yet; I'm tutoring her."

When he escorted me to the staircase, the door next to his opened slightly and that very same young woman peered out. She was not only plump but heavily made-up, with lined eyebrows; she was still in her dressing gown, and behind her one could glimpse her unmade bed and water splashed on the floor under her decorated washbasin.

"I'll be right there, Valentinochka," Marko said to her.

Two weeks later I went to visit some friends and learned that an announcement of the war would appear in the newspapers the following morning. The excitement at the table was palpable—and now, it's clear, especially from such a distance—the excitement was also peculiar: it's unlikely that this psychological moment has been repeated among educated society in any other country. The family was native Russian, of a progressive nature in favor of the zemstvo, and almost all the guests were, too. But this war excited them not as their own personal event but as something occurring nearby, very close, before their very eyes, but still not quite here. It was as if a roommate had fallen ill, or as if some drama on stage had struck them, seizing them to the depths of their soul: they were sitting in the orchestra, a few feet from the footlights but on the other side of the action.

The most peculiar thing of all was that no one knew anything. Knowledge about Japan came from distant textbooks: people were accustomed to consider it a small country, on the order of Holland; they didn't understand how such a runt nation would dare wage war on Russia; and they opened their eyes wide when they suddenly learned that more than fifty million people lived there. They also couldn't conceive that Russia wasn't the same kind of giant in the Far East—that only a thin thread of a single pitiful railway track led there over thousands of miles, along which platoon after platoon would trickle slowly, and even more stingily—provisions and ammunition. They knew even less, of course, where Manchuria was and who needed it: if they did know something, it was gossip about some Abaza,[2] or some Bezobrazov,[3] who either made a mess of things there, or stole things—but what or how, was unknown.

And, in spite of this (as of this morning) still unquestioned disparity between the runt and the giant, for some reason everyone was making spirited predictions: they would defeat our troops and no one in the whole house was saddened by this certainty. There, on the stage, the Japanese would defeat them; here, among us, in the auditorium, our urgent worries lay elsewhere—if the play flops and the whole enterprise collapses, then we'd be better off. . . . At the time, of course, none of this struck me in the least: I didn't expect anything different; only now, looking back, do I realize how strange it all was, how much age-old alienation must have accumulated for this fundamental, involuntary, original response of the national organism to this thorn piercing the body to be so misinterpreted.

The night before, Marko and I had agreed to meet the day after to-morrow for *pirozhki*[4] at Filippov's; of course, he was an hour late, but I knew he would be. I had no reason to complain: I met an acquaintance at Filippov's, a major writer from the capital. I won't name him, but everyone remembers him. He was, in my opinion (even though the general opinion remains different to this day), a man not authentically talented, but, on the other hand, he had specks of true genius:

[2] Identity unknown.
[3] Probably refers to Aleksandr Bezobrazov (1853–1931), who was involved in Russian activities in the Far East before the Russo-Japanese War.
[4] Meat-filled pastries.

a most unlucky and unfortunate combination. Talent consists of a high level of ability to do something well; in my opinion, however, he didn't know how to do anything well, and all of his big books about Russian novelists and Italian painters, intensely meditative but leading nowhere, will be forgotten. But he was sometimes able to astound and even stagger with a single line—all of a sudden to lift the lid of something unknown and reveal for a moment the reflection of primordial nature in a drop of ordinary rainwater. Once (but we were speaking of another author), I heard a fine phrase from him to characterize this ability: "a shaft of light into eternity." He was a product of the Jewish primary school and spoke with that accent. It was a great pleasure to converse with him, especially when he was in good form: recalling last summer, it was like that night at sea when we were splashing about in the phosphorescent water.

That day he was not merely in good form, he was trembling with excitement. I sat down next to him and expected that I would hear views very different from those I'd heard the day before. All his life he'd been digging passionately into the most minute twists and turns of the Russian soul and Russian thought; he could devote a whole page to learned discourse on the significance of black hair on some character in *Devils* ("a lifeless cover between consciousness and infinity");[5] he once delivered a lecture in Odessa (in Odessa, no less!) about some icon named "Wider than the Heavens," and another one called, perhaps, "Panagea"—and in general about the difference between Byzantine and Slavic iconography (he donated all the proceeds to the victims of the Kishinev pogrom); it was then we became acquainted. I expected, in the simplicity of my soul, that such a man, especially by the Jewish straightforwardness of these ardent natures, would stand up for Russia organically, blindly, and *quand même.*

Instead, he prophesied "a crushing defeat," "a predestined crushing defeat. And not at all because the regime is bad: the race itself is ill fated."

"Are you really saying that? You, who . . ."

"Oh, don't confuse two different hypostases of our national countenance. On the heights, Russians ignite incomparable universal fires, but in the flats, splinters flicker. This is the token of their great-

---

[5] *Devils (Besy)*, also known in English as *The Possessed* and *The Demons*, is a novel written by Fyodor Dostoevsky (1821–81) and published in 1871–72.

ness: the sluggish slow-wittedness of millions—so that the spirit of the race would be concentrated more brilliantly in a chosen few. It's the complete opposite with us Jews: among us talent is widely distributed; everyone has some gifts, but there are no geniuses; even Spinoza was only a jeweler of thought, and Marx was simply a conjurer."

"Why then couldn't some military leader of genius appear among them?"

"Contemporary warfare is like contemporary industry: no Colbert[6] would help, not even a Suvorov.[7] What's needed is the initiative of each and every officer, and more than simply native wit—what's needed is a spark of the conscious will to victory in every anonymous soul."

"Isn't it there already—even in some unconscious form?"

"No, it isn't. Russians are a god-bearing people; it's a trite phrase, yet true. But the highest divine service, as in ancient Israel, is performed only three times a year, no more. The god of the Japanese is an earthly god: the state. It's a convenient god, in every soldier's knapsack, always at your service."

"Well," I said consolingly, "many hope that a defeat might bring us a constitution."

"What banality! I wouldn't take all the parliaments of the world in exchange for the life of one Yaroslavl peasant. It's shameful even to think about that: to discount bloody bills."

"Lord, but if the Yaroslavl peasant has to suffer, it shouldn't be in vain . . ."

"Torments are always 'not in vain.' All torments are always and everywhere specific to the race—but of invisible races, where new stages of penetration arise, new acts of aboveground tragedies, but not new measures of well-being."

It was becoming difficult for me to understand his metaphysics, and I don't recall the rest; but soon Marko arrived, and at last I found the first real patriot in all St. Petersburg. He didn't even apologize for his lateness; he sat there with his collar raised, because the porter at the military office had let him know that his undershirt was showing

---

[6] Jean-Baptiste Colbert (1619–83) was a French statesman who significantly developed the economy and military capability of France.

[7] Aleksandr Suvorov (1729–1800) was a Russian field marshal with a distinguished military record in several wars.

beneath his jacket, and he'd forgotten to put on a shirt—obviously he'd left the house even before the leisurely Valentinochka had gotten up.

"Excuse me, why the military office?"

As it turned out, he'd decided to go to war as a volunteer: that morning he'd rushed off to make inquiries but still hadn't managed to locate the precise room necessary, and suffered many setbacks as he wandered from office to office; but it was clear that he was accepting his suffering with gladness. As far as being a soldier, he'd decided once and for all: he was writing home today; tomorrow he'd return to the office with a school-friend of his—i.e., she wasn't taking any courses yet, but . . . and so on and so forth—she was a capable person and would locate the appropriate table immediately, where they would administer the oath, provide weapons, and pack him off on a train. That is, of course, there'd be a period of training; but it needn't be long—don't you see, "he'd learned to shoot" when he took part in the self-defense effort, back in Heinrich's apartment.

My interlocutor knew him from a distance, had met him at religious-philosophical discussions. He delicately expressed doubt that the fatherland was in need of volunteers at this time; Marko, in reply, approached the subject from a broader point of view—concerning Odin and Zeus, Saint Augustine and Buddha, Shintoism and Russia's providential mediation. A conversation ensued between the two of them that was not for my obtuse mind; I remained silent and thought about Anna Mikhailovna. Serezha, it's true, had written to me that "Marusya's Argonaut" had sailed off so far without incident, but that "the ancestral ghost of the Milgroms was wandering nightly through the resonant galleries of the patriarchal castle and every midnight would wail in a treble voice: 'Gevalt!'" Things were not very cheerful with Marusya; Lika was still Lika; and Serezha was Serezha; at the mention of his name his mother's wise, patient eyes would grow sad when she was alone with me. It was no longer merry in their merry home, previously so full of laughter; and now this blockhead wanted to add even more joy. An idea occurred to me; I left them to their *pirozhki* and their efforts to comprehend God, and I went to Marko's apartment.

Valentinochka was embarrassed but welcomed me joyfully: Marko had praised me. By now things had already been tidied up over there; I saw the same suburban luxury as at Marko's place, without any books, of course, but with teapots, little teacups, and a canary. Rouge had been applied again and heavily, a velvet ribbon attached to her light brown curls, another ribbon on her shoulder. She insisted that I have some more tea with jam, in spite of the feast at Filippov's; she turned out to be a native Odessan—judging by her accent, from Peresyp. "I don't like to go out," she explained, pouring tea. "People are so vile, always pestering me. Of course, now, as soon as anything happens, I instantly move a good ways away." She repeated the word "now" in almost every sentence that had autobiographical content: it was clear that previously and "now" (as she herself said) were "two big differences."

"Is Marko preparing you to take university courses?" I asked sympathetically. "Frebelichka,[8] Bestuzhev's courses,[9] or something else?"

She looked at me distrustfully, wondering if I was making fun of her; in fact, I was stupid. There was no need to ask.

"Mark Ignatievich is a kind soul," she said, and suddenly her voice trembled. "He would pick a sparrow up off the street and would make him over into, I don't know what; a peacock. No way I'm going to take any courses; I want to learn how to sew, but I still can't get up early in the morning. He took me to the Art Theater when the Muscovites came to perform—but I requested, and with difficulty, received permission to leave."

I liked her sincerity; without beating around the bush, I got down to business. I asked her to prevent Marko from going into the military and made her understand that she was our only hope.

Valentinochka literally grew fierce; loud tones resounded in her voice, evidently carried over from her "previous" existence.

"Send him off to shoot? And I would have to take him to that office? I'd scratch his eyes out. . . . Him! If there's a puddle on Kolontaevsky Street, and he's over on Kanatsky Street—without fail he'll manage to fall into that puddle. Excuse me, how do you say it in your language: *schlimazel*.[10] Or, in the theater I heard how Muscovites say it: "twenty-two misfortunes."[11] Why even here during training he'd be struck by a Japanese bullet! I'll let him have it . . ."

---

[8] A young woman receiving training to become a nanny in courses organized according to the principles of Friedrich Fröbel (1782–1852), German educator and founder of the kindergarten.

[9] The only form of higher education open to women.

[10] Yiddish. A chronically unlucky person; a born loser.

[11] The comic nickname of the character Semyon Yepikhodov in *The Cherry Orchard* (1904) by Anton Chekhov (1860–1904).

It was in the bag: Marko was saved. I marveled at the twisted paths of Providence—you can never guess what will turn out to be a calamity or a blessing. I made her promise that Marko wouldn't find out about our conversation.

"Don't worry," she replied militantly, "I'll swear at him so lustily, I'll forget all about you."

I didn't see Marko any more during that month; I soon departed for the south and there discovered that at home they hadn't heard a word about this latest idea of his: Valentinochka had managed it all so quickly; he didn't even have time to write.

We met up again in St. Petersburg during the summer of that year. I wrote to him and gave him my address; the following day, around three o'clock, he rushed in to see me, not quite himself from happiness; he grabbed hold of both my arms, pulled me from the vestibule into my room and said, gasping for breath:

"Do you know what just happened half an hour ago? Plehve[12] was assassinated by a bomb!"

And, tossing his cap up to the ceiling, he shouted:

"Banzai!"

This cheer in the language of the samurais and geishas was then the most popular exclamation in the mouths of literate, protesting Russians, and merited a whole confession. Even through my own sincere joy at his striking news, I couldn't help marveling at the powerful sweep of his spiritual pendulum.

We decided to go for a walk and listen to what was being said on the street. But this didn't prove to be easy: his cap, it turned out, had sailed not up to the ceiling but onto the top of my enormous wardrobe. It was impossible to reach from a chair; we had to move the table over; but at long last we headed out.

The street turned out to be in the same mood as Marko and I were. Some people walked in pairs, smiling and nodding their heads approvingly; others met and stopped to shake each other by the hand and utter as their greeting: "Well done!" But we didn't manage to eavesdrop on any real conversations: Marko kept interfering. All along the way he kept talking about himself. He had definitely decided to become a Brahmin. In addition, now he was studying the art of breathing with a genuine yogi. This, you see, was the most impor-

[12] Vyacheslav Plehve (1846–1904) was a Russian statesman who pursued reactionary policies in a number of important government positions.

tant thing on earth—to draw oxygen into every nook and cranny of the respiratory system; this cleans not only the blood but also the gray matter of the brain, and the mind itself. Every morning—ten minutes of exercise; it's even better if two people do it together, but it must absolutely be done in the morning, and if someone gets up late, then it's so much the worse for him . . .

───ᴠᴠᴠ─ XVIII ─ᴠᴠᴠ───

Potemkin Day

A year later I recall an important and horrible day; all of Odessa and all of Russia recall it, too.

I spent the autumn, winter, and spring on trains, but occasionally I came home and would visit Anna Mikhailovna. The good Lord had sent her some respite. Lika was a student (in Paris, where she'd transferred from Bern); she wrote infrequently and coldly, but she was, thank heavens, there, and not here. Serezha was finishing his third year at the university and was leading a multifaceted existence but, at least, outside the field of vision of my colleague Shtrok.

Marko had already spent an entire year without undertaking any dangerous new projects—he was in good hands; however, he wasn't completely without projects. He came home for the Easter holidays, and that was the time he had the distressing incident with the Mesaksudi tobacco factory. He learned that if you sent in several thousand empty packets of their brand of cigarettes, this firm would reward the loyal client (or, let's say his lady friend) with one month's vacation in Yalta. Ever since autumn, having rejected his theory of breath, Marko had become an insane smoker, even though he still hadn't learned to inhale; he assessed all his acquaintances in Odessa with a duty on their cigarette packets; at this time he became especially close to the two brothers and grain dealers, Abram Moiseevich and Boris Mavrikievich, who lit each cigarette from the burning end of the previous one. But after he'd packed up the heavy load with his own hands and personally delivered it to the post office and sent it off to the Mesaksudi office, he received an indignant letter back stating that there was no such offer—where on earth had he heard that? He then confessed to me that he'd heard it in St. Petersburg from a waiter in a Greek restaurant; he was very embarrassed and crushed, and soon left for the north to recuperate.

There was a new generation of "sightseers" gathered around Marusya, just as merry as the previous group, although these were legal assistants and doctors-in-training; however, for some reason, it seemed to me that she kept them in a separate railway carriage, so to speak, and didn't allow them into her own coupé; or, if she did, it was only infrequently. About Runitsky, she once managed to say that his mother and sister had moved to their estate near Chernigov, and he spent his infrequent shore leaves out there but didn't say any more about him to me, and didn't reveal the contents of his letters which arrived occasionally bearing exotic stamps.

"Thank heaven," Anna Mikhailovna confessed to me once, "because last summer, when they were living near here, you know, I turned gray."

Of course, I didn't inquire further but learned from her fragmentary remarks that there was a month when she was awaiting an "earthquake" at any moment. Marusya would go off with him, just the two of them, on a rowboat, and return just before dawn. One time there was a storm, and Anna Mikhailovna sat up the whole night and didn't go to bed; Marusya returned to the dacha early the next morning in a cab and said that the previous evening, as soon as the water had become rough, they'd returned to shore. Her mother asked anxiously: but . . . where were you all that time? Marusya replied that they'd sat and chatted in a valley on the Langeron, near Prokudin's dacha, where his family lived at that time. It was a bit painful for me, but, after all, the republic of Lukaniya was no longer mine.

Samoilo Kozodoi had also left Odessa: he bought his own "pharmacological" business in Ovidiopol, on the shore of the Dnestr estuary. Serezha once visited him there and brought home a poem about him of which I remember only one verse:

> Since language is not the same in different parts,
> But it's whimsical and different—
> He abandoned a pharmacy here,
> And opened a pharmacy there.

Torik, as always, was impeccably irreproachable. That summer he was promoted to the eighth grade and worked diligently to earn a medal; in general, he read and studied a great deal. Once I was completely astonished to see on his desk an Old Testament in the original and a textbook of biblical language with a mass of pencil annotations: this spirit never existed in his family or in his milieu, and I myself never even attempted to speak about these matters with them.

"It's only natural," he explained in reply to my wide-eyed stare. "I'm a Jew, after all, and that means I'm supposed to know all this; but the language is a bit tedious."

"Are you a Zionist, or what?

"How can I explain? I'm as much a Zionist as I am a proponent of Home Rule for Ireland: if Redmond[1] requires autonomy and you need Palestine—then I vote in favor; but I won't go there myself; I have no reason to."

His close friendship with Abram Moiseevich did not diminish. The childless old man (his son, Syoma, had died from scarlet fever when he was in the fifth grade) was extremely fond of Torik. On his behalf he forgot all about his contempt for "education," believed in him, and consulted him about business matters. He told me:

"This young man will grow up to be the best lawyer in all of Odessa. He never makes judgments just by guessing or joking; he's not, if you'll excuse me, a newspaperman. He has to study everything thoroughly beforehand. He's a serious fellow, very solid."

In the evenings in the small living room, apart from the young people, just as before, the two brothers played cards with Ignats Albertovich and other grain dealers, or else they talked about the harvest or argued about who was the best tenor of all during the last forty years at the municipal theater. Boris Mavrikievich would bang on the table and assert:

"There never was and never will be another such as Abramburo."

"Beiresh, you're a cow," Abram Moiseevich would reply, "You've forgotten all about Giannini in *The Huguenots*."

Then both of them, studying their cards and wiggling their brows, hummed "Charles has enemies," and Ignats Albertovich quoted

---

[1] John Edward Redmond (1856–1918) was an Irish nationalist leader who served in the British Parliament as a "home rule" member.

something appropriate from the German poet Zschokke,[2] who had lived, they say, some one hundred years before the tenor Abramburo.

Nyura and Nyuta visited often, just as before dressed like twins from head to toe, and both, as if from some invisible tickling, giggled softly at every word Serezha uttered. Someone told me that they had family quarrels at home with their father, but they never brought him along.

———

One can't possibly recount all the events of an important day in one chapter: as I've already done once for an important night, I'll need two; this is merely the beginning.

It was summertime. Anna Mikhailovna had left with her husband for Karlsbad or somewhere; the children were still living in the apartment in town.

At noon, when I was on my way to the editorial office, my door-man—the very same Khoma—muttered to me as I was leaving:

"There's no need to hang around town today."

I didn't ask what was wrong with today; but, as a matter of fact, on the streets, something unusual was happening; in the editorial office I was told that a mutinous battleship stood at the roadstead conducting some sort of negotiations with the authorities and was threatening to shell the city. My colleague Shtrok had already been to the port and seen everything: sailors from the ship had arrived in a launch, spread out a canvas and laid out their deceased comrade; mercantile sailors were scurrying along piers, as well as boatmen, factory workers, stevedores, loaders, and simply tramps, but there were no police. A crowd of young people constantly streamed from the statue of the duke, down the steps, and back up again—at first it was just the city, then even the suburbs got involved and nobody interfered. Only on the boulevard around the palace of the governor-general stood a large detail of soldiers. Shtrok already knew for certain what was in the telegram they'd sent off to the authorities in St. Petersburg, and, even though they'd yet to receive an answer, Shtrok knew what it would say; and he knew what the town governor had told the chief of police ("I myself don't know what to do"); and who killed the sailor, and why there was a rebellion, and everything else.

———

[2] Johann Heinrich Zschokke (1771–1848) was a popular and prolific German writer of novels, short stories, and autobiography.

Shtrok hurried; he wanted to dash it off at once with all the conversations in quotation marks; he had to be calmed down—the censor had already called to say that nothing whatever should be printed about it; Shtrok sighed and nonetheless sat down to write; his soul demanded it.

During this time the first of two barrages thundered intermittently through Odessa, fired on the city from the battleship *Potemkin*. For almost all the inhabitants this was the first time we'd heard such a sound: both in our editorial offices as well as in the farthest outskirts, it seemed to people that shells were exploding right in their own courtyards. We came running out into the streets. Enormous crowds were swarming: it was the first time I saw thousands of people in the same frame of mind. It was as if some finger were singling us out, choosing this city of ours from all the cities in Russia. "It has begun," and the honor fell to us. All faces, as if one, were agitated and anxiously jubilant. Classes mixed freely, grain dealers forgot about the trading floor, workers spilled out of factories, women in hats and women in kerchiefs were crowded closely together; they say that even thieves in the crowd ceased stealing things—perhaps it was even true. The police, as a matter of fact, were not there; but it seemed that no force could have coped: where and why people surged, they themselves didn't know—for some reason the crowd moved toward the monument of Catherine the Great—but wherever they went, they forced their way through and didn't retreat.

Of course, it merely seemed like that. Before reaching the monument, the crowd suddenly rushed backwards: Cossacks came galloping along the pavement. I was pressed up against a tree, and there I suddenly caught sight of Runitsky and Marusya. Apparently, they were crossing the pavement when a crowd of people started to run; he stopped directly in the path of the oncoming Cossacks, put his arm around Marusya's shoulder, and drew her to himself. Her face, too, didn't show any fear; she righted her broad hat that someone had knocked to one side in running past. Glimpsing the sailor's double-breasted jacket, the Cossacks divided and galloped around them; as he rode by, a Cossack lieutenant leaned over and said something to Aleksei Dmitrievich, pointing with his whip in the direction of the duke and the port.

After the Cossacks turned into Deribasov Street, Marusya ran up to me, and Runitsky followed behind. It turned out that his ship had docked an hour ago, she was meeting him, forced him to walk around the entire port, and they had seen and heard everything. She repeated the story I'd heard from my colleague Shtrok, but now with added details: orators were perched everywhere on boxes and barrels and saying the strangest things! There was even a young lady speaking, with a little snub nose and glasses.

"It won't have any effect, unfortunately," Runitsky said sharply all of a sudden.

Why it wouldn't have any effect, he didn't specify: but he said it so clearly, as if he'd tapped it out on a telegraph line (I didn't know Morse code, but there's no other comparison); I read beneath his abrupt irritation: it won't have any effect because all the orators are from "your people"—or something even more accurate. In general it was obvious that he was irritated, and Marusya, with her tone of voice and demeanor, was trying to comfort or cajole him.

He looked at his watch, then at Marusya inquiringly. She said to me:

"Promise Aleksei Dmitrievich, you won't leave me alone and you'll see me home in a cab. He has to go to the office and report—and he's afraid that I might sail away on some battleship."

I replied as requested; he said good-bye, without even arranging with Marusya when and where they'd next meet. That could mean either that they'd quarreled, or they'd already arranged it; I imagined that the latter was more likely.

As soon as he'd left us, it was as if the winding mechanism had vanished from Marusya. Crushed and distraught, she sat in the carriage and was silent; I, too, was silent. Only the telegraph in her mind clicked inaudibly, and it seemed that I understood once again. She probably felt that I was following her thoughts because not far from her home she suddenly began talking again, without looking at me:

"You were right."

I turned to her but made no further inquiries. There was no need to ask: everything was clear. Marusya, your semigifts are ill-suited to the nature of the wide steppe and the open sea; it's either all, or . . .

A moment later she said, more to herself than to me:

"But I can't behave any differently."

I was silent.

"Such is my soul, lacking breadth, even in the long run," she added spitefully.

I was silent. She didn't stir, sitting next to me, my arm around her waist, but the impression was that she was tossing about. A minute later she whispered to me with infinite anguish:

"Give me some advice . . . if you dare."

"I dare," I replied sharply. "Is he here for long?"

"He plans to leave for Chernigov tomorrow."

"Then order me immediately, in this very cab, to take you away to Ovidiopol; and tomorrow to your mama in Karlsbad."

Her shoulders flinched and she ceased talking. We arrived at her house; after ringing the doorbell, she flung at me:

"By the way, Ovidiopol is also here today."

—⁓—

I don't like to recall the events of that day: I don't like to do it for superstitious reasons—from that time forward there began that dark plague around the family that had become like my own family; in three years it was destined to transform Anna Mikhailovna into Niobe,[3] and to surround the paths of my friends with other graveside inscriptions. But I don't like that day for reasons other than this personal pain. We greeted it reverentially; we believed that it—this dawn of dawns, was the beginning of long-awaited events. Perhaps, historically this was actually the case; but we stupid, inexperienced, young people didn't foresee that its chorale, having begun as an alarm bell, would be deflected that very evening into a howl of drunken derangement.

[3] In Greek mythology, Niobe was queen of Thebes. She boasted of having many children, whereas Leto had only two. Apollo and Artemis, angry at this insult to their mother, killed all of Niobe's children and turned her into a stone statue of perpetual weeping.

—ᴠᴠᴠ— XIX —ᴠᴠᴠ—

Potemkin Night

That evening at home, Samoilo stopped in to see me: he'd also happened to come to town to make some purchases for his store and had arrived for the holiday. It was his first time at my place; he refused to sit down; his whole group of friends was waiting for him outside; they'd decided to go to the park and observe from the cliff what was going to take place in the harbor; in town they were saying that "something was going to take place." Everyone was there already, only Serezha, the rascal, had gone to the harbor for the third time that day, climbing down the massifs; all other ways down were now blocked by the police; but he'd also promised to come to the park.

Something had delayed me for about five minutes; Samoilo waited, but still didn't sit down. Today the sound of the telegraph that was so clear to me was also tapping loudly in his head in a very restless fashion. I said nothing; he looked out the window and refused to sit down. All of a sudden, he said:

"Monsieur Runitsky has also arrived today from Shanghai, for one day only; tomorrow morning he's leaving for his mother's country estate."

I heard the tapping of the telegraph. Worst of all—precisely that "for one day only." If he'd come for a while, perhaps it could all be resolved in time; but since he had to bid farewell the next morning, fate absolutely had to turn one way or the other within the space of one day and one night. But nothing whatever was expressed on

122

Samoilo's face; it was sewn together from sturdy skin and muscles; I also made no reply.

In that part of the park over the precipice, there's a hillock or embankment, and on it a wall with wide, latticed arcades; we called it the "fortress." We'd all settled down there somehow right on the lawn. Crowds of such spectators sat everywhere along the cliff, or along the slope among the bushes, and conversed with restraint. The night was hot and dark; as usual, far below us in the port, all the lights at sea and on land were shining, shimmering with reflections, and far away in the gulf, a mile or more out, a stationary group of lights stood all alone; people pointed it out to all the new arrivals: it was the battleship. Sometimes shadows scurried about under the harbor lights, but none of us had brought along binoculars. Nyura and Nyuta said: "We thought about it, but it seemed odd; this isn't the opera." A muffled, steady roar came from the port, but it was impossible to make anything out. Sometimes we could hear separate cries, also indecipherable. Twice loud shouts resounded, and then everyone on the cliff fell silent and waited; interrupted conversations would resume only gradually.

Marusya and Runitsky sat at opposite ends of our group. I wondered: maybe they haven't made up yet? Or are they being diplomatic? In reply to Nyura's and Nyuta's questions, where was such and such pier, and where was the tent with the deceased, Runitsky said very little. Marusya chatted softly, in her usual way, with the neighbors in her retinue—and once again I thought: this woman's also made of strong stuff! Samoilo as usual was silent, and as usual, no one talked to him.

Suddenly the crowd all around roared, hundreds of hands pointed somewhere below: a small fiery spot gradually spread, and from there, after a moment, an enormous roar ensued, this time prolonged, deafening, and all-encompassing; from the nature of the sound, no words were needed to know that it was a triumphant roar.

"They've set fire to the grain elevators," Aleksei Dmitrievich said sharply, "and they're rejoicing." He turned to Marusya: "I told you earlier today, Marya Ignatievna, that the rabble would get totally drunk and begin carrying on outrageously. Our emancipators . . ."

It was strange: we, too, felt sorry for the port and sorry about the portentous day that was unfolding in a manner that was less than grand: but on that warm night we all suddenly felt the chill emanating toward us from Runitsky. Each of us would have said the same thing, the very same words, with the same irritation—but that wasn't the point: his words seemed to be uttered in another language, as a challenge. I'm certain that at that moment one and the same idea flashed through everyone's mind: he's not one of us. Perhaps it was because of that, either intentionally or unconsciously, that Marusya stood up and went over to sit beside him.

Serezha came up from behind; he'd just been down below; he was looking for us along the cliff and finally found us. He was in civilian clothes, without a hat, and today he had the appearance of the common people: he must have dressed like that on purpose. In the darkness behind him there appeared another demotic silhouette, but it remained some distance apart. Serezha was weary, not at all cheerful, unlike his usual self; only his speech remained colorful. He confirmed that ever since sunset rivers of vodka had been flowing into the harbor; that the deceived agitators had long since given up and retreated to town, "because their young ladies were about to be consumed as hors d'oeuvres"; there were no sailors left, either from the Potemkin or from other trading ships and boats—they'd all scurried back on board. He'd seen the grain stores set on fire; it was done joyfully with cries of "Lift slowly, lads!" They were still setting things on fire. They were sure that the shelling would soon begin from all the cliffs, but what the hell—they were at least having fun.

The silhouette behind me suddenly touched me on the shoulder and beckoned with his finger: it was Motya Banabak. I followed him some distance away from the others. He remembered me from the self-defense league and obviously had decided to share with me that which was offending him, a worldly-wise fellow, most bitterly of all:

"Tell your folks: six of 'em. Or else, they should hand out rattles again. Because, ya' know why they're making such a racket? It's about the Yids, a plague on 'em."

Serezha came up to us. Motya Banabak said to him:

"Well, Serezha, I'm off."

"Go on then," Serezha gave his blessing. After he'd departed, Serezha provided me with the following information in clarification: "He's off to see whether he can fatten himself up in the crowd with all those watches and wallets; the climate's just right for that."

We returned to the group; by now there were fires burning in three new locations. Serezha sat down between Nyura and Nyuta and chatted with them about something unrelated, not softly, as we'd been talking before, but loudly; suddenly I noticed that the entire crowd along the cliff and on the slopes was talking noisily and excitedly. The inherent thread that since morning had connected all thoughts to the mutinous ship with some semiconscious anticipation had snapped; this had passed, the sensation that something important was about to happen was no longer present; there remained only an unusual circus, never before seen by anyone—pity that we hadn't brought along our binoculars. Laughter could already be heard in some quarters, especially down below, from the bushes on the slope, and a shrill note could sometimes be detected in young girls' voices—from the usual scale of very dark and very ordinary nights.

The crowd fell silent again for another moment when from the left side below, not far off in the distance, the first staccato of gunfire resounded; but that was only for a moment; soon everyone started humming again in a lively and merry way. Marusya asked:

"Aleksei Dmitrievich, are those machine guns?"

"No, they're rifles; it's called 'bursts.'"

But she asked using a special tone, as if stroking him affectionately; she inquired not to find out whether they were machine guns or bursts of rifle fire but rather to touch him with her words; and in his reply there was no sound of that previous clacking—it was a signal soft as velvet, long-awaited. Suddenly I noticed that Serezha's two arms were wrapped around the waists of Nyura and Nyuta, and those two, murmuring something together in soft, joyous unison, were leaning their shoulders up against his: this had never happened. Before this they'd often revealed themselves by their voices, sometimes their glances, but not by their actions. The general pendulum, previously about to ascend into the pure radiance of the heights, now swiftly fell back into the atmosphere of street dust. Or no, more profoundly: I even felt within myself certain fetters coming undone, not only today's special ones, but even yesterday's ordinary ones. Now, not only things that had been "permitted" yesterday evening were allowed, but even many things that had never before been permitted. I could slide right down the slope and join that group laughing during the sound of the shooting, that same group that had been whispering only a mere half hour ago, and those men and women would receive me as one of their own, and would continue to spew witticisms; the young lawyer, whom we'd brought along with us, had already done so. What sort of fetters could there be, what rules, when nothing really mattered, when the earth was made of filth and slush; pendulums always return, the dream ends in mockery; when you see an apple, pick it, all else is mockery. If Marusya had asked my advice now . . .

The "bursts" rattled first nearer, then farther away; Runitsky identified the locations by sound: that's from Gavan Street, that's from Nadezhdin. But all the while during this naming of streets that cerebral telegraph was once again tapping out its different letters so distinctly, that beside me, at least two others must have heard it, too: leave them, my dear, leave all of it, the acacia's in bloom down in our valley, and today you love me as I would like.

Marusya stood up.

"Let's go, Alesha; take me away somewhere so we won't hear the shooting."

He stood up, said nothing, once again so nice, timid, sensitive, just as I'd seen him several years ago at his mother's house. Marusya used her parasol to adjust her creased light dress. Aleksei Dmitrievich said goodbye; Nyura and Nyuta, whom he'd obviously informed about his departure the next day, politely wished him a good journey, and the others joined in. The last person he approached was Samoilo; he said something amiable to him; Samoilo extended his hand in silence. Runitsky carefully descended several steps to bid farewell to our lawyer who'd slid down the slope, and everyone was looking in that direction. Suddenly Marusya's changed facial expression struck me: she stood apart and, with lips open, breathing heavily, stared at Samoilo as intently as if he'd somehow suddenly chained her eyes to him.

But he didn't even look at her; he merely stood before her, lit by the street lamp, eyes downcast, standing squarely, solidly, awkwardly; he stood, his arms dangling, clumsy, second-rate, dressed ineptly and tastelessly, befitting a small-town pharmacist; he didn't move, hardly breathed, not a muscle stirred. There were many small wrinkles around his eyes, also along the sides of his untrimmed mustache; he looked much older than thirty. I couldn't read his expression at once; the man simply stood there in silence and wasn't looking at anything: yet all of a sudden I realized that I couldn't take my eyes off his withdrawn, inscrutable face. If you could take away one thing after another, and, after a lengthy process of training the will, combine every-thing that a person can reveal through movements of his soul: to wait without showing, to strive without telling, to blunder without blink-ing, to stake everything in silence, to accept both failure and loss, and thus year after year—then this person's face would take shape with-out any need for expressions; even eyes would be unnecessary. It would be sufficient for the person observing this face to have a set of eyes: he'd be able to read everything written there, etched once and for all, eaten into the very fabric once and for all. An apathetic face, and mute, like thick oak gates—that the owner has intentionally con-structed to be so heavy: an inert face, like a fetish carved by a savage, one which when guilt-stricken women regard it, they begin to foam at the mouth; so inert, that I suddenly recalled his own words: death grip.

"Why not, go for a ride," he said to her simply, as if she'd asked his permission. And, after saying this, without raising his eyes, he turned away and went to sit down in his previous place with the look of a man who'd completed his business: the necessary instructions had been given and would be implemented precisely. You can "go for a ride," please do. You may release the cabby at the gates of the Prokudin dacha and, making your way through the scattered houses, descend the overgrown cliff to the unpopulated valley where no one goes even by day, and now it's nighttime. Please. Samoilo doesn't re-ally mind how you've grown used to spending moonlit or dark hours there; some time ago he dismissed it from his own consciousness once and for all. That on which Samoilo would silently stamp "no" is never going to happen: this "no" had been absorbed into your soul like a death grip and would stand between the two of you like a wall of ice. Go on; you may play, Samoilo won't interfere, but the play re-mains a game and it'll never be anything more.

—⁓—

I never dream, but in those years I would devise dreams for myself until the moment I fell asleep. That night the following dream oc-curred to me:

The next morning I wake up and go to the editorial office; at the gate Khoma informs me, of course, that he didn't approve of all that had happened, and also didn't approve of me; on the street, near Quarantine gully, two carts drive past with a load concealed by a can-vas cover; from under it bare blue arms and legs were sticking out.

The entire editorial staff had assembled and the noise they were making could be heard on the staircase. In my dream I could determine precisely what the nonpartisan editor was saying about yesterday's events, what the headline-writer said (he was a populist), what the feuilletonist on serious themes thought (that's what he was called as opposed to me, and he was a supporter of Lenin's Iskra[1]), and what the reporters who were more literate thought. Only the main person was missing: Shtrok's friends from the police had called him early that day to inform him of another sensational event he would be allowed to write about—it would take place in such and such a place, and he should take a cab and go there.

At last Shtrok returned and set about writing immediately; his look was consequential. He whispered to me apart from the others: "Read column after column as I write—you'll find it particularly interesting; in return you can help put pressure on the supervisor of the chronicle so that this time he won't mangle my style."

I began to read column after column, the last lines still moist from his ink. So it was: suicide on Langeron Street. A junior assistant captain in the Volunteer Navy; his family was well known in Odessa, his father was a councilman during the Novoselsky[2] period (Shtrok wrote, that's what I saw distinctly in my "dream": "the memorable Novoselsky period, coinciding with the first dawn of the all-Russian period of great reforms"). The body, in a merchant naval uniform, was found today at dawn by the boatman Avtonom Chubchik in an isolated, thickly overgrown gully halfway between Langeron Street and the Prokudin dacha. "The cold hand of the ill-fated man was still holding the lethal weapon in its final spasm. In the opinion of the police doctor, death occurred between three and four o'clock in the morning. Semyon Pozdnyurk, the doorman at the Prokudin dacha, indicated that the deceased had driven up to the gates of the dacha the previous evening around ten o'clock in the company of a young lady; he knew both of them well, since the departed ("the sailor who departed so tragically") had spent the previous summer with his mother and sisters, and the young lady had been a frequent visitor. At approximately two o'clock in the morning, Semyon Pozdnyurk

---

[1] An unofficial organization formed by Lenin in 1900 within the Social Democratic Party to unite more orthodox Marxists. The leaders went abroad and published an influential newspaper, *Iskra* (The Spark).

[2] See above, chap. 9, n. 1.

was roused by a bell ("a commanding bell"). The sailor ("above whose head the wings of willful and premature death were already hovering") ordered the doorman to unlock the gates; he sat the young lady in a cab that was already waiting outside, and she left; then, after tipping Semyon one ruble, he remained at the dacha ("and disappeared into the shadows of the spreading avenue of trees, never to return again"). "What transpired between these two participants in this mysterious drama from ten o'clock until one in the morning, will forever remain hidden by the darkness of uncertainty; that which occurred after the young lady's departure—unfortunately, is all too clear."

In fact, of course, everything happened not at all the way I "dreamed" it. Aleksei Dmitrievich was too decent a man to associate his departure from life in such an obvious way with Marusya. My colleague Shtrok never got the chance to write about the episode: four months later, the telegraph agency informed us of his accidental death somewhere en route to Bombay—he was washed overboard in a storm; meanwhile Marusya was already married and living in Ovidiopol.

$\overline{\ \ }\!\!\!\!\sim\!\!\sim$ **XX** $\sim\!\!\sim\!\!\!\!\overline{\ \ }$

The Wrong Way

I said that Anna Mikhailovna's tale was almost like that of Niobe; now I've reached the story of the first arrow shot by a wicked deity. I don't recall in precisely which year it occurred; I only know that it was during the winter, near the very end of it, almost at the beginning of St. Petersburg spring when the ice on the Neva was just starting to break up.

Of course, I myself didn't witness it. I'm writing from the testimony of two women: the first was an eyewitness (in part: even she didn't see the end of it, and no one knows), and I heard it from her directly; the second woman, whose version was set forth in a clerk's handwriting, was shown to me by the officer on duty at the police station where I went for more information; she had nothing whatever to do with the affair and couldn't have had, and that shows the unmitigated bitter absurdity of the whole terrible business.

In any case, it occurred after the events of October 1905 because at that time Marko was undoubtedly taking part in the celebrations in St. Petersburg over the constitutional manifesto.[1] My friends told me all about it: one of the street demonstrations was proceeding along Kamennoostrov Prospect, and all of a sudden someone shouted out:

"Pobedonostsev[2] lives right here in this house!"

---

[1] On October 17, 1905, responding to considerable political pressure, Tsar Nicholas II signed a manifesto transforming Russia into a constitutional monarchy, an event that marked the end of unlimited autocracy in Russia.

[2] Konstantin Pobedonostsev (1827–1907) was a Russian statesman and jurist, procurator of the Holy Synod, and a strong proponent of Russification of subject peoples.

A roar of hostile shouts went up, someone even hurled a stone at his window; the crowd stopped, turned toward the house, and formed a circle around it; those in front made threatening gestures with their fists, those in the rear pressed forward—gradually the circle reached the steps of the porch and someone, rushing forward, climbed the stairs and banged loudly on the carved wooden doors with a truncheon.

At that moment, pushing through the ranks, a student with bulging eyes ran up onto the porch, pushed away the fellow who was knocking, and stood in front of the door, his face toward the demonstrators, his arms extended in the shape of a cross:

"Comrades!" he shouted. "I protest. Don't you see, we mustn't finish off the vanquished enemy. There's only one fitting sentence for him: contempt and oblivion!"

The reaction of the crowd then was extremely lofty; it's said they listened to him, even though up to that point they'd roughed him up a bit while trying to pull him away from the door, but he fought them off with his arms and legs, crying:

"I won't allow it!"

By that time, apparently, Marko had already forsaken the Rigveda and was now engaged in politics. There's even some proof that he was attracted not merely by the spirit of liberation but even to one particular faction. It was he who played a decisive role at the famous meeting of dentists on Vasilievsky Island where a stubborn struggle emerged between two competing resolutions, one proposed by a Marxist speaker, the other, by a populist. How and why Marko turned up among the practitioners of that profession remains his secret; but people at the meeting told me that it was precisely he, stepping onto the tribune, who ensured victory for the second of the two resolutions, and thus was it put to a vote: "We, the workers of the dental profession on Vasilievsky Island, regarding ourselves as an indissoluble part of the laboring peasant class . . ."

Afterwards, and perhaps even simultaneously, Marko participated in spiritual circles and also attended lectures about Tibetan medicine according to the teachings of the Mongolian healer Badmaev; in the course of the last few months before the events on the Neva, he also became a passionate collector of postage stamps. In fact, Valentinochka sent Anna Mikhailovna a thick album almost completely filled up; once I saw it and recall that a splendidly engraved stamp from one of the South American republics, with the country indecipherable under the heavy postmark but with the label "Correos"—which in their language, it seems, means "Post"—decorated a blank square on the page designated for Korea.

The first eyewitness of the definitive events, known to the sanitation inspectorate of the capital police, was the Odessan petty bourgeois Valentina Kukuruza, who testified at the police station (in fact, I learned what had happened from the newspaper account of her report), and then in person; I'll relate her account—more in my own words—as well as I can recall it.

This is what happened: that April evening she took Marko along as a guest to visit a friend who'd married a telegraph clerk. They spent a pleasant evening: the host played music on a guitar, Marko tried to demonstrate table-turning, but it didn't work; then for the most part, they played cards—a skill that, by her request, Marko had recently acquired. They ate pancakes. Did they drink? In a manner of speaking: that is, they drank, but only a little. Are you asking mainly about Marko? He couldn't drink much: after only two shots he'd suffer a headache for the whole next day, therefore she always made sure that people didn't encourage him; otherwise Marko, in his kindness, would consider it impolite to lag behind the group, no matter how much he disliked vodka. In a word—he did drink but only a little; of course, what was for him only a little might be a whole bottle for someone else. In any case, when they left, and it was already past one in the morning, no one was drunk, but Marko was—well, very merry. He walked arm in arm with her, not staggering at all, stepping once or twice on her bunions, but he always did that anyway when they walked arm in arm. He rattled off the names of all the stars to her, pointing to each, and said that he planned to transfer to a different department to study astronomy. In general, this time she expressed herself more accurately, even though it was not without her native Odessan irregularities.

The telegraph clerk lived in the Vyborg section, and their small apartment (they'd long since left their rooms and moved in together) was on Znamen Street. They didn't want to hire a sleigh—both thought it useful to get some fresh air in view of their previous activity, and therefore they made their way through the totally deserted area along the Bolshaya Nevka River, planning to cross the Neva by the Aleksandrov Bridge; they got as far as the military hospital where the Nevka flows into the Neva, when all of a sudden they heard a woman's desperate cry in the distance.

It was impossible to tell from afar what the woman was shouting, but it was clear she was calling for help. Her cry was repeated with short interruptions. They stopped; Marko listened and said:

"Valentinochka, it's coming from the middle of the ice—on the Neva. Is someone drowning?"

Valentinochka, on the other hand, thought that the sound was coming from the right, the Nevka, and from so far away that it probably wasn't from the middle of the ice—the Nevka wasn't that wide, so it was most likely coming from the other side.

"Some cavalier's battering his dame," she suggested. "They're sloshed, streetwalking scum; let's go on."

Valentinochka had assumed of late a very stern attitude toward streetwalking types in general, especially those belonging to the female sex.

They walked on, but after a few steps, Marko stopped again: the cry was repeated, even more desperate. Now she was even more convinced that it was coming from the canal; but Marko even more insistently maintained that it was coming from the river. They approached the parapet to the river, "by the street light," and below, right in front of them, they saw the numerous temporary bridges set up over the Neva for the winter. The first planks near the shore had already been dismantled in view of the impending thaw; but the workers either hadn't had time, or, plague on them, they'd run off to a tavern—and had removed only the first few yards; up ahead, still somewhat intact, the bridges stretched away into the darkness.

"Do you know what, Valentinochka?" Marko started to say. "You wait here, and I'll go ahead a little way and have a look."

"But it's not coming from over there."

"Yes, it is: there—you hear?"

Once again she was ready to swear that it was from the right; once more he assured her that it was coming from the Neva, precisely from the place the bridges led.

"You're drunk or you're mad; the ice is already starting to break up!"

"Not at all, Valentinochka; I'll stay on the bridges and go on only twenty paces or so; well, maybe fifty; I'll be able to hear it better from over there. What if she's slipped, and there really is a crack in the ice?

That is, somewhere over on the side, near the bridges; I'll be able to pull her out, don't you see, from the bridges."

Valentinochka kept a firm hold on his sleeve with both her hands; but then a cry sounded once again and Marko, tearing himself away, climbed over the parapet, stumbled, slipped, fell on the ice, stood up, ran along the vacant space until he reached the bridges and started walking across the planks.

She wanted to run after him, but then she saw, only three street lamps away, the figure of a policeman. Relying more on the power of authority than on her own, she rushed to meet the officer; she ran and shouted with all her might, "Help!" The policeman, now hearing women's cries from both sides, apparently, was befuddled and stopped. When she reached him and dragged him toward the bridges, explaining that a man had lost his mind, had gotten drunk from drinking only one glass, and that the officer should give him a good smack and haul him off to the police station . . .

No one could be seen on the planks in the dim light cast by the street lamp; once Marko's voice emerged from the darkness, calling, "Where are you? I'm coming to save you!" After that, he wasn't heard again; and he didn't return.

It was strange: neither later that night, nor the next morning, nor even the following week did they find even one crack in the ice near the bridges. The water was showing through in several places, but in small puddles, only an inch or so deep. There was an ice hole on one side but far from the bridges, twenty yards or more off to the right.

And even stranger: spring arrived, the ice melted, the river became clear, but Marko's body never washed up on shore, neither on the islands, nor on the Strelka, nor in the canals, nor in the branches of the Neva: nowhere. They found tramps and women, they found a man who'd declared bankruptcy and disappeared without a trace, but they didn't find a student dressed as Valentinochka had described him. Marko had gone so far astray that he left no trace.

And the most bizarre thing of all: that woman, as a matter of fact, wasn't shouting from the ice on the Neva, but precisely from where Valentinochka had heard the sound—on the right, across the Bolshaya Nevka, not far from the Samson Bridge. The clerk at the police station had recorded it all accurately: her name was Marya Petrova, a peasant girl from the Pskov district, twenty-eight years old; she'd been given a beating on the embankment by her lover, Ivan Sidorov or Sidor Ivanov; the beating was fierce; they brought her to the police station covered in blood; a gentleman who'd walked past had decided to intervene, and, to discourage him from so doing, Marya and Ivan had both hurled themselves at him with their fists and obscene words, thrown him down into the snow, broken his eyeglasses, torn off his fur coat—and that was the only reason they wound up in the police station; to this day Marya Petrova still doesn't know and never will find out how a confused, simple fool ran across the bridges "to save her," ran the wrong way, and, listening (he once said about himself, "I'm someone who listens")—called into the empty darkness: "I'm coming to save you!"

Broad Jewish Natures

It had become dark and uncomfortable in Anna Mikhailovna's house. Ignats Albertovich had begun to stoop noticeably; he said that it was written somewhere in the Midrash[1]—or, perhaps it was in the sayings of the old Volynian sages: man has two mothers. The first is his birth mother and the second, mother earth. When he's little, he listens to his first mother's voice, but she's taller than he is, so he has to lift his head up; at the approach of old age, his second mother begins talking to him, and the man has to lean over to hear her whisper. Anna Mikhailovna, on the other hand, didn't attempt to explain away the increase in her gray hair. It was gloomy in the house and they entertained only older guests; even Nyura and Nyuta appeared infrequently—Serezha, now without Marusya, stopped gathering his friends; after supper, around ten o'clock, he'd set off alone, while the staid Torik sat in his own room poring over his books.

Ignats Albertovich's business affairs also began to deteriorate. Whether it was because the padishah closed the Dardenelles too frequently, or because the towns of Kherson, after dredging the Dnepr "inlets," and Nikolaev, at the wide estuary, had begun to overtake the arid Odessa, or because of some other reason—Quarantine harbor began to be noticeably deserted, the boats on the Platonov and Androsov piers were fewer, and the prosperous hubbub of brokers at the stock exchange and on the sidewalk in front of the cafés Robin

---

[1] Ancient Jewish commentary on some portion of the Hebrew scriptures.

and Fankoni (the illegal but genuine stock exchange that everyone referred to as "Greek"), if it hadn't actually fallen silent, it had begun to sound anxious. At Ignats Albertovich's table in the evening Abram Moiseevich and Boris Mavrikievich would argue even more fractiously; the older brother was especially irritated by the new phrase "state of the market" which "Beiresh" would find in the lead article of my newspaper and pronounce in his own way, something like "sta-mark"; while he himself, the older brother, blamed the "banks" for all their misfortune.

"Hey, young man!" he'd say to me. "You should've seen what was happening on the Dnepr some thirty years ago, when there were only two rulers all the way from the rapids to our grain elevator: one was Webster-Kovalenko, and the other, even more important, was the "Russian Company." The Jew Ionya, the main buyer for "Ropit," would travel up from Kherson on a paddle-wheel steamboat; black beard, gold-frame eyeglasses, and a belly to match. He makes his way, like a tzaddik[2] among Hassidim, with a retinue of some fifty people—bookkeepers, brokers, assayers, and miscellaneous scroungers. They serve tea all along the way, and sometimes even a glass of vodka with a spice cake; they play cards until three in the morning—and do you know, they would lose up to five hundred rubles; I myself have known some idiots who even paid to enter the game! The landings go by—Bolshaya Lepetikha, Malaya, Berislav, Kakhovka, Nikopol, up to Aleksandovsk. Three hours before Ionya arrives at each pier, even the governor himself couldn't push his way through the crowd: agents, brokers, secondhand dealers, horses pulling carts, ox-cart drivers, the whole square is piled with sacks, wagons, and oxen in the back. What do you think—Ionya didn't sleep all night, so he's tired? As soon as he sees the pier, he shouts to the sailor: "Yurka, over here—swing it! He shoves his own head under the spout, Yurka starts to pump water, and splashes half the Dnepr onto his bald pate, and once again Ionya's ready, even for a wedding. He stands on deck and shouts from afar: "How goes it, Stavro Lefterevich, how're you? I see you've put on some weight; this summer let's go to Marienbad together." "Hey, Kurolapchenko, what did I hear in Kakhovka, you've given birth to another daughter? Your seventh? Christen her Sofiya—it's time to make 'sofas!'" "Shalom aleichem, Monsieur Gro-

---

[2] Hebrew. A most righteous man, upright and honorable.

bokopatel; hurry up, you numskull, you! Open up that shop!" He had a kind word for each person; they stood there and laughed, ready to kiss his hand. . . . That was the Dnepr then, but now, excuse me. And it's all because of the banks."

"But what do the banks have to do with it?"

"They began loaning money to every Tom, Dick, and Harry instead of 'Ropit' and Webster-Kovalenko, a bunch of small fry—'Mr. Exporter,' but he wears pants with a fringe, his uncle's pants at that. They themselves have nothing to eat, and the larger companies are also left with neither water nor air. It's time to die, Ignats Albertovich; but, you, Beiresh, should please die first."

In general, it became uncomfortable in Odessa. I had trouble recognizing our city, which only a short while ago had been so free and easy and good-natured. Now it was swept by malice that, they say, had previously never affected our mild southern metropolis, created over the course of centuries through the harmonious and loving efforts of four peaceful races. They'd always quarreled and cursed each other as rogues or idiots, and had sometimes even fought; but in all my memory there'd never been any authentic, ferocious hostility. Now all this had changed. The first sign of benevolence among men had disappeared—that is, the southern custom of considering the street as your home. Nowadays we walked the streets with caution, hurried along at night, and drew closer to the shadows . . .

The issue, however, was no longer limited to a mere tribal feud. Two years ago, when we all read about the first heroic raids from the underground on convoys of government gold, no one suspected to what extent the system of financial, nonmonetary transactions was gradually being democratized. Now it was referred to in Odessa by the shorthand of "ex" and had been adapted simply and openly for the replenishment of the raiders' personal benefit. At first, they would send a threatening letter or flash a revolver and mention some unnamed "party"; but soon they ceased doing that and merely began plundering openly. As for the breadth of their appetite, they were distinguished by their Spartan modesty: although there were a few attempts to extort large sums of money from a particular frightened wealthy individual, the usual type of "ex" took the form of a visit by two men to a grocery store and the confiscation of the morning's proceeds to the tune of two rubles plus change. The most curious thing of all was that this "ex" raged in our city only among Jews: Jews were its objects, rich and poor, and, as the victims swore, all of them, without exception, were also its subjects. "They thrash the Jewish population with two whips," recorded my colleague at the newspaper with melancholy, the feuilletonist who wrote about serious themes: at night, with foreign swine, truncheons, and during the day, our own swine.

Our Abram, a worker at the newspaper, reported that a student by the name of Viktor Ignatievich, was asking to see me.

In general, Torik rarely visited anyone, and that was the very first time he'd come to see me. I realized that it must be important and told Abram not to let anyone else into the reception room. As it turned out, it was no laughing matter, though at first it was a bit amusing. Torik related it systematically, all the events and discoveries in chronological order, one after another, without jumping ahead; nor did I have to urge him on: he was a very sound, well-organized young man.

An "ex" had taken place yesterday at Abram Moiseevich's. Two young men showed up, one belonging to the common people, the other, better "educated"; they brandished a document with a stamp as well as two "pistols with large cylinders," and demanded five thousand rubles—if not, Abram Moiseevich would die. He looked at them, thought for a moment, and asked:

"How did you know I was back in town? I just returned from Marienbad yesterday."

The youths proudly explained that the committee knows everything: that was the system of shadowing now in place.

He thought for a bit, suddenly burst out laughing, and then said to them:

"Listen, you young men: how'd you like to get fifteen thousand rubles instead of five? Go to my brother Beiresh, show him your guns, and get ten from him. Then come back to me: if you show me his ten, I'll turn over my five to you then."

Their eyes bulged; of course they suspected he'd send for the police. They thanked him for his advice and agreed to go to "Beiresh," but he still had to pay up on the spot, now.

"Hey," he replied, "when people treat you with respect, don't behave like kikes. My word is good. Every banker in Odessa would hand over fifty thousand rubles on my say-so without a receipt, and here are two snivelers. Get out of here or else, do as I say! Your pistols? I don't give a damn about 'em. I'm not afraid of no bombs (Torik related the most characteristic parts of the story with grammatical fidelity to the original). And if you do me this favor with regard to Beiresh, then your 'yes' is worth five thousand rubles: please go."

They conferred in a whisper in the corner and decided that they needed to confer with members of their "committee" by telephone. The one who belonged to the common people led Abram away to another room and locked the heavy door behind them, while the more educated one stayed behind to use the telephone. Ten minutes later he called them back and told them the committee's decision: they'd agreed, but while he went to see Beiresh, the other one would have to stay here in the room with Abram.

"Fine," said Abram Moiseevich. "Does he smoke cigars? I brought back some excellent ones."

So the member of the common people remained behind with Abram Moiseevich for two hours, they smoked cigars, and gradually got to chatting amicably. He said that he wasn't really a swindler but a decent fellow and a good Jew; he'd participated in the self-defense of 1905, had even contributed an entire militia unit, and then, after the manifesto, had worked diligently during the month of October. (I stopped smiling as he told this part of the story: something foul had begun to emerge as I listened.) In a word, the more educated one returned after two hours and displayed the ten thousand rubles; Abram Moiseevich opened his safe immediately and calmly extracted a packet of bills, counted out five thousand right in front of them, thought a bit, and added another thousand; then he put the rest of his money away—it never occurred to them to interfere—and he locked his safe.

"Good-bye and good luck," he said to them. "You'll end up in Siberia, but you've made me happy."

Right after this Abram Moiseevich summoned Torik and shared the following reflections with him. In the first place, it was very odd that they'd come to see him only one day after his arrival from Marienbad: who could've informed them? In the second place, they hadn't even asked for "Beiresh's" address: and he, too, had moved into a new apartment only a week ago. In the third place, his conversation partner, the member of the common people, bragging about his own exploits and relaying how he'd been praised by the organizers of the self-defense leagues, happened to say that his name was

Motya—and Abram Moiseevich had heard that name somewhere before. Finally, when they were whispering in the corner, it seemed to him that he'd heard one more name.

"Serezha?!"

"Not exactly, even worse: 'Sirozhka.'[3] The clues were flimsy, as you can see; but Abram Moiseevich believed in his own intuition. 'I'm an old horse thief,' he said, 'and for that reason alone, when a mare's taken away, I can sniff out who's taken it.' He'd stake his own life that the educated fellow hadn't called the committee at all but had called the number 9-62."

Torik himself had conducted a small inquiry at home. He didn't find Serezha there but carefully interrogated the maid. She said that around eleven in the morning Sergei Ignatievich had been called to the telephone, that he'd sent her out of his father's study where she'd been dusting, and he'd locked the door.

Torik related this story to me in such a way that I became interested unwittingly, even though I had better things to think about. He told it with just the right amount of anguish needed and the right amount of humor possible, given the level of anguish. He said not one accusatory word against his own brother: it was as if he were talking about a person who was ill, who had to be treated but not judged. And he'd come to see me because, in Marusya's absence, for Serezha I was the only one who could . . .

---

[3] An extremely informal diminutive form of the name Sergei.

—ᄿᄿ— XXII —ᄿᄿ—

One More Confession

That evening I went to talk to Serezha. Torik had informed me that his parents were going to the opera, that he himself would also leave, and there'd be no one at home to interfere; Serezha wouldn't be going out before ten p.m. In fact, I heard Serezha's voice as I entered the hallway: he was playing the piano and singing.

"My friend brought back a lovely little ditty from Paris," he said to me, beaming. "Janneton prend sa faucille pour aller couper les jones."[1] They say it's a very old song. I've been sweating over it for an hour; I want to translate it. Do you like the beginning?

> It was hot July,
> Sap was flowing in the trees.
> Tanya went out for an hour
> To stroll in the woods near her dacha.

"I've come to see you about something else: Serezha, I have a serious matter to discuss with you, and it's not pleasant."

"Wait a minute, right away; it's so hard to capture all the rhymes; it's not merely '-ok,' but '-sok,' avec la consonne d'appui. Listen:

> Suddenly she met a foursome:
> Each was well built and very tall.

---

[1] A racy French popular song of the eighteenth century titled "Jeanneton Takes up Her Sickle [to Go Cut Rushes]."

The first was modest, at the start,
He pinched her . . . temple.

"You can't pinch a temple, but that's for your chaste ears: in fact, I
have a different rhyme, more pinchable. The rest isn't ready yet. I'm
listening; but don't holler if I suddenly jump up for a moment to sing
the final couplet. What's new on the Rialto?"

I closed the door of the living room and said very simply:

"Today Motya Banabak and one of his comrades carried out an 'ex'
at Abram Moiseevich's house; and they did it on your orders. Do you
know what that smacks of?"

He stood before me, smart, graceful, elegantly dressed in something particularly domestic, one hand in his pocket, a cigarette in the
other. Not a brow twitched, but his train of thought was clearly reflected on his face. At first he wondered how I could've found out and
wanted to deny it; then he realized it wasn't worth it; he smiled sincerely and asked in a tone of affectionate dexterity:

"What does it smack of?"

"Whatever you prefer, from the penal battalion to the firing
squad."

"*Caballero*, I spent four years in the law faculty. The venerable grain
dealer Avraamii, son of Moisei, will remain silent as a mackerel, mute
from birth, caught, stuffed, grilled, eaten, and digested."

"Don't count on it!"

"I do. He can't prove that the visit was made on my initiative; on
the other hand, there are two witnesses who'll testify that he incited
them to launch a raid on his brother Beiresh, son of Mavrikii, and that
he even paid them six thousand rubles to do so. Do you know what
that smacks of?"

This was sound logic, indisputably. For his own self-preservation,
he'd repelled my first assault. For a moment I lost my train of
thought; I stood there and for some reason thought about the fact that
today he was speaking only *Russian*, without his usual port slang, and
that this had been true from the moment I'd arrived: had he sensed
that I'd come about no joking matter?

"It's not just this one case, Serezha," I said, getting back on track.
"I have no doubt that you're implicated with these raiders in general.
You've no justification; you're not doing it for the 'party'—especially
using Motya. It's simply despicable meanness."

He squinted and replied deliberately:

"I could, strictly speaking, show you to the door and even assist you in making use of that particular opening."

I replied again very simply:

"Don't be an idiot, Serezha."

He shrugged his shoulders; he didn't say anything for a few minutes, merely tapped his foot; suddenly he wiped his forehead, beamed, nodded to me happily, sat down at the piano, and (saying, "One moment!"), burst into song, tapping on the keys:

—But the second one was bold, and boldly
Threw Tanya down onto the sand.
The third deftly and skillfully
Unfastened her belt,
While the fourth . . .

"Now it's only the fourth one, damn it, that I can't get. '*Ce que fit le quatrième . . .*'"

I was furious inside; true, I wasn't worried about him. Let the devil take him: Anna Mikhailovna hadn't left my thoughts that entire day, my oldest and first love in that house. It was only for her sake, so I wouldn't be ashamed to look her in the eye, that I'd said, "Mind" to Marusya that time in Lukaniya and never laid a finger on her: it's time to tell the truth, it was only for her sake. A woman with an astonishing genius for understanding, accepting her powerlessness without complaint—the powerlessness of all mothers and fathers in that generation of crisis and collapse; a woman stretched on the rack by God, the further she went, the worse it got; and now this charming scoundrel was preparing yet another turn of the rack for her, pulling at the ropes. Oh! I also knew some port slang, the latest words, the rudest ones: I desperately wanted to shout them all in his face and to spit at him as well, really spit, and then leave. But I had enough sense, thank heaven, to behave differently. I gathered in my throat the most affectionate, most musical, and intimate tones of voice, and said to him:

"Serezha, we've been friends for so many years. If you don't hear the cry of pain I feel now in my soul, then you're deaf. For God's sake, Serezha!"

He turned toward me slowly on the rotating piano stool, leaned his elbow on the echoing keys, and looked at me in his usual way, with the open, honest gaze of his bold and boundless nature.

"This is the second time you want to rescue me," he said with a sense of profound, disheartened friendship. "And for the second time I'm asking, believe me, not to mock you but with total sincerity: What's wrong? Why is it forbidden? It's not as if I'm stealing from a beggar. Perhaps I'm morally deaf, but it's a birth defect, an organic disability, and not a fault."

"But why, why?"

He lowered his head and thought for a minute. Then he began speaking, absentmindedly tapping his fingers lightly on the keys; I recall his entire speech through the soft sound of the intermittent rumble of the piano, just as I remember Marusya's confession through the moonlight and verdant rustling. Whether he was unconsciously playing a favorite melody, or his talented fingers were simply composing one involuntarily, even I, who usually responded to music only with difficulty, was strangely seized by it and submitted to the muffled murmur; his words poured effortlessly into my consciousness along with the music.

"It doesn't matter, my dear friend," he said. "I'm done for. I'm not fit for life. This sounds mad when you're talking about a person who's so richly endowed with semitalents: piano, drawing, verse, wit, what have you. Perhaps that's where my illness lies, when a person can do everything he sets his mind to: like the tsar whose touch turned everything to gold and who died from hunger."

"That's not true: you'd have made an excellent lawyer . . ."

"But I'm already someone's assistant—I've even made a note somewhere of whose assistant I am. But nothing will come of it: I'm unable to work. I can't bear even easy work: it's not a matter of effort—I can haul heavy sacks all day long if it's a game; but if it's not a game, if it's 'necessary,' then I can't do it. Have you read Weininger?"[2]

"'M' or 'F'? What of it?"

"'F.' I know that it's even crazier to say this about a young fellow with such broad shoulders; I'm a good gymnast, and, to be frank, I'm

---

[2] Otto Weininger (1880–1903), Austrian philosopher whose single work *Sex and Character* (1903) served as a source of anti-Semitic propaganda. He advanced the thesis that all living things combined varying proportions of masculine (positive) and feminine (negative) elements.

completely normal in that other—you know what I mean—specific sense; but, as a matter of fact, I'm really a woman, a female butterfly born only to be taken care of, amused, and pampered. If I'd been born a girl, no one would've reproached me for the fact that I'm not cut out to earn a living: it's in the order of things, as long as the girl's appearance is pleasing. Then someone would feed me and dress me to adorn their life and their house, and would thank me every day for allowing it. Then I'd be 'kept.' . . . Shall I confess something to you? That phrase, 'to be kept,' that sounds so vile to every real man, doesn't irritate me at all. Several times I've been on the verge of this experience; for some reason, I didn't submit, I don't know why; but it's still possible."

I nearly moaned: my rage had long since passed, and there remained only dull, heavy pain. I said:

"Now you're talking as if you're a beggar."

"I am a beggar. I don't know where my money goes. I had a cup of coffee this morning for twenty-five kopecks, bought nothing much, and somehow spent five rubles. That's also characteristic of a young lady: black magic would come more easily to her than the arithmetic of her own purse. That's what the word 'beggar' means: a person over whose soul there hangs every moment the vile, base worry—how can I get more? For a lady it's simple: she rubs her shoulder up against her father's, her husband's, or her friend's, and she says nicely: 'Give me.' Even if they sometimes refuse—she's not ashamed. But I wear trousers and a necktie, so I'm considered a man. Papa *c'est un chic type*, he brings home a check on the first and the fifteenth of each month, and for me that's like a whiplash across the face. I'm good for nothing; I'm done for, no matter what; it's not worth your pain."

We were both silent; suddenly he spoke more boldly, and the accompaniment on the piano was louder:

"By the way, this escapade with Avraamii is a first in my biography. It suddenly occurred to me. I haven't touched his money yet; strictly speaking, it's because I haven't got used to accepting cash from my friend Motya Banabak's hand—I'm used to the opposite. It's a prejudice . . ."

He turned to the piano and began playing more attentively, muttering something, wiping his forehead with one hand, knitting his brow, and nodding to me absentmindedly: "Forgive me," he said and started singing again, at first in a low voice, but by the second line, more forcefully:

> —And the fourth . . . But we must
> Omit a section of the drama,
> So that when our ladies find out
> They won't run off into the woods.

And he was completely transformed. He pushed off with his foot, twirled around three times on his piano stool, and came to rest right in front of me: his face shone with genuine, unadulterated joy; he ran his thumbnail forcefully across every key, playing all the sharps and flats, and cried out:

"Done! Do you like it? Don't agonize: for the second time I promise you in all honesty—it won't happen again. That—it won't happen. I don't want you to leave so sad. As for me—I'm done for."

—ᴠᴠ— XXIII —ᴠᴠ—

Visiting Marusya

I saw Marusya only one more time (although once afterwards I planned to visit her but was late). I had a lecture in Akerman, and from there Samoilo and Marusya took me across the estuary to their house in Ovidiopol.

I found myself almost writing: "I didn't recognize her." That wouldn't be true: Marusya hadn't changed at all. What I "didn't recognize" wasn't the old Marusya I'd known before but the new one I'd unconsciously expected to find in this new setting. Before our meeting, apparently, I'd been thinking thus: she must be missing something here that she'd grown used to—as a result, I'd observe some yearning in her. As it turned out, nothing of the sort occurred.

Nothing about her had changed, except that now she'd become a very efficient manager of the household, but that wasn't really unexpected; we all knew that Marusya would master whatever she set her mind to. Once, several years ago, she came to see me, wrung her hands at the disarray she found (though in my opinion, there was no disarray whatever), gave me a tongue-lashing, tied up her hair in a kerchief, scurried around for two hours, swept up and wiped down everything, moved things around, tossed out photographs of all women ("What a gallery of monsters this lad has assembled!"), with the exception of the genuinely fine ones and her own ("In my opinion, I'm the best of the lot"); and the result was so blissful that afterwards I regretted having to wash my hands in the basin—she'd draped the pitcher so cozily with a towel. So it was no wonder that things turned out even better in her own home; the maid understood her every desire, dinner was tasty, there were flowers on the table, and the baby was happy, rosy-cheeked, and well brought up for his eighteen months. It wasn't even a wonder that Samoilo had become more human, no longer so maladroit and awkward: I wasn't surprised by this at all; that means, I'd foreseen it subconsciously, knowing from afar how Marusya wins people over.

This is what was surprising: she spoke, laughed, and sparkled exactly as she had during the first years of our acquaintanceship, before all the business with Runitsky. Guests arrived that evening, a Greek neighbor and his wife named Kalliopa Nestorovna (the husband was, apparently, the owner of melon plantations in the vicinity); and a German pharmacist from Gross-Libenthal, who came in his own carriage, and who also brought along his wife and two lovely daughters, staid and stupid. They talked about cucumbers and watermelons, about scarlet fever and country doctors: that is, in essence, the same kind of everyday matters that were talked about in Anna Mikhailovna's living room—except back in those days, their everyday themes were one level higher; there one could discern the presence of a major theater, Thursdays in the literary circle, a university. But here, too, Marusya was like a fish in water: not one false note, everything as it should be, and the whole room was alive with the ringing of her little bells: just as if Marusya'd been born and grown up here and had no need for anything else.

I observed how she behaved with her husband and her child: there was nothing to report, nothing new. She talked with Samoilo as she had at one time with me or with those aristocratic students of reactionary views: impassioned when the subject was silliness but efficient when it was business. She tended to her child just as equably as necessary, since there was no nanny, but somehow didn't leave the impression that she was "fussing" over him; she raised her voice, made jokes, soothed him when he fell, but in no way was she indulgent; and when he fell asleep for his nap, she said sincerely: "Oh! I've had enough of you, Prince Charmant; I'd give a hundred rubles if you don't wake up until half past four." She gave me a tug, grabbed me by the hand, led me out into the garden, and said:

"Samoilo, go on to the pharmacy. We have no need of you: we're going to continue our affair."

I spent two days at their place and all the while followed Marusya around the house and garden like a little puppy dog. In the morning she put on a loose, light, colored garment: she referred to it as her "coverall" and assured me that in such a garment it was more convenient to whip up something for the baby, although it always seemed to me that her wide, dangling sleeves could catch fire at any moment from the kerosene flames. I even followed her into the kitchen: "the cook's godfather-fireman," she kept saying with a laugh. After feeding her son, she fastened a kerchief around her red hair, put on an apron, and straightened up the apartment along with the maid, while I helped—I myself wiped the dust off the shiny frame around the mirror; but I refrained from wiping any uneven surfaces, and didn't let Marusya do it either, because it couldn't be seen anyway. And she, bustling about, twittered nonstop, calling me incompetent and laughing, as before, a little hoarsely.

"I can't quite figure it out, Marusya: have you changed or not?"

She thought a bit and decided that she had but only in one respect. She reminded me: once, a long time ago, when I "reprimanded" her for her too free use of language, she'd explained to me her classification of indecent expressions. There are those that children shouldn't know, and there's a category of indecencies that children are not only allowed to know, but it's even inevitable that they will. In society where there are both men and women, "childish" indecencies are strictly forbidden, and a different tone prevails; but those that aren't for children's ears—be my guest.

"And now," she confessed, "I can inadvertently regale you with an anecdote from the category of infantile liberties, although I'll try to restrain myself. It's hard, you understand, when I spend my whole day with a year-and-a-half-old infant."

She suddenly drew me close to her and whispered into my ear:

"In five months there'll be a second one."

"I never would've guessed!"

She turned her profile toward me and asked merrily, observing my expression:

"Doesn't it show?"

I honestly replied no, but she noticed something in my eyes.

"What are you laughing at?"

After bursting into laughter, I confessed:

"I remember. Once, after my other 'reprimand' on a different theme about your . . . taking liberties, you also turned your profile toward me then but asked me the opposite: 'Well, is there any less of me?'"

She gave me a kiss for this bit of information and fell silent for a moment, her head resting on my shoulder.

"Do you still meet my 'sightseers?'" she asked.

Odessa was not that far away, but she rarely went there; more often Anna Mikhailovna visited her; and, when she did stay with her mother, she didn't see any of her previous friends. I had to tell her who was still there, who'd left, who'd found work or was in training; that everyone I met to this day still talks not about his or her former youth but about Marusya. She listened attentively and seemed touched, inquired about each, recalled various phrases, escapades, eccentricities, and recited from memory Serezha's "portrait" of each and every one:

> He entered like a god, scented with bergamot,
> And once in the room, one could smell an idiot.

"They're all so dear to me," she said sincerely. "It was marvelous to be with them; I'd give each one a kiss now—just like you. Don't be jealous."

"Marusya, don't you ever yearn for it?" I asked, getting bolder.

"No," she replied simply, shaking her head. "It was like swimming: it's lovely to plunge into the sea, but then, after a little while, you've had enough; after getting out of the water and putting on your shoes and hat and everything else, who could possibly long for more water?"

She showed me a small room, a sort of boudoir ("my personal lair"); there on a little desk I saw a photo of Runitsky, but she didn't mention him at all, nor did I.

The second day, right after breakfast, Samoilo left to purchase something in Odessa and said that he'd return late, after midnight: he had an assistant apprentice in the pharmacy. Although he'd become much nicer of late, I felt much freer in his absence; but Marusya, in my opinion, didn't seem any different—only, understandably, she had more time to talk with me one on one; but she spoke just as she had the previous evening.

I went to bed at ten—I had to leave early the next morning; I fell asleep very quickly. The sound of a child's crying woke me; in a moment I heard the sound of bare feet and Marusya's reassuring voice. Although she was speaking to him in a half-whisper so it wouldn't wake me, I could hear all her words clearly—though half of them didn't make any sense: it was all in the language of that enchanted land to which the gods carry away young women transformed by their first experience of motherhood. A-ba-le-ba-le-ba-le. . . . A-gud-gud-gud-gud. . . . Sometimes, however, the words were Russian, but such as I'd never heard before: "a silvery thin silk thread," "a sweet little firefly," "a tiny little petal." . . . Then she sang softly:

> Uli-lyuli-lyuli,
> Pears for other children,
> But for ours, sweet rolls
> So they won't whimper at night.

At last he quieted down; the bare feet shuffled over to my door and Marusya whispered:

"Are you asleep?"

I replied; she came in, her hair in a braid, wearing that coverall over a nightgown, and said "Move over." She sat down, put her feet on my bed, and began talking:

"I'm supposed to say I'm sorry we woke you, but actually I'm very glad: while I was rocking that sweet little thing back to sleep, all the while I was praying to God that you'd wake up. Somehow during that time I came to miss 'you' more than ever since the creation of the world."

"Obviously, I haven't finished saying good-bye. God knows when I'll get to see you again—my youth . . ."

It wasn't completely dark, but light from a kerosene street lamp poured in obliquely. She stared at me fixedly; she extended her arms, stroked my hair, then took hold of my ears; I recalled, read somewhere, that women in ancient Rome also took hold of men's ears when they kissed them—Marusya leaned forward slightly, as if wanting to kiss me, and her braids fell across my forehead; but she reconsidered, moved away, and commanded: "Give me another pillow." She placed it behind her back and leaned up against it.

I said, not to provoke repudiation, but in all honesty:

"Why worry about your youth, Marusya? You're just fine in this new youth of yours, a hundred times better: I don't know how it happened; I'd never have believed it, but it's as if you were born for this life, and had been preparing for it all these years, in your own special way. Your mother knew it—long ago she predicted it would happen, though she never mentioned Samoilo."

Marusya was silent, then replied:

"Mama's a very clever woman. She and I never talked about it— but she knew even earlier than I did.

"And how long have you known?"

"I don't remember, so help me God. Always. Papa brought him to us; I was still a schoolgirl and helped prepare him for his exams; I was terribly impressed that he knew how to concentrate on one thing and sweep aside everything else, and that you couldn't deceive him in any way or charm him. He has a soul made of metal, perhaps, oak. It was probably then I decided; but I don't remember the moment."

She suddenly burst out laughing:

"You know what? Samoilo, in his own way, is just as keenly clever as my mama (it's in their blood—after all, he's related to her, not to Papa). Once he said to me: 'If you ever try to flirt with me, I'll leave you once and for all. I don't care if you carry on with others, but never with me. It doesn't matter if a person whistles outside on the street— as long as he understands that he doesn't whistle in the synagogue.'"

Then she corrected herself, without looking at me:

"Actually he said: 'I don't care if you carry on with others—except for Runitsky.'"

Her voice trembled slightly; I instinctively withdrew my hands from under my head and extended them toward her—she intertwined her fingers with mine and didn't let go for a long time. We were silent—I'd read somewhere, or else I thought it up myself and wrote it down: to be silent in unison—that's when people communicate with each other through their thoughts. Therefore, it occurred not at all "suddenly," but naturally, in the course of and according to the logic of this implicit conversation, and with her implicit permission, that I asked:

"What really happened that time in the valley of Lukaniya?"

Marusya pressed up against me, wound my arms tightly around her, wove her hands into my hair, pressed her lips to my ear, and whispered:

"It was a terrible thing. I went there feeling possessed, I ran from the cliff like a madwoman: I knew it was all over, that in a moment

I'd be Alesha's wife, I wanted it so much and it was so necessary, let it be painful and terrible and let everything fall to pieces once and for all. That's what I said to Alesha down below, at the same place where you judged me and forgave me; I didn't even say it to him, I commanded him. Suddenly—I don't even know how to explain it—it was as if a spring broke inside of me; I wasn't myself but someone else, a strange person with another strange person. He'd only just extended his arms to me—then withdrew immediately and understood everything all at once. He didn't say another word, led me back up, found a cab, and took me home; I remember my teeth were chattering. At the entrance to the house he helped me find the key in my bag, opened the door himself, and removed my hat. I wanted to say 'Forgive me, for Christ's sake'—a half hour before that in my own mind I'd already been baptized and married in church. I said nothing, nor did he."

Marusya withdrew from me, sat down again, leaned against the other pillow, and tossed her head back; then she raised her hands and looked at them for a long time in the dim light of the street lamp.

"Strictly speaking," she said loudly, indifferently, even chuckling, "I have blood on my hands, strictly speaking."

"Don't talk nonsense," I replied angrily.

"Oh, it doesn't torment me." As a matter of fact, she spoke very calmly. "Perhaps, it's the age we're living in: all these guns, gallows, pogroms. Blood doesn't frighten me. I'm only worried about Mama."

I didn't understand. "About Mama? What for?"

She explained slowly, with long pauses, choosing her words carefully; once again she spoke very calmly, evidently not experiencing the terror that her strange ideas produced in me. Strange? I'm not sure that they were completely unexpected: in this tale the name Niobe has already appeared several times, and now I don't recall whether it occurred in my own consciousness only after this conversation and after everything else—or, like Marusya's foreboding, much earlier, "just so," "for some reason or other."

"Just so, for some reason or other," said Marusya. "For some reason it seems to me that all of Mama's children will come to grief; that is, except for Torik—he's not one of us. Marko's already done for, in a totally hideous way, unlike anyone ever before. Lika—she's a cutthroat to the roots of her hair, to the chewed off ends of her fingernails; I don't know whether she'll strangle someone or be strangled, but some time ago I crossed her off the list. And Serezha—he once dragged me to a Caucasian tavern where a Circassian danced holding five daggers in his mouth: that's our Serezha—oh, he'll cut himself. And the worst thing is this: Mama knows it, she thinks about it all the time."

I was silent, so crushed that I didn't even try to protest with an appropriate indignant remark, such as, "What nonsense!" or something of the sort.

"Except for Torik," she repeated. "And I omitted Marusya. I'm a little beast without claws; I won't strangle anyone and we have no daggers here in our house; but kill me, too—somehow I can't imagine myself as an old woman, or even middle-aged. You once read me some of your verses: 'Lilac blossom, you've lost your vernal attire, when did springtime pass?'"

At last I regained control of myself:

"I'm extremely flattered: they were my verses; but it turns out that you, my friend, are a clandestine hysterical woman. You need some hydrotherapy: there's only one answer to such fancy—cold water, or else, yanking on your braids."

Marusya was already laughing, mussing up my hair:

"That's true; most likely I don't believe it myself, or else I wouldn't be living in such a carefree manner as I am now. Tomorrow morning I'll forget everything I've predicted."

I said: "If you like, I'll tell you what I've 'divined' here, during the last two days."

"Yes, please."

"You once said to me in Lukaniya: if you had a singer's talent or some other gift, you'd hide away from the whole world, all alone or with your slave owner. Now I ask: maybe women exist whose sublime song, their song of songs, is a husband and a child, and in general, the entire bathtub of serene tenderness in which you're living?"

"'I'm extremely flattered,'" she said, echoing my previous phrase, but her eyes looked very serious.

"You realize," I insisted, "that once upon a time there lived a man, who was an artist from birth but who didn't know that he was one; for some reason he always spoiled other people's wallpaper, drawing arabesques on them. All of a sudden they took him on as an apprentice, gave him a canvas and paint: all day long his hands and face and even his nose were covered in paint, and he didn't need anything else in the whole world. Or, once upon a time there lived a young woman, who from birth had an unprecedented, incalculable supply of affection in her soul; she scattered this affection to the right and the left, without calculating or stinting, and without deciding whether it was all worth it, until . . ."

"Until she fell into a bathtub? Perhaps."

She yawned and jumped off the bed.

"One thing's certain: my apparel's better suited for the bath than for a visit. Once again we've returned to the beginning of the beginning—to the story of how your heroine 'scatters affection.' That means our circle of subjects is complete, and I'm going to bed. I'll make you some coffee in the morning; there won't be any rolls, but I'll warm up some rusks for you. How would you like your eggs—soft boiled or scrambled?"

She continued to stand next to my bed for another minute, shaking my hand while saying good-bye; she looked at me pensively, inclining her head to one side and tickling her lips with the fuzzy end of one of her braids; once more she seemed to want to bend down but changed her mind.

"What are you being so quiet about in your indecision, Marusya?"

She made no reply, freed her hand, and went to the door, but stopped and turned to face me.

"What about?"

She started laughing and answered as if she were twenty years old again, once more a reddish kitten in a muff, as if she hadn't learned anything or forgotten anything:

"I'll confess. I was standing here thinking: I ought to say farewell to him in a special way—perhaps we'll never meet again. But, as you can see, I've reconsidered. You and I have missed all our deadlines; in general, it's unnecessary; let things remain as they've been. Mona Vanna (she yawned again) offers humble thanks to Zhofru Rudel, but I may be confusing two operas. Go to sleep, my dear. 'Dream me,' if one can say that."

She left. Somewhere a clock struck one a.m.; afterwards I heard her go downstairs on tiptoe but no longer barefoot; she'd obviously decided to wait up for her husband. Then Samoilo came back; then I fell asleep. In the morning they made me coffee, scrambled eggs, crispy hot rusks, and both saw me off affectionately. The carriage took me to Lyustford, and from there I took a streetcar to Bolshoi Fontan and on to Odessa; the next day I left for St. Petersburg.

⚉ XXIV ⚉

Mademoiselle and Signor

That year Lina Cavalieri[1] came to St. Petersburg on tour; someone invited me to enjoy a performance of this famous beauty, either in *Lakmé* or *Thaïs*. As a matter of fact, it wasn't just someone. It was an old friend I've mentioned twice before in this tale, without naming him; and even now I don't want to reveal his name. It was he who once said to me that the stumpy "dregs," the girlfriends of the revolutionary external students of 1902, were disguised daughters of the biblical Judith; and it was he who, a year or even less after that performance by Lina Cavalieri, perished by order of the tsar on the gallows near Sestroretsk. Before then he was living incognito in the capital: a native of Odessa, my former fellow student in the gymnasium, he was passing himself off as an Italian, a correspondent for a conservative Roman newspaper, pretending not to know a word of Russian; he spoke Italian like a Florentine and French with an irreproachably fabricated Italian accent; he curled and dyed his mustache, wore a bowler hat, and sported a pin with a bauble in his tie— in general, he acted out this comedy flawlessly. When we met somewhere for the first time, I, who'd sat next to him on the same school bench for years (afterwards we'd continued to meet often, even recently), simply didn't recognize him and never even suspected who he was: he guarded his own appearance, intonation, and gestures so

---

[1] Lina Cavalieri (1874–1944) was an Italian lyric soprano whose voice was especially suited for French opera.

carefully. He revealed his identity to me—he required my assistance abroad on some matter; but his self-possession had so convinced me and disciplined me, that even when I was alone with him, I never spoke Russian to him. He was a great devotee of the opera and a great fan of Lina Cavalieri; besides, as he explained to me without batting an eye, "She's my compatriot, after all."

"You may call me a traitor," (in Russian we addressed each other informally) he whispered to me during intermission, "but I think the woman sitting in that box is even finer than Lina."

I glanced at that box and agreed with him privately; I was not surprised—I'd known for some time that I'd never meet another woman as beautiful as the one sitting there; at least, it didn't happen to me, either before or afterwards. She had black hair and the profile of a Greek statue; her forehead and nose merged into one feature without interruption, and her splendid shoulders (I recalled them as slender when she was a girl) sloped like the outline of an amphora where the mouth gradually turns into the neck of the vessel. She had a tiara in her hair; something was also sparkling on her bosom; she wore an evening gown, "immodest" by local standards, from a major designer, the way we wear our jackets—simply, as a matter of habit, imperceptibly. "She's lived in the beau monde," I marveled, remembering the past. She wore high gloves on her bare arms; I wondered if her fingernails were still bitten off, or whether they'd been neatly trimmed by a manicurist? I didn't see her eyes at first; she was facing away from me; then she turned her head, saying something to her companion in tails, and her deep blue eyes became visible; they were of some unprecedented, implausible blueness. I remembered the color, but here's what was new and what struck me: the expression of those eyes. I'm not a great reader of physiognomy and glances, but it was apparent even to a nearsighted person, that enormous love was clearly reflected in them: a strange love, rare in human practice, a selfish love, powerful, intolerant, strict, but at the same time, tender and obedient. Then she glanced up at the hall; my neighbor bowed to her, she nodded with stately courtesy, and then her eyes met mine. Something whispered to me: don't acknowledge her, she doesn't want it. As a matter of fact, she turned her glance away coolly. But at that moment her cavalier, who earlier had been sitting with his back to us, turned around, and I uttered his name aloud involuntarily:

"Doctor Vernicci?"

"Is that so?" asked my neighbor with curiosity. "You know him, do you? And her—can it be that you don't recognize her?"

Vernicci, seeing us both, nodded cheerfully and began to motion us over to his box. I had no desire whatever to comply, in the first place, because of her, but in addition—acquaintances of mine might be in the hall for whom his profession was no secret. But my neighbor muttered a Roman curse under his mustache:

"*Accidenti a li mortacci sui.*[2] I must . . ."

"Tell him I have to call my editorial office," I begged, "or whatever you want to say, but rescue me. His signora is hardly eager to see me."

After the performance we spent a long time in a cab getting to the Restaurant Vienna, and he told me all about this couple. In line with his designation as a conservative journalist, he visited Vernicci in Paris where he, of course, was passing himself off as a representative of the fourth estate; but through the really seditious nature of his profession, he knew well the true profession of his Roman acquaintance.

"His bosses," he said, "value him highly; but in my opinion, he's what Bismarck once said about the young Napoleon: 'major, but unrecognized lack of talent.'"

"Why lack of talent?"

"If only for this reason: do you believe that to this day he doesn't suspect that Mademoiselle Lapervanche is your compatriot?"

I recalled that in Bern, when we'd met at the bank and then sat together at the café, her name had not been given, and she'd immediately passed herself off as a foreigner. It turned out, according to my friend's account, that for some time now in Paris she'd been considered Vernicci's official friend and traveled with him in the capacity of "secretary" throughout Europe, wherever his investigative service led him; she was called Madeline Lapervanche, or even de Lapervanche; her papers were in order and she'd received a visa to enter Russia.

"And she doesn't speak a word of Russian, just like me."

He fell silent, then all of a sudden leaned over to my ear and, for the first time in all these months, whispered in Russian:

"She's an important woman. After the revolution, history will record such figures on a board of honor."

I was totally astonished and looked at him inquisitively; however,

---

[2] "Damn your dead relatives."

he nodded with a look that clearly indicated: "Don't ask; I have no right to explain; you should even forget what I just said to you."

We remained silent for the rest of the trip; I tried my best to construct from these fragments a portrait of the new Lika. On a board of honor? Coming from him, that could mean only one thing: as before Lika was working for some underground organization. At the same time—the tiara, the necklace, that weasel's kept woman. . . . Strictly speaking, what was it he did? A foreigner, unable to insinuate himself into the good graces of anyone in the political emigration—of what use was he to the investigative service? What did they pay him for? But obviously, they did pay him; and, to all accounts, he was the right hand of that very Signor M.-M., that polite, affable convert to Christianity who was so highly valued by the Russian secret police. So Vernicci came in handy, too; but what was Lika doing here? What sort of role was this strange girl playing with this insidious man, a girl who at one time responded only to rancorous voices of hatred but who's now obviously clinging to this man? I couldn't come up with anything; no portrait emerged. I merely sensed vaguely that I'd gotten to some murky business, perhaps sacred, but insidious.

In the Restaurant Vienna, as always at night, there was a huge crowd. I don't recall how we spent our time there, who sat down with us, and why we stayed for so long; I only recall that my companion acted his role as a foreigner astonishingly well for other people. The following episode even occurred (perhaps, not this time, but that doesn't matter): another journalist arrived after a night's work, also a native of Odessa, also our classmate; he sat down at our table and spent an hour with us; I introduced them and acted as their interpreter; the new arrival, in the middle of our conversation, suddenly said to me: "There's something about him that reminds me of L, isn't there?" I confirmed that there was; then he left, without ever guessing that my companion was none other than L. himself.

Suddenly, very late in the evening, the public began to stir, necks stretched, heads turned; I also turned around—the maître d'hôtel was ceremoniously leading Vernicci and Lika to a free table. She had a very expensive fur stole draped over her shoulders and she moved serenely and effortlessly through the ranks of admiring glances. The man escorting them had already indicated with a gesture of supreme elegance a very special table, but at that moment Vernicci spied us. He rushed toward me with his usual expansiveness, once again took my hand and shook it endlessly with both of his, in a minute pronounced a long speech about how glad he was to meet me, and then pointed to Lika:

"Can it be that you don't recognize Mademoiselle Madeline? It was you who introduced us."

"Hello, monsieur," she said in French, extending her hand. Her voice sounded courteous and nonchalant, her eyes regarded me serenely and confidently. I muttered:

"Mademoiselle de Lapervanche has changed considerably . . ." Then I recalled that on such an occasion, in the presence of an Italian, one must offer some compliment, so I added: "The star has become the sun," or something like that.

"May we join you? Merci, maître d'hôtel, we'll stay here."

I'd already dismissed internally the fear that people would see me, a liberal journalist, in such friendly contact with a man about whom they might have heard; but I was in a cold sweat from the muddle that had ensued. There were now two poseurs at my table, and all three of us were deceiving the fourth person; it was worth it, and I didn't feel sorry for him, but would I, a complete novice, be able to uphold my role in this act of dissembling? And for what? What did any of this have to do with me? It occurred to me to excuse myself, to say I had work, and then leave; but everyone knows how hard that is. Actors in the Solovtsovsky troupe, with whom at one time I'd been close in Odessa, had explained to me that on stage the most difficult thing to do is to know how to "bow out"—to take one's leave without awkwardness, without tripping; in life it's even more complicated than on the stage. I stayed there, took control of myself, and decided to say as little as possible, so as not to betray my disguised fellow Odessans. It turned out not to be that hard—Vernicci talked nonstop, my friend was almost as bad, so my cooperation was almost unnecessary.

Vernicci turned out to be an interesting and charming conversationalist. Of course, I don't remember exactly what he talked about, but it included world politics, all the latest books that had been published in the West, the decline of Eleonora Duse[3] and Marinetti's school,[4] and twenty or so anecdotes about kings and ministers, each

---

[3] Eleonora Duse (1858–1924) was a very popular Italian actress.
[4] Filippo Marinetti (1876–1944) was an Italian novelist, poet, dramatist, and the

one funnier than the last. At the same time he chose a special bottle from the wine list; the maître d'hôtel even stood at attention while taking the order. All my bourgeois prejudices immediately began grumbling inside me: drink out of *his bottle*? But my friend came to my rescue: he declared categorically that at this table we were the hosts, he would allow no objections, and "when we meet in Paris, you can seek your revenge . . ." I felt much better, and in my joy drank more than the rest; we ordered a second bottle and a third, and gradually my quandary subsided.

I recall the following moment: Lika was chatting with my friend; Vernicci wanted to say something to her and placed his hand on hers. She turned her head to him and listened, but looked at his hand rather than at him: once again in her eyes and in her face I could see the imprint of that same expression, "I'm yours," grasping and submissive, slavish and slave-owning, that had struck me earlier in the theater. "Good Lord!" I thought, really wracking my brains over this puzzle, "is she in love like a gypsy girl—and is she lying to him like a gypsy girl? What's going on?"

He said what he intended to and then removed his hand; she began talking again with my friend, all in French, "Monsieur," "Mademoiselle." Vernicci turned to me but was silent at first; suddenly he raised his eyes and, in spite of all my expectations, had the genuine, cordial look of a very sincere, very nice fellow.

"You," he said in a low voice, "without even knowing it yourself, have made me happy for the rest of my life."

It must have been a result of the wine, but I was deeply moved: his words touched me directly. Feeling guilty without guilt, I felt shame in my soul: I couldn't figure out who was deceiving whom more, who was digging a deeper hole for whom, but today I was also helping make a fool of this goy,[5] whoever he was. "Happy for the rest of his life . . ." actually, since he was sitting at my table and drinking my wine, it might even be appropriate to hint that his happiness wasn't going to last for long, that a rusty needle was already lodged somewhere in his feather-bed—I didn't know what kind of needle, but the rust was poisonous, and the result would be unfortunate. Of course,

---

ideological founder of Futurism, an early-twentieth-century literary, artistic, and political movement.

[5] Yiddish. A Gentile, i.e., anyone who is not a Jew; here, someone who is dull, insensitive, heartless.

I said nothing to him; in silence I let him shake my hand again, and drowned my embarrassment with a fifth or sixth glass of wine.

At the end I remember a moment when Vernicci and my friend left and I remained alone with Lika, We sat opposite; she motioned to Vernicci's chair—"Come closer." I obeyed. We were surrounded by half-drunken conversation; no one paid us any attention. She began speaking Russian, barely audibly:

"When did you arrive from Odessa?"

I replied in the same low voice, that everyone was well (I don't recall whether Marko was still alive); I spoke about Marusya and the baby in Ovidiopol.

"You get high marks," she said. "At first I was afraid you'd somehow misspeak. Don't tell my family about this meeting either."

Her tone, even though she was talking to me now about her secrets, was her old one, cold, dismissive—and I thought: "It's like she's talking to a servant, telling him to take away the leftovers." All of a sudden I was struck by a surge of malice—the enmity of my whole life, the whole mutual polarity of our dispositions, all my dismay in the face of a soul that held nothing sacred and recognized no categories of good and evil; perhaps, I confess, I was even more struck by those countless glasses of *vendage* 1872. I replied to her sharply:

"Not only won't I tell them, but I myself will try to forget this nightmare. You're a monster, Lika: you live with a spy, you're in love with him like a kitten, and you spy on him for others. I don't believe that even a good cause is worth that kind of service."

Her blue eyes looked at me haughtily and apathetically; she replied slowly and very serenely:

"It is."

Vernicci's career came to an abrupt end a year later; an accident, the details of which remain unknown to this day, almost toppled his boss as well, the convert Signor M.-M. I don't know exactly what kind of foul deeds they cooked up together; they say that Evno Azef[6] was also involved, that they were trying to arrange a major assassination attempt, to thwart it at the last moment, to catch a large number of valuable people from a militant organization, perhaps, and perhaps

---

[6] Evno Azef (1869–1918) was one of the few Jews in the Russian Social Revolutionary Party and the leader of its terrorist arm; he was subsequently unmasked as a police informer.

not. But something large was organized, and the threads led from Paris; on the eve of the denouement, the entire plan, for which Vernicci was responsible, was exposed in the illegal press. Vernicci disappeared from that day on; even in Italy no one heard anything more about him. Someone told me that supposedly he'd left for Argentina and had vanished there. Perhaps it was along the way that he'd disappeared, also allowing some wave to wash him overboard? Perhaps because he'd so confidently admitted over the wine: "Happy for the rest of my life."

Not one word about Madeline de Lapervanche found its way into the press. Once Anna Mikhailovna let me know that Lika had left for Paris, though her exact whereabouts were unknown; while saying this, Anna Mikhailovna's head, which had turned completely gray, shook like an old woman's head. I would've inquired about Lika from my friend, but very soon he was followed and arrested, still in possession of an Italian passport; now he's no longer among the living.

---⁓⁓― **XXV** ―⁓⁓---

Gomorrah

The Turks, it seems, even to the present (I've boasted about this before), refer to Odessa in their official documents as Khodzha-bei, the
ancient name of this location on the shores of the Black Sea. Here in
town that name has been preserved only in the designation of one estuary: the Khadzhi-bei. On it, in the summer of 1909 approximately,
my beloved Serezha met his end; that is to say, he remained alive in
the technical sense, and, while his parents still lived, of course, he was
not abandoned; I think he won't ever be abandoned as long as Torik
survives; but whether Anna Mikhailovna, Ignats Albertovich, Torik,
or Serezha himself is still alive—I don't know. I haven't been back to
Russia since 1915, and no one has written to me since 1917. In any
case, at that time, on the Khadzhi-bei estuary, he was still technically
alive, but for himself and everyone else, he was already dead. I
haven't seen him since that time. For a few months after the episode
he still lived at his father's house but didn't show himself to anyone,
not even to me; then he left home and hid away in some hole, no one
knows where, without acquaintances, without books, living alone in
eternal darkness. If he's still alive, then today, perhaps, he's tearing
his hair out or moaning softly, whispering: if I'd only moved another
half inch, either to the right or the left . . .

A famous Odessa lawyer, the one who defended Rovensky[1] (and
who, in fact, secured him such a lenient sentence—only a year and a

---

[1] The surname of Nyura's husband and Nyuta's father.

half in a penal battalion, if I remember correctly), was my close acquaintance. After the trial I spent a long evening at his house, almost the whole night, and questioned him about the one thing I couldn't understand. Not about Serezha's role, of course: for Serezha, this unusual occurrence, until it ended in such terrible retribution, must have been just another curious experience among the unlimited possibilities of life; in having that experience, probably, he was neither shaken nor seized by its monstrous unnaturalness—Serezha, most likely, was simply amusing himself again; an hour after the beginning of this "experience," he was already suppressing a slight internal yawn. But the two women? How could it happen? I'd known them for a long time, since my first visit to Anna Mikhailovna; I knew that our whole circle and the "entire town" made fun of their caprices, of their accentuated similarity and their identical dress, even of their infatuation with Serezha, which, by the end, had become quite obvious; but I'd known them a long time and thought I knew them thoroughly; I was aware of their impeccable, refined restraint—and it seemed to me that never (except for that drunken "Potemkin" night in the Aleksandrov Park near the fortress—but at that moment the foundations of our whole world were being shaken), never did I see even the slightest indication of familiarity on their part; then, all of a sudden . . .

I didn't understand anything.

"The crux of the matter is gradualism," the lawyer kept insisting. "Gradualism, and another little phrase, an interrogative consisting of a few short words. You just admitted you heard this very phrase uttered by Sergei Milgrom himself—when he was young and you were trying to dissuade him from having contact with some cardsharps. The point, however, is not Sergei Milgrom; the point is that this phrase is typical, truly typical of his entire generation. The phrase is: "But why is it forbidden?" Let me assure you that no power of agitation can be compared to this question in its devastating impact. From time immemorial the moral equilibrium of humanity has rested on the fact that we hold certain axioms: some closed doors bear the inscription "Forbidden." Simply "forbidden," with no explanation; these axioms stand firm, doors are locked, floorboards don't crack, and planets continue to revolve around the sun according to the established order. But if only once you pose the question: "But why is it forbidden?"—these axioms come crashing down. It's a mistake to think that an axiom is obvious, that it's "not worth" proving because it's clear to everyone; no, my friend, an axiom is defined as a proposition that is *inconceivable* to prove; inconceivable, even if the whole world were to rise up in rebellion and demand: "Prove it!" And, as soon as this question is posed—it's all over. This little phrase is like an incantation: in its presence all locked doors are smashed to smithereens; there's no more "forbidden" and everything becomes "permitted." Not only the rules of conventional morality, such as "don't steal" or "don't lie," but even the most instinctive, most innate (as in this matter) reactions of human nature—shame, physical squeamishness, the voice of blood—everything dissolves into dust. For our moral foundations this one question is just like that little bottle of sulfuric acid thrown at someone's face and eyes. Your Sergei Milgrom merely received a dose of what he himself had first tossed somewhere he shouldn't have."

The lawyer was a remarkable orator; I knew that considerable patience was required in conversation with such types. They always have an inner supply of unutilized eloquence available: they have to be allowed free rein before their conversation really gets down to business. They're like hot water faucets: at first they run cold, for a long time. But perhaps it was because I loved Sergei Milgrom so much that I was so irritated at hearing this truth.

"And the second point is—gradualism," continued the lawyer. "There's no task so difficult that it's impossible to overcome with the secret of gradual pressure. One must merely investigate closely the concept of 'difficulty,' divide it into separate components, not tackle it all at once, but take things in order, one at a time: at first spray that same acid on one thing, wait until it works and the pain passes, then move on to the second, in its turn. Allow me to pose an indiscreet question, since we're alone: have you ever—I'm searching for the right words—*débaucher une jeune fille très pure* [corrupted a very innocent young girl]? Perhaps it's better to leave our personal secrets alone, and turn to literature instead: what was Don Juan all about? Not Byron's character,[2] nor the one depicted by Tirso de Molina[3] or even later by Zorrilla y Moral:[4] that individual acts by force, by

---

[2] The hero of the narrative poem *Don Juan* (1819–24) by the English romantic poet Lord Byron (1788–1824).

[3] Tirso de Molina (c. 1580–1648) was a Spanish playwright best known for his treatment of the Don Juan legend in *The Seducer of Seville* (1634).

[4] Zorrilla y Moral (1817–93) was a Spanish poet whose play *Don Juan Tenorio* (1844) was also based on the national legend.

charm; it's enough for him to utter one monologue—the purest maiden is smitten after only a dozen or so lines. That's nonsense. No, try to imagine the actual, "historical" Don Juan: Juan Tenorio, son of an impoverished landowner near Seville, a spendthrift and swashbuckler but by no means an Adonis. How did he achieve his conquests? One thousand and three victims in Spain alone, not even counting those abroad, and among that number such untouchables as Donna Anna: how did he conquer them, one after another?"

(My interlocutor knew Spanish well and pronounced Donna Anna correctly, but we aren't obliged to do the same.)

"I assure you: it wasn't charm," he continued, "but exclusively gradualism. Donna Anna says: 'I don't want to listen to you. It's forbidden!' Don Juan asks: 'But why is it forbidden?' And sure enough—after two days she's listening to him. But she has a second strategy: 'I won't agree to a rendezvous with you at night for anything on earth—that's really forbidden! Once again: 'But why is it forbidden?' And three days later, at their secret rendezvous, he begins to apply the same magic to kissing her hands, her cheek, then every button and buckle of her intricate attire . . ."

I lost my patience and interrupted him:

"But there was always only one Donna Anna, not two at the same time! And not a mother and daughter!"

"The difference, if you think about it, lies in the fact that two pairs of ears were listening to your friend's syllogism instead of one; but it's not hard to devise syllogisms on this theme, too. All the more so, since both were undoubtedly in love with him; and there was so much time. Their friendship had been going on for eight years. It's very easy for me to imagine all the developmental stages of this ménage à trois. At first, let's say, the three of them are sitting together on a cliff, somewhere along the sea coast in the moonlight, and so on; he's in the middle; he takes both of them by the hands, Mama Nyura in his right, and her daughter Nyuta in his left; he holds them fast and doesn't let them go. The first time, they may even pull their hands away, Mama Nyura, probably, wags her finger at him: it's forbidden. He's offended, distressed, and sulks. But why is it forbidden? Prove it. Of course, it's impossible to prove; the next time their hands remain in his. In a month—or a year, there was plenty of time—his arms are already wound around both their waists; at first, without any pressure applied, then with. . . . It's not worth continuing; you can finish it all yourself, I'm feeling sick to my stomach. But you must understand one thing: if this is all done carefully, gradually, slowly, so that both women get used to it and grow comfortable with the increase in their threefold intimacy, then, of course, strangers would notice nothing at all. You wondered before how no one could have been struck by anything unusual for so many years? People are 'struck' only by sudden, sharp changes: the only ones who give themselves away are those who don't get used to a new situation; gradualism, on the other hand, is a guarantee of complete composure. They've probably spent Athenian nights together—Sodomite nights, if you like—in various hotels, in that same setting described in breathless terms by the unfortunate Rovensky. . . . Brrr! And the very next day, in public, in your presence, there were no immodest implications, no unnecessary touching, only innocent, loving feminine eyes . . . your Sergei himself, of course, was never the least bit 'in love.'"

I started pacing the room, trying to formulate a question that, for some reason at that very moment, seemed both most important and most horrible; but I couldn't conceive of anything, so I stopped and asked point-blank:

"Is it true they gave him money?"

He replied:

"Undoubtedly. It's an established fact. Just between us—although I consider Rovensky a very decent person—I have the distinct impression that for him it was precisely this aspect of the whole affair that was the last straw. Not as a result of his miserliness: he's not a miser at all, nor even a penny pincher; he's a typical Jewish merchant from Odessa who, at some point, made it here as a pauper from the village of Volegotsulovo, fell into our port city whirlwind of rainbow-colored, hundred-ruble bills and promissory notes, of people arriving and departing, and he immediately lost track of money. You must surely have noticed that our grandfather Shylock died a long time ago and unfortunately left no heirs? There's not, in all the Orthodox world, in spite of the broad expanse of the Slavic soul, such a hopeless spendthrift—or, as they say in Odessa, a "charlatan"—as this type of half-Russified Jew. If your Nyura and Nyuta brought him to ruin over diamonds, Rovensky would merely have groaned and signed the promissory notes. But that—brrr!"

At this point he remembered to glance over at me and must have noticed what was going on inside. I was hiding in the farthest corner of the room; if I could have, I'd have crawled into the woodwork as a result of my pain and shame. It's true that Serezha once told me this about himself, in their living room, in the pauses between couplets of a French song: *Si vous le saviez, mesdames, vous iriez couper les joncs*— even then he'd said, or hinted, that he wasn't the least bit frightened by these feminine gifts; and, at the time, I thought I believed him. Now it was clear I didn't: I believed everything, but not that . . .

My interlocutor was a kind, sincere man; it isn't fair that so many annoying comments about him have crept in previously, as if it was his fault that my favorite, Serezha, had gone crazy. He began talking in a different way, sympathetically:

"Look at all this in another light. The same question and, probably, the same gradualism, but now seen not from his point of view. The first time he said to Nyura and Nyuta with a guffaw, 'I've lost everything playing cards! All I can do is shoot myself!'—they offered him help immediately. He made fun of them, perhaps even pulling their ears a little, if they were already close enough for such a rebuke to their absurd proposal. At this point, either Nyura or Nyuta, or both, managed to ask: 'Serezha, if you please, what's the matter—but why is it forbidden?' His own weapon, don't you see? A month passed, or a year, or three, the acid had its effect, the prejudice was relaxed (you know, it's really only a prejudice—that money doesn't smell; it's an olfactory and chemical lie; but, as a matter of fact, money has no gender). In a word—the moment inevitably arrived when it appeared that it was indeed 'permitted' . . ."

"That word 'permitted' is horrible," he said later, almost at dawn. "And here's what I can tell you; if you repeat it, don't attribute it to me. You know that a long time ago I changed the designation of my own religious persuasion in my passport. Thus I gave up the right to judge my former community; on principle, as you know, I'm not a person who holds the same views as you; I believe in assimilation and consciously desire it. But it's impossible to ignore the fact that the initial stages of mass assimilation are very difficult. Russian culture is as great and as deep as the ocean, and as pure; but when you enter the water from the shore, for a while you must swim through putrid slime, wood chips, and watermelon rinds. . . . Assimilation begins precisely with the relaxation of old prejudices; but a prejudice is a sacred thing, as the poet Baratynsky[5] once wrote: 'It's a fragment of an-

---

[5] Evgeny Baratynsky (1800–44), a contemporary of Pushkin, was a leading philosophical poet who combined spiritual melancholy with an elegant style.

cient truth.' Perhaps the genuine meaning of morality, even the concept of cultural level, consists of prejudices; every culture has its own, original prejudices; during a transition, a lengthy interruption occurs—old prejudices have fallen away, while new ones have yet to be adopted; it takes a long time, perhaps not just one or two generations, but more. And do you know what? Don't get angry—you're such a patriot—just as I am—but it's true, nevertheless: in all of Russia there's not a better example of this interruption in cultural succession than in our own dear, happy Odessa. I'm not talking only about the Jews: it's the same with Greeks, Italians, Poles, even with 'Russians'— even they, en masse, are born dumb Ukrainians, who merely 'turn themselves into Russian butchers'; most clearly of all, of course, this is manifested in the Jews. As a result of this, probably, comes the special, provocative quick-wittedness of the local milieu, at which all Russia pokes fun, and which both you and I love so much: after all, it often happens that periods of disintegrating foundations are considered ones of brilliance. But our underhandedness also results from this, our affectionate relationship to the blatant lies of everyday life and trade, and the fact that for every ten maidens from respectable households, there are nine semivirgins, and the tenth one is . . . not; and your Sergei comes from this milieu, too, as do Nyura and Nyuta."

"How did it happen?" I asked. The town governor had prohibited newspapers from describing the details of the affair on the Khadzhibei estuary; the trial took place behind closed doors; the reporter Shtrok from our editorial office knew everything, of course, and tried to tell me, too, but I threw him out. I don't know why I even asked now; I recall the lawyer's answer very clearly, but I don't feel like recounting it in detail, merely in a few broad strokes. Rovensky had procured a bottle of acid three months before; the man had suffered a great deal, hadn't spoken to his wife or daughter for almost a year, tried to stay away from home on business, most often without any real need. That evening he told the maid he was leaving town but hid out in a coffeehouse on Langeron Street, diagonally across from his own house; he saw Sergei pull up in his dashing cab, and saw him leave with both ladies. He followed them to the estuary and then to a hotel; he hung about under the illuminated windows for an hour or two, until the kerosene lamp was extinguished. Then he rang the bell, rented a room for himself, went through the corridor in his stocking feet with the bottle of acid in his left hand, a hammer he'd brought along in his right; using it, he smashed the cheap, rickety lock and burst into the room. They had extinguished the lamp, but a stearin candle was burning on the table. Seeing the hammer and his insane eyes, Serezha jumped up and rushed to grab it; Rovensky didn't struggle; he stepped back but shifted the vial from his left hand to his right, and then threw the acid in Serezha's face. He admitted that he wanted to do the same to his own wife, while he "just wanted to strangle" his daughter Nyuta, but didn't have the strength to raise his hand; or else, he "suddenly went numb," as he admitted later at the trial.

Anna Mikhailovna was already a little old lady when I saw her later, although she could've been taken for Marusya's older sister only about five years before. I sat around their house quite a while, like a fool, unable to utter a word; she was silent, too. Ignats Albertovich, whose appearance was also quite changed by it all, was somehow managing to cope: he tried to sustain a conversation on peripheral matters and quoted long passages from Wieland's "Oberon,"[6] and even from Klopstock.[7]

---

[6] A verse fairy tale (1780) by the German novelist, poet, and translator Christoph Wieland (1733–1813).

[7] Friedrich Klopstock (1724–1803) was a lyric poet who helped inaugurate the golden age of German literature.

—–∿– XXVI –∿–—

Something Bad

The letter, under the influence of which I was preparing to visit Marusya again, was long and confused. Of course, I no longer remember its exact words, and there's no reason to pretend that I do; nevertheless, it's still so vivid in my memory, that I'll try to recollect not only its ideas but also the sound of the letter accurately.

"Dear friend, dear friend, for some reason I don't feel quite right. Samoilo's a sweetheart, a fine soul, and a gentleman, not commonly found; he even knows how to do something that no one else can do—to fall silent and be inconspicuous when I'm angry at the whole world. He probably thinks that I'm most angry with him: that's not true, on my word of honor. Sometimes I think to myself: of all those whom I could've married, whom should I have chosen? I couldn't have chosen a better man. He even gets angry in an attractive way, like a born nobleman. We have not fallen out of love with each other, and we still have completely intoxicated encounters. It's not appropriate to report to those young fellows I knew, but 'Everything's permitted to Marusya.' Samoilo has nothing to do with it.

"My children are both even better. The elder one's already a helper, pushing a little broom around or fetching me matches: he brings them when I sweep, or else, brings the broom when I'm heating the milk; he has the very best intentions. He looks me right in the eye as he's doing all this with the earnest look of a loyal dog . . . my soul leaps inside me. And he has such amusing speech—half Ukrainian (as a result of our maid Gapka); he uses all his verbs in the feminine form because he's accustomed to female company. He bursts into the bedroom and announces: 'Hi, Mama, it's me!' The younger, during the ritual of disenfranchisement according to the laws of our people, was nicknamed Zhorzhik; his major contribution to the welfare of our family consists in the fact that he never cries, even when he gets soap in his eyes: he's a reserved little lad, like his grandfather; we'll have to invite a Fräulein who knows the verses *Leier und Schwert*,[1] I don't remember by whom. But there's still a long time until his first birthday.

"I feel awfully cozy with all three of them. I don't need anything else. I have no curiosity left for anything except what Mishka will be like a month from now and what Zhorzhik will be like a week from now (for each that's a whole new stage in life). I could sit down and write a book: 'Housekeeping of a Happy Woman.' Every word in it would be the sacred truth; but the whole work, on the other hand, would hardly be true.

"'I don't need anything else.' That's true. But here's the quandary: people think that 'I don't need anything else' means the same as 'It's enough.' I don't know. . . . Sometimes it happens that Mishka has no appetite, but that doesn't mean he's full.

"The capital city of Ovidiopol is also not to blame. Last winter when you weren't around, I spent a month in Odessa; I visited all the theaters and attended two balls: it wasn't bad, I wasn't bored, but I left for home with pleasure. 'I don't need anything else.'

"I've become so much prettier; many young people come here in the summer, most of them Russians—I have great success among them, but no one dares court me in earnest: I have a reputation as a good family person. And thank heaven: I know that now (tear up this letter and burn all the pieces), by wagging his little finger, any man at all, as long as he's neat and clean, could take me down from the shelf of faithful wives, probably even without any former 'limits,' and carry me right to seventh heaven. And that's not at all because I feel drawn to seventh heaven: I said that I have no curiosity left whatever: it's just so. A person walks along the road, the road leads exactly where he has to go and where he wants to go; suddenly there's a path

---

[1] *Lyre and Sword* (1814), a collection of poems by Theodor Körner (1791–1813), a German patriotic poet of the war of liberation against Napoleon. After his death at the age of 22, his father collected the best of his works and published them in one volume.

off to the right, the most ordinary path, not at all picturesque, not mysterious in any way; perhaps it even says on the path 'dead-end.' All of a sudden the person stops and thinks: shall I turn here? Why turn, where to turn, he himself doesn't know; but I don't guarantee that he won't turn. Isn't that what clever people describe as a 'lost soul'?

"I'm philosophizing about myself a great deal right now; don't be angry if it seems incoherent. Perhaps there are some souls who have no place on earth after their youth. 'Youth'—that means a time when nothing has been resolved, therefore everything can still be resolved just as you like, or that's how it seems. You stand on the threshold of the whole world, there are a hundred doors before you, and you can open any one you like, peek in without entering—and, if you don't like it, you can slam it shut and try another. This gives you a terrible feeling of omnipotence: youth is omnipotence. Afterwards, when this has all passed, you feel as if all of a sudden the emperor's crown has been taken off your head. All people come to terms with this, that is, they never even suspect that there once was a crown and that it was removed; there are, of course, exceptions. Sometimes it seems to me that there are many deposed kings in history, but they were all left with one important consolation—the dream of revenge. But imagine a king who was absent from his kingdom for a minute—and his kingdom up and drowned, just like Atlantis. He continues to live on, demoted for the rest of his life, and has nothing left to dream of. It must be that all this passes sometime around the age of thirty-five.

"Dear friend, come visit me, even if only for a week. This may sound suspicious after what I just wrote about any little finger that could take me down from that shelf; but we both know already that for some reason the good Lord has decided that *this* affair would never be consummated. I often think that's odd and too bad. He completed one chapter of it and that night was the best one of my life. But there will be no sequel to it—have no fear and come visit me. You can't help in any way, because it's impossible to cure a person when there's no illness; but I would like a week's vacation."

I still recall that around that same time I once went to Fonberg's barbershop on Richelieu Street; the apprentice Kuba, as he fastened the smock, for the hundredth time said to me sympathetically:

"It's a mistake to shave you: your hair's wiry, but your skin's tender."

At that moment, from the next chair in the shop, someone said, "Hello." Turning to look around, I recognized Abram Moiseevich from under his ample wig of shampoo bubbles. We started chatting, at first about neutral subjects, because we were in a public place.

"How's your brother, Boris Mavrikievich?"

"Beiresh? He's in Italy, no more, no less. He couldn't go to Marienbad like everyone else; he just had to go to Italy. What an aristocrat. He writes letters with long descriptions."

In spite of the fact that we were in a public place, Abram Moiseevich pulled out a postcard from his pocket and, interfering with the apprentice's work, read me aloud Beiresh's composition. There really were descriptions of cathedrals and canals, in a very elevated style, but I don't recall them. I remember only two sentences, something like:

"On the other hand, the food isn't very good, especially the meat: today they served entrecôte—I suspect it was horsemeat, not beefsteak."

"Give my very best regards to Ignats and especially to the unforgettable Anyuta; I'm totally devastated by grief over the matter of the misunderstanding with Serezha, although he was always such a good-for-nothing."

His signature: "Your ever-so-devoted brother, Bor."

When we left, I escorted him to his home on Kolontaev Street, and all along the way he talked about various members of the Milgrom family; he spoke with great feeling.

"A good-for-nothing, he was such a good-for-nothing, I, too, still haven't forgiven him for that 'ex,' although, of course, it gave me great pleasure when they also stole from Beiresh. But you have to be a cow like Beiresh to write like that now. As if the sum total of Serezha's worth is that he's a 'good-for-nothing.' I tell you, Serezha was merely born thirty years too late, or perhaps, fifty years. When I was still a child, it was only that kind of person that was able to establish a career here in Odessa. One got rich on contraband, another by loading one third rubbish along with grain into his sacks, and the third simply bribed the inspector, received back used bills of lading, wiped away the seal with solvent, and then sold them to those fools in Kherson—that's what Kherson's all about. On the other hand, they themselves were rich and a hundred or so souls were supported around each one of them. On my word of honor, it was better back then. In a port town that wants to grow, you need crooks, six fingers on every hand, and a hook on every finger. You also need wealthy men, not honest calves like Beiresh and me or Milgrom—our place is in the be-smedresh,[2] studying the Mishnah[3], not trading grain. Just look, Odessa used to be the most important town in all Russia, and now it's in decline; it envies the likes of Nikolaev, and tomorrow it will envy Ochakov. Forty years ago this Serezha would probably have been the wealthiest man on the whole Black Sea, and Beiresh and I would have been his apprentices—and that blockhead Rovensky, too, in spite of everything."

Then he told me about Anna Mikhailovna: it was odd that before this conversation I hadn't known anything about her previous life.

"Hey, what are all your liberal rules, as if one has to marry for love. It's the same if you choose the fabric for a jacket blindfolded. When a young man and a young woman fall in love, that means both of them are blind. Would you like to know how Anyuta Falk got married? The old man Falk was a clever man; he could look at a person and imme-diately draw up a ledger of his entire worth. Once he was traveling from Kiev to Odessa; opposite him sat a young man reading a Ger-man newspaper. They got to talking. At one station Falk wanted to go to the buffet, but the young man said, 'There's no need. I have enough for two.' He took a basket down from the shelf: he had a teapot, some rolls, salt pork, Warsaw sausage, hard-boiled eggs, knives, forks, plates, all tied up with straps. Falk had a snack, and then asked, 'What's your name?' 'Milgrom.' 'Which branch of Mil-groms—from Volynia or Tavrida?' 'From Zhitomir.' 'Single?' 'Sin-gle.' 'Listen, don't go to a hotel, come stay with us: I'll take a look, and maybe I'll give you my daughter in marriage; she's nineteen, has com-pleted the gymnasium, plays the piano (though not every day), and her dowry's twenty thousand.' A month later, they had a wedding and the result was the most loving couple in the whole town. I've been in all the best houses, lawyers' and doctors', and even in the house of the leading broker: I always feel that it's enough for the wife to say the most ordinary word—let's say, 'lid'—and the master of the house gets angry because this 'lid' reminds him of some fight they had the year before last. But at the Milgroms—that never happens.

[2] Hebrew. House of prayer and study or small Orthodox synagogue.
[3] Hebrew. Collection of binding precepts that forms the basis of the Talmud and embodies the content of oral law.

"And what they've endured! Right after the wedding the old Falk went bankrupt; it was the time of the Turkish War and the Dardanelles were closed. Of course, he said not one word about it to his son-in-law or daughter. But they thought about it, kept silent, and on the third day went to the theater to see some comedy or other, by Ostrovsky,[4] or whatever his name is; they went up to the gallery; at that time they lived modestly, in an apartment on Kuznechnaya Street. The comedy, obviously, was very much to the point: it really affected both of them deeply; they left the theater and decided to return the entire twenty thousand to Falk. You'll say: 'Was it Ignats'? I tell you: 'It was she.' In general you should know, once and for all, about all Jewish households: if something very difficult has to be decided, 'she' is always the one to do it. My wife, Leah, has always been as dumb as an ox, but it would never have occurred to me, let's say, to buy a barge or sell the house on Slobodka Romanovka, if she hadn't said, 'What do I know? Do what you think.' When Marusya was born, not only didn't they have a nanny, they didn't even have a maid; Anyuta herself used to go shopping at the market . . ."

Toward the end he got on to his favorite theme:

"I tell you, Torik will repay them for all their grief. Do you want to know about Torik? I have an employee, a little worm of a fellow, with a demeaning name: Funtik. I've sent him to Torik a few times with papers. Last week his son had his bar mitzvah. What does Torik do? He sends him a congratulatory letter and a velvet sack for his tefillin;[5] but that's not the main thing. In the letter he called both Funtik himself and Madam Funtik by their first name and patronymic (I've know them for a hundred years and I never knew that either one had a father). That's Torik for you: everything's written down, he's polite to everyone, no matter what, Ashkenazi, or Brodsky, or someone's tenth shop assistant. And what a head for business! When he writes a document, he knows beforehand how the person will respond—and he inserts traps so that the respondent will say something stupid. Torik will be a very important person in Odessa: it's really a shame he's a Jew—or else he'd become mayor or even a minister. He'll pay his parents back for everything; for that little 'misunderstanding'

[4] Aleksandr Ostrovsky (1823–86) was a leading playwright whose characters and themes were drawn principally from the Russian merchant class.

[5] Two small leather cases that contain slips inscribed with biblical verses and are worn by Orthodox Jews during prayers.

with Serezha (How do you like my Beiresh? God has given him the talent of finding the most appropriate word, to the letter); and as for Lika, if she doesn't come back here first to hang us all, beginning with her own parents; and as for Marko, who ran after every bell, without knowing where it was ringing, and even in the next world, no doubt he can't tell the difference between the Garden of Eden and the devils; and as for Marusya . . ."

I pricked up my ears:

"What's wrong with Marusya?"

"I don't know what's wrong. They say they're doing all right. But I wouldn't give you a kopeck for their 'all right.' I'm very stubborn, but if you put an even more stubborn man next to me who'll stare at me out of the corner for ten years—not aloud, God forbid—but just in silence, 'to think about me': *'Become* a maker of watches,' 'Become a maker,' 'Become . . .' in the last analysis, so help me God, even I'd begin to mend gears and repair springs; but, excuse me, nothing good will come of it. That's how this Samoilo has refashioned her. Ignats is a fool, and so's Anyuta: they should have done what old Falk did, chosen someone for her who would know how to do a somersault at least once a month for no good reason at all. . . . Someone like you."

After escorting him home, I went to the post office and sent Marusya a telegram: "I'm coming next Tuesday for a week."

The End of Marusya

I reconstructed the circumstances of this event immediately on site—I arrived in Ovidiopol one day after it happened. I was helped by our reporter Shtrok who was specially dispatched to cover it. He was so shaken, he felt the grief so personally, that for once in his life he forgot all embellishments and flourishes; he simply interrogated everyone possible and conveyed everything to me in detail. There was only one eyewitness, that Greek neighbor named Kalliopa Nestorovna, and even she couldn't see everything—the windows of her apartment and those of Samoilo Kozodoi's on the second floor didn't face each other directly but were at an angle. I spoke with Kalliopa Nestorovna after Shtrok had questioned her but gave up after only ten minutes and said good-bye: I didn't have the strength to torment the young woman whose lips and hands began trembling as a result of the ordeal three days after it had happened. On the other hand, the maid Gapka willingly and loquaciously described it all: even though she wasn't there at the time, the circumstances in which this all occurred became clear from her account; and I myself also recalled one detail—during my first and only visit, Marusya was in the kitchen, wearing the same loose "coverall," heating milk for their first child. In a word, I could see the whole picture in my mind's eye, and I was sure that I was right. But I don't feel like relating all of it; the shorter the better . . .

First of all, I need to explain the layout of their little house. On the ground floor were the pharmacy and the storeroom, as well as one large room that they'd made into a dining room where guests were received. Above was a bedroom, nursery, and two small rooms: one was Marusya's "den," and the other, where they'd housed me that time; there was also a fairly large kitchen, with even a sleeping bench, or as it was referred to locally, the "mezzanine," where Gapka slept. The window in the kitchen was diagonally across from Kalliopa Nestorovna's; the door opened into the hall, and there, next to it, stood a large trunk, a little lower than an ordinary chair, precisely on the side of the door where the handle was located.

In the mornings now, when the weather was fine, Marusya would send Gapka to take the year-and-a-half old infant for an outing; the older one, who was three, was beginning to reveal his own character. Mishka was a very active child—may God forgive him this decisive attribute. Some time ago he'd learned to navigate his way up the wooden stairs to the second floor without any help. His main achievement was that he could open the door to the kitchen all by himself. Of course, he couldn't reach from the floor to the handle, but he devised a scheme: he climbed onto the trunk and from there, panting and puffing, squeezed the door handle with both his hands, opened the door, climbed down from the trunk, entered the kitchen, and announced:

"Look, Mama (or, Gapka)—I oh-pen!"

When Marusya was busy at the oil stove in the kitchen, and Mishka was in there with her, he was forbidden to approach the corner where Mama was working so that he wouldn't burn himself, and he'd learned to obey this rule very strictly: he would play over by the door, for the most part left open (so he could run into the hall without making Marusya open it—there was no trunk on the inside): he'd build castles using bars of kitchen soap or else gallop around on the broomstick.

That day was hot but breezy, and the windows were wide open. Samoilo wasn't at home, the apprentice was dozing in the pharmacy, Gapka had gone out to push Zhorzhik in the baby carriage, the older child was in the garden, and Marusya went upstairs to the kitchen. She placed herself near the window—sideways, next to the stove—so she could see Kalliopa Nestorovna who was sewing something, sitting alone on the windowsill; they were engaged in spirited conversation across the quiet narrow street. The kerosene cooker stood on the stove.

The Greek woman told Shtrok that on that morning ("for the hundredth time") "she laughed with Marya Ignatievna," about why she insisted on heating the child's milk three times. "They must've really convinced you about sterilization in the gymnasium! What nonsense—how did you and I ever grow up into such competent mothers without this technique?" Marusya, also for the hundredth time, replied with a phrase from some children's card trick: "Science has many mums"—there was no such word as "mums," it was a trick—but the meaning was that if the doctors so ordered, they were the learned ones, and it's not for the likes of us to argue with them.

Then something stirred in the hall, probably the familiar panting could be heard, the door opened, and in walked Mishka; he announced, most likely, "I oh-pen!" And, just as he was supposed to do, he didn't approach the area where his mother was working and where the fire was lit; instead he kept himself busy near the threshold. Kalliopa Nestorovna could see him all the time from her window seat: she recalled, and told Shtrok, that until the second boiling time was finished—he was prancing around on the broomstick; afterwards, when he'd had enough, he threw the broom on the floor, the broad, shaggy crosspiece facing him, and the end of the handle, stretching across the kitchen toward Marusya. He left the door open and the day was breezy.

The milk started to foam, Marusya removed the saucepan, cooled the milk (completely? or a little? I don't know what science requires), and once again placed it on the fire, turning her back to the cooker, leaning her shoulder against the window frame, and continued chatting with her neighbor. Then all of a sudden it seemed to Kalliopa Nestorovna that in a draft the flame stuck out its silken tongue and licked the sleeve of Marusya's coverall. I don't know the name of the material it was made of, but one thing I remember well—from when Marusya was clinging to me and whispering in my ear about that night in the valley of Lukaniya: it was gossamer thin.

Later, as Shtrok related, the neighbor was unable to convey the rest in a coherent manner: she mixed everything up, describing things earlier that according to the course of events could only have happened later, and vice versa. But she clearly recalled that she was even unable to scream in time: so quickly did she understand what had to follow that she lost the power of speech; apparently Marusya realized that her dress was on fire only from the distorted face of the Greek woman. Kalliopa Nestorovna was sure that Marusya only realized it and didn't feel it: even though she turned quickly and backed away, it was clear from her face that she still didn't feel any pain.

Kalliopa Nestorovna vouched for one more thing: in the very second before she began to tear off her coverall, Marusya rushed over to where the broom lay, bent down, grabbed the end of the handle, "swept the child out into the hall," and slammed the door behind her with the brush end of the broom.

Only after taking this action, did she try to do something about her own clothes; but it was already too late. Kalliopa Nestorovna had recovered her voice and was already shouting; through her shouts she could hear Marusya moaning: she saw how, still standing in the middle of the kitchen, she was twisting and flailing her arms hopelessly, grabbing her chest, then her knees. A second later she began to scream, but the Greek woman was shouting herself and couldn't understand anything. At first Marusya seemed to run to the window, perhaps wanting to throw herself out, but didn't dare, and only then did she start rolling on the floor; or else, at first she fell down, then jumped up, and leaned out the window—one couldn't make sense of the neighbor's account.

Nervously tugging at his sparse mustache and without looking at me, Shtrok explained what Kalliopa Nestorovna hadn't seen; it was something that perhaps had never been seen on earth before, and I don't believe that it will ever be seen again: there will never be another Marusya.

"This is the main thing: when the apprentice climbed the stairs, the door to the kitchen was locked from the inside with a key; subsequently it was found on the street. Do you understand? There, at the door, stood the frightened Mishka; and he'd found that damned trunk and, I suppose, had already climbed onto it and was planning to 'oh-pen.'" That means: she must have made it over to the door— or else, perhaps, could only crawl on all fours—and turned the key in the lock. The first thing I would've done is to go rushing out of the kitchen, to find other people: but she locked the door with the key because Mishka was out there in the hall. Wait a moment: that's still not the main thing. How did the key wind up on the street? It's clear. At such a moment anyone, not merely you and I, would first of all want to escape. Madam Kozodoi is, after all, also only a human being, and she, too, wanted to escape; the worse it grew, the more she would want to escape, or else, let's say, crawl out. We're not even talking about seconds, but a smaller fraction of a second; but for her, every fraction was an age, and with each one, everything was becoming clearer to her: I won't make it. I'll try to escape! But Mishka's out there. Let's say the key was still in her hand. Perhaps it was different: the key was still in the lock, and a fraction of a second arrived when her hand all on its own was stretching out to reach it. Then Madam Kozodoi says to herself: "No. It's forbidden." And, so there wouldn't be any argument, she hurls the key onto the street. That's probably the meaning of the part in the neighbor's story when: "she ran over to the window."

The pharmacist's apprentice was, as appropriate for such a position, a narrow-shouldered young man with slender arms who was unable to break down the door. Much time elapsed until other tradesmen arrived and they managed to break through the door. The local doctor explained the situation to me from the point of view of the fire-resistance of various fabrics. The coverall was in and of itself not such a terrible thing: it didn't last long. But Marusya had received her nightgowns as part of her dowry, and Anna Mikhailovna had carefully chosen the most expensive fabric: it was sturdy, substantial, and would burn slowly. Marusya was also wearing a brassiere; after the birth of her second child she was worried about her figure, and would put it on first thing in the morning; the brassiere was also of high quality.

"I've seen lots of things," the local doctor told me, "but I've never encountered such thorough, conscientious, godly work, to the last hair on her head, to the last nail on her foot."

Marusya died about three hours after they picked her up. Samoilo had rushed home shortly before her end: he listened, frowned, went in to see her, looked, and frowned even more; he went to the pharmacy, selected what was needed, and returned to his wife to apply some lotion or to give her an injection, whatever was appropriate.

That morning the doctor was called away; when he returned, Marusya was no longer alive. I didn't have the courage to ask Samoilo if Marusya was still conscious when he'd come home—so I really don't know. But Shtrok, a person who's not especially tactful, asked him in my presence: "Did Madam Kozodoi suffer a great deal?" Samoilo didn't answer him. Then, when he was left alone with me, all of sudden he said abruptly:

"What a fool. She suffered until I came home. When I arrived and saw the situation, I decided, enough's enough: then her suffering ended. Her husband is a pharmacologist; or, as Serezha used to say, 'pharmaconomist.'"

"Dream me . . ." I've already written that: as a matter of fact, I never have any dreams; on the other hand, as I sing myself to sleep, I sometimes devise them for myself. Or else, let's say, I compose letters that no one's ever sent me; for example, a letter from the other world. I've "dreamt" one so many times that even now I can remember every word of it by heart; it's odd—not all the details correspond to my colleague Shtrok's reconstruction of the incident, and for some reason the Greek woman has a different patronymic. In general, it's a little silly that I want to append this "letter," but I will nevertheless; not the whole thing, just the last few pages:

"The first thing I noticed was Kalliopa Stamatievna's shock: her face became distorted, her voice broke off, she reached her hand toward me, pointing with her index finger, leaned forward, almost tumbling out her window; she was still a very young woman. I looked at myself: I saw that my left sleeve had caught on a nail on the cupboard and that the flame from the spirit lamp was licking at it. You know, the first thing I thought was: Samoilo will say, 'Aha! What did I tell you? You mustn't wear that gossamer coverall in the kitchen!' I began to unhook my sleeve from the nail; it was my own foolish fastidiousness—I should have simply torn it and jumped away; however, even that might not have helped; it all happened so quickly. In a word . . . well, let's pass on, I'm not good at describing things.

"I myself don't know why I thought of the broom at that moment; but I can swear that I thought about it, not about Mishka; it was the same with the key. I'd swear in court that the thought of Mishka never even entered my head all that time; to tell the truth—I didn't have time to think about him; it's a terribly nasty, completely insane thing.

"My dear, please don't think I'm being falsely modest or posturing when I say 'nasty' instead of 'painful.' Of course, it's really 'painful,' but that's not even the right word. Has it ever entered your head that 'pain' is a repulsive, demeaning concept? It's the most passive suffering on earth, somehow servile: you mean nothing at all, no one asks you, someone's mocking you. That's really why I disliked giving birth, out of a sense of offense or outrage. As a result you become rude, a beast without shame; let everyone gawk at you, let the whole town hear you . . . it's so unnecessary, my dear, don't ask me about it. It wasn't nice at all. I rushed to the faucet, but it wouldn't turn on; Kalliopa Stamatievna was shouting, I was, too. . . . It wasn't nice at all.

"One thing's strange: how slowly a person guesses that something irrevocable has taken place. I think that's what happens when a serious illness begins—like cancer: 'Do I really have it? It couldn't be!' You've known it for a long time, yet you still don't believe it. The word 'slowly' really doesn't fit here—most likely the good Lord didn't need even sixty seconds for this whole episode with Marusya; nevertheless, it was slowly. My hair was already sizzling, and everywhere I was feeling—well, 'pain'—meanwhile I was still chuckling to myself: just as if I'd spilled borscht on a new dress and was wiping off the stain and thinking that perhaps I could clean the spot with boiling water and then go visiting, and that everything would soon get back to normal—isn't it true, everything would get back to normal? Samoilo, Mishka, and Mama, all you heavenly angels, tell me it's nothing, that it's just so, that soon everything will be just as it was before . . .

"In a word—it's all over, and it's not worth talking about.

"There's one thing that is worth talking about. Of course, I understand that people call this a 'heroic woman.' . . . The first word is beside the point; the second goes to the heart of the matter. Sitting there in Ovidiopol, I thought a great deal about women. I wrote you: there were moments when for one piece of candy, and even the candy was unnecessary, I could've been an unfaithful wife, just so, not for any particular reason. Afterwards, I would've shaken myself off, powdered my nose, and run off to heat the milk without any pangs of remorse. Do you know what? Don't think I'm merely blaspheming: I consider my mother sacred. But if it could be proven that during her life my mama had accepted such a piece of candy, I wouldn't be very upset; I wouldn't even be very surprised. That's not the heart of the matter: faithful, unfaithful, serious, depraved. . . . We're all, how shall I say it, 'loyal.' All of us: Mama, Marko's Valentinochka, and Lika in her own way—Lika, if she's not loyal to people, then let's say she's loyal to some idol of hers, one that doesn't even exist on earth. Everyone I know is like that; probably even Nyura and Nyuta, if one were to get to know them (I really didn't—how could one ever talk to them since they were always together?) I can't define what loyalty is, but I can tell you one thing for sure: if sometime, my dear, everything on earth cracks and collapses, everyone else betrays you and runs away, and there's nothing to count on—find a woman and lean on her. I'm not bragging, God forbid, and I'm not getting a swelled head for our gender: it's merely the truth.

"That's all there is to it, my friend. Don't regret that when you responded to my invitation to visit, I didn't wait for you. It's better this way—I was in such a strange mood then; perhaps I wouldn't have kept my word that I'd given you in my letter, and we both would've been not quite ourselves. So it's better this way; farewell, my dear."

—⁓— XXVIII —⁓—

The Beginning of Torik

Half of Odessa came to the funeral: there were six carriages with wreaths and almost a full page of announcements in the newspaper. No one ever suspected that so many people had heard of Marusya. Our editor who'd never set eyes on her, and who generally liked to be thought of as an unfeeling man, also attended and then wrote in the paper (although he'd long since stopped writing): "It seemed as if complete strangers showed up, not only to pay their respects to the majesty of her self-sacrifice but simply to bid farewell to this splendid embodiment of youth, grace, and of everything good and pure in life."

The first to stagger behind the coffin was a pitiful, perplexed little old man, with a face of long-standing destitution; still, he was dressed appropriately for such an occasion according to the rules of his generation, a person who'd been brought up on respectable and staid German literature—he wore a top hat and black gloves. Abram Moiseevich, also in a top hat, supported him by the arm. Anna Mikhailovna remained at home; the doctor had ordered her not to get up, and they say she herself didn't even attempt to go; in general, she said nothing to anyone. For some reason I don't recall Samoilo at the funeral, although, of course, he was there. I remember Torik: he was pale and stern, and kept order inconspicuously but precisely. He'd arranged for the transport of the body and everything else, had gone to the brotherhood to secure the best place in the cemetery and the best cantor; all the undertakers followed his orders.

". . . And give her refuge on high, where the holy and pure reside, radiant as the shining of the heavens . . ."

We have some fine prayers. But another one was strange, even senseless, in which there was no mention of loss, merely resigned praise of God-the-offender. Listening to how first Samoilo and then Ignats Albertovich muttered the words of this prayer, I bit my lips in rage and thought to myself:

"I'd cast a stone at You, oh Lord, if You weren't hiding so far away."

From the cemetery I rode in a carriage together with Abram Moiseevich; I don't recall what we talked about at first; only one thing struck me. I said to him, thinking that it would cheer him up:

"You're right. Torik is golden. Tried and true."

Suddenly I noticed that his face had become distorted. All the while he'd been sincerely overwhelmed, what's called vanquished, but he'd endured: now I felt the old man was about to break down in tears or collapse into unconsciousness. But he gained control of himself and merely uttered a completely unexpected phrase:

"He's a slippery, slimy snake . . ."

Even though I wasn't concerned about Torik at the time and I wasn't eager to quarrel, my eyes opened wide at hearing this opinion of his long-time favorite. But then it seems I decided not to inquire further; or else, perhaps, I did ask what the issue was, but he didn't reply.

The next day, or the day after that, I went to visit the aging parents. An efficient nurse, recruited from a private hospital, wouldn't let me in to see Anna Mikhailovna; Ignats Albertovich, as prescribed, sat on the floor in the living room, unshaven according to the rules of mourning, reading the book of Job from a thick Bible with a Russian translation. He received me serenely and spoke softly, not about Marusya, mainly about Job.

"A remarkable book. Of course, only now do I understand it well. The main thing in it is the following question: if something like this happens, what should a person do—rebel, summon God to a court of honor, or else stand at attention like a soldier, hands at his sides, or salute, and shout to the whole world: 'Very pleased to suffer, Your Excellency!' The question, in my opinion, is to be understood not from the point of view of justice or injustice but altogether differently: from the point of view of pride. Human pride, Job's (of course, he pronounced his name, 'Iov'), yours and mine. Do you understand: which is prouder—to declare a rebellion or to salute? What do you think?"

Of course, I didn't "think" anything and had never read the book of Job; I made no reply, so he answered himself:

"It turns out it's prouder to salute. Why? Because: if you rebel, that means only nonsense can result, as if a cart loaded with manure happened to drive by and for no particular reason crushed a snail or a cockroach; it means all your suffering isn't worth much, an accidental absurdity, and you're just like a cockroach."

I began to understand and listen more attentively, and remembered that at one time I'd considered these people from the grain exchange to be men of great experience, and the school of "business affairs," a very large school.

"But if only Job had found in himself the strength to shout 'Very pleased to suffer' (but this is hard, very hard indeed)—then things would've been completely different. Then, it would mean that everything went according to plan and there was no accidental manure cart. Everything according to plan: there was the creation of the world, the great flood, well, the destruction of the temple, the crusades, Yermak[1] conquered Siberia, the Bastille fell, and so on, all of history, and included in that was the misfortune in the household of one Mr. Job. Not a manure cart, in other words, but all according to plan; it's also a note in the larger opera—not such an important note as Napoleon but a note nonetheless, deliberately written by the selfsame Verdi. That means, you aren't really a snail, you're a martyr in an opera, without you the chorus wouldn't be complete; you're a person, a coworker of this same Lord; you salute not only Him but also yourself, that is, all this isn't specified in these words, but the entire argument is precisely about this subject. A remarkable book."

After a short silence, he began again precisely about the prayer that had so infuriated me at the cemetery:

"Take the Kaddish itself—the prayer for the dead, the principal one, recited at every funeral; according to our laws no other prayer is needed. And its content—'Magnified and sanctified be the great name of God,' and nothing more. Not only is there no mention of the deceased, there's simply no indication of what's happening; no mention of 'I submit to Your will'—not even that. In general, if you like,

[1] Yermak Timofeyevich (d. 1584) was a Cossack headman who in 1581 invaded the Siberian khanate, conquered its capital, and enabled Muscovy to annex western Siberia.

it's an absurd choice of words: 'Hallowed and honored, extolled and exalted'—and five more compliments of this sort. It's just like 'Beiresh'—Boris Mavrikievich, you know—just like he wrote to Anna Mikhailovna from Italy: 'Dearest, kindest, most celebrated Anyutochka . . .' It seems that if the Lord had a stomach, He'd feel nauseous from so much deference. But as a matter of fact, it's not nonsense at all: he's doing it all deliberately; he's teasing the devil."

"Who's 'he'? Why the devil?"

"He's the one who composed the prayer: Rabbi Akiba,[2] if I remember correctly; a very clever man, indeed. He reasoned as follows: here now, a misfortune has occurred, some orphaned merchant of the second guild stands before the abyss, everything's lost and there's no reason to live. He stands before the abyss and mentally presents God with an account of his damages and losses; he's so angry—he's just about to raise his fists and curse the heavens. Satan squats right behind the next grave marker, waiting for this very moment: that he would begin to curse and would acknowledge openly, once and for all: 'You, Lord, excuse me for saying so, are simply a petty tyrant and a lout, in addition, You're heartless. Get out of here. I don't even want to know You!' Satan's merely waiting for this: as soon as he hears it, he'll record it, fly off to paradise, and report to God: 'Well then? You got Your ears boxed, didn't You? And from whom? A Jew—one of Your own representatives and managers! Time to retire, old man; now I'm the boss.' That's what Satan's waiting for; and that merchant of the second guild, standing over the grave, already feels this. He feels it and asks himself: 'Is it really the case that I'll make Satan rejoice? Make the devil lord of the world? No, excuse me. I'll show him.' And then, you understand, he begins to assign to the Lord the highest possible marks, one after another; without any sense—what good is sense? Merely to offend the devil, humiliate him, annihilate him once and for all. In other words: 'You, Satan, don't interfere. Whatever accounts I have with God—that's our own business; He and I have been partners for a long time, and we'll straighten it out somehow, don't stick your nose in here.' It's the very same idea, you understand, as in the book of Job: the Jew is God's partner."

Undoubtedly I saw Anna Mikhailovna after this, and more than

---

[2] Akiba ben Joseph (AD c. 40–135) was a Jewish sage and the principal founder of rabbinical Judaism.

once; but, strange to say, I don't remember anything about it. In fact, I don't recall anything even from earlier days: since Serezha's calamity. Most likely that's the way my memory works. Once Lika, while still an adolescent, in the one conversation she granted me in all those years, explained the difference between white memory and black: and she was proud of the fact that her memory was "black"—it retained only the distressing aspects. Whereas I have a "white" memory: it tosses away the most painful impressions, removing them cleanly and without trace; I've observed this a number of times. It's nothing to brag about—it may be that Lika was right in her own way, considering her own memory a higher order.

I don't recall anything about my Niobe from the time of these two blows; not even how her relations with her blinded son were managed; nor whether she latched on to her last child, Torik—during that short month or two that he still granted her.

—ᴧᴧᴧ—

Torik waited the requisite seven days while his father sat on the floor in mourning. On the eighth day Ignats Albertovich took a bath, shaved, and went to the exchange; Torik telephoned me at the editorial office and told me that he wanted to see me that evening to talk about a personal and important matter.

I remember him well, especially that evening. I seem to have written about him several times: irreproachable or "impeccable"—truly, without mockery. I've really never met anyone like him: whether you love him or not, there's nothing to find fault with; it was impossible to find fault even with this irreproachable nature of his—it wasn't artificial, and he didn't flaunt it in any way, it was simply that his nature was "couth," without a hitch, incapable of either cheating at cards, telling a lie, stealing some one else's property, or merely overdoing it in any way, outwardly or inwardly.

He came to confide some important news and to ask that I assume the responsibility of preparing his parents.

"You're the second person in our circle to whom I'm telling this. The first was Abram Moiseevich: in the first place, he was the one to whom I felt morally obligated—I think you know the reasons why. Besides, I thought I'd ask him to conduct the negotiations with my papa; but he took the news very badly, so I decided not to ask him."

I was silent, staring at the rug. He was also silent, then suddenly began to speak:

"I'd like it if you understood me: not 'excused' me, but understood me. If you're willing to hear me out, I'll try to explain my position with complete fidelity, without shifting a single center of gravity: it's not difficult; I thought it all through a long time ago and from all different angles: back in fifth grade in the gymnasium. You don't have anything against it?"

I remembered that it was approximately when he was in fifth grade that I came upon him poring over a Yiddish language textbook or Grätz's *History*, something like that. He was a solid young man, conscientious: if it was necessary to "think through" something, he'd begin with a study of original sources. How many years was he pondering such contraband—and no one noticed, not even his friend Abram Moiseevich, wise as a serpent, who sees through each and every person, knowing from afar what was going on in that happy little house in Ovidiopol. I replied, without looking at him, "I'm listening."

"I'll begin with one *mise au point*: I wouldn't like to create the impression that this decision has 'cost me dearly,' as they say, or that I had to 'struggle' with myself. I have no emotional relationship to this category of questions; from early childhood I've had only a rational relationship to it. But it's precisely in this rational approach that special vigilance is required; and this approach, for me at least, doesn't free a person from the ethical obligation of being decent. For example: it seems to me that if I were in a shipwreck, I wouldn't leap into a lifeboat before all the women, children, old folk, and cripples had been taken care of; at least, I hope I'd have the strength not to. But, it's a different matter altogether when everyone else has already jumped ship or has inwardly resolved to; besides, there are plenty of lifeboats all around and there's room for everybody; and the ship isn't really sinking; it's merely uncomfortable, dirty and crowded, it isn't going anywhere, and everyone's sick and tired of it."

I shrugged my shoulders:

"How do you know? Here in Odessa you've never even seen a genuine ghetto."

"Yes, I have: from childhood and until recently, like almost all my comrades, I've been preparing external students for their exams—'emigrants from the Pinsk swamp,' as Marusya used to call them. It seems to me that this is a very accurate means of studying this milieu: by example. Perhaps it's much more accurate than viewing this milieu from within, when you can't distinguish anything because of the commotion and crowd. An intelligent chemist in a laboratory, busy drawing a patient's blood, will find out more about the illness than the doctor who's treating the living person with all his whims, paroxysms, and respites. And my diagnosis is established irrevocably: disintegration. The Jewish people is dispersing every which way, and it won't ever return to its previous state."

"And Zionism? Or even the Bund?"

"The Bund and Zionism, if you reason clinically, are one and the same. The Bund is like a preparatory class, let's say, or a public grade school: it readies you for Zionism. Plekhanov, it seems, said about the Bund—'They're Zionists who fear rough seas.' And Zionism is like a gymnasium: it prepares you for university. And the 'university' toward which they're all are subconsciously heading and where they'll finally wind up is called assimilation. Gradual, unwilling, dismal, for the most part even immediately disadvantageous, but inevitable and irrevocable, with conversions, mixed marriages, and the complete annihilation of the race. There's no other way. The Bund clings to Yiddish; they say, it's the most amazing language on earth—I know only a little of it, but my external students, for example, quote a word used by Yiddish speakers in Whitechapel: 'boychikel'—simple little lad. Why that's a real tour de force: elements of three languages in one short word, and it sounds so natural, an ideal amalgam; but twenty-five years from now there won't be any Yiddish left. And Zion won't exist; only one thing will remain—the desire 'to be like all other peoples.'"

I could ask another twenty questions: what about religion? Anti-Semitism? But he undoubtedly had foolproof answers for all of them. I remained silent and he continued:

"The best school for all this, in my opinion, is our family: the children, the five of us. Each one of us was a valuable person in his or her own way, only without dogma: and look at what's happened to us. I don't want to speak about each one of us individually; I merely want to defend myself so you don't think I'm unaware of Marusya's worth. I know it well: it was worth it, it was worth it a thousand times over for the Lord God to create the world with all its abominations, and it was worth it for a whole people to drag itself through trials, tribulations, and demoralization, if for this price, only once in a generation one such lovely cornflower could blossom on earth, a being possessed by one concern—to embrace everyone and give comfort to all. But you yourself know that Marusya, too, was a flower of decadence."

I was silent for a while and then asked:

"What's the hurry? God willing, your parents will die soon; you have lots of time ahead of you."

"I don't know if there's so much time. They say the Ministry of Internal Affairs is now negotiating with the Synod and wants to introduce new regulations that would really complicate this whole procedure and, in any case, would delay the awarding of full rights. But that's not the point, believe me. By nature I'm a builder, a person with a plan and a schedule; I have a grand plan, for the long term; I'll graduate this year and have to start building. I can't tread water—even worse, wait impatiently until I bury my mama, father, and Abram Moiseevich."

"What does he have to do with it?"

"As a matter of fact, he's the sorest point of all; that's why I told him first. The thing is, long ago he made me the benefactor of his will; and a fat sum it is. And it's because he didn't know: if he had, he'd sooner have left his money to a shelter for homeless dogs, like that crazy Greek Ralli (it's his legacy that paid for all those green water bowls under the acacias throughout our city with the inscription, 'For dogs.') So—why remain silent? To rob a man? That's not to my taste: I went to him and told him in order to give him time to change his will; most likely, he's already done so."

I looked at him at that moment and our eyes met—apparently, he hadn't lifted his gaze from me all the while he spoke. His look was direct, his eyes, those of a decent fellow with nothing to hide; not a shade of posing—he was telling me, in essence, about his very fine and noble act, but telling me simply, as if it was something completely understandable, in and of itself. He was dressed well, with none of Serezha's foppishness, just well, "*standesgemäß*,"[3] fitting a young member of the intelligentsia who inspires hope and would become a personage, but who, for the time being, has yet to accomplish anything special and knows that himself. No rings, no bracelets, a pin with a matte finish holding his gray tie—probably not inexpensive, but small and discretely matte.

---

[3] German. In accordance with or appropriate to one's class or rank.

"Have you chosen a church?"

"Yes. At first I thought about the Armenian priest in Akkerman who's simplified the ceremony considerably; but that would be too exotic. I'll do as everyone else does; I'll go to the local pastor Pirkho in Vyborg; I've already exchanged letters with him."

L'envoi

I'll probably never get to see Odessa again. It's a pity, because I love the place. I was indifferent to Russia even in my youth: I recall that I always got pleasantly agitated when leaving for Europe and would return only reluctantly. But Odessa—that's another matter: arriving at the Razdelnaya Station, I would already begin to be joyfully excited. If I arrived nowadays, my hands would probably tremble. I'm not indifferent only to Russia; in general I'm not really "attached" to any country; at one time I was in love with Rome, and it lasted a long time, but even that passed. Odessa's a different matter: it hasn't ever passed and it won't.

If it were possible, I'd like to arrive not at the Razdelnaya Station but on a steamship, in summer, of course, and early in the morning. I'd rise before dawn, while the lighthouse on Bolshoi Fontan was still shining, and I'd stand all alone on deck and look at the shore. It would still be covered in mist, but by seven o'clock two colors would emerge: the reddish yellow clay and the barely grayish greenery. I'd try to pick out by memory various locales: Bolshoi Fontan, Srednii, Arcadia, Malyi; then the Langeron, and beyond it, the park. From the sea, if I recall correctly, the black column of Alexander II is visible from afar; well, they've probably removed it by now, but I'm talking about old Odessa.

Then the details of the harbor would begin to appear. First the sea wall and then the breakwater (no one living in the city knew the difference, but I did); Quarantine Harbor and beyond it, a piece of the stockade—we're heading for the Quarantine. The piers on the right are smaller, for our Russian ships, and even more, for oak sailboats, and simply barges and launches: Platonov pier, Androsov, and one more. In my childhood, when Odessa was queen, chimneys and masts stood like a forest in all the harbors; then the forest became sparser, much sparser. But I want it to be as it was in my childhood: a forest, and everywhere sailors calling to one another, boatmen, stevedores; if it were possible to listen in, you could hear the finest song of mankind: one hundred different languages.

Do I still remember the buildings high on the hill when approaching from the water? The Duma was a white, one-story structure, built according to a simple Greek design; several days ago in the American city of Richmond I saw an inexpensive, regional capital building, somewhat like our Duma, and for an hour afterwards I walked around in a daze. On the right stood a line of graceful palaces along the boulevard—I don't recall whether you could see them from the water behind the maples on the boulevard; I'm sure you could see the last one on the right, Vorontsov's palace with its semicircular portico above the rich verdure on the cliff. And the grand staircase, as wide as a broad street, two hundred low, lordly steps; it seems there's no other one like it in the world, and if you tell me there is, I wouldn't go to see it. Above the staircase, the stone duke—his arm extended and his finger pointed at all those arriving: he was called Du Plessis de Richelieu—just remember how many different peoples had gathered here from all corners of Europe to build this one city.

They say that people regard even the name Odessa as something of an amusing joke. To tell the truth, I'm not offended: of course, it isn't really worth revealing one's own sorrows, but I don't take offense for a risible relationship to my homeland. Perhaps it really was an amusing city; perhaps it was so because it laughed so readily. Ten tribes converged, each and every one so fascinating, one more interesting than the next: it all began when these tribes started laughing at one another, then they learned to laugh at themselves, and then at everything on earth, even at what hurt and at what they loved. Gradually their customs rubbed up against each other and they ceased regarding their own sacred altars in such a serious manner; they gradually discovered a very important secret in this world: that what you hold sacred your neighbor thinks is rubbish, and that your neighbor isn't a thief or a vagrant; perhaps he's right, perhaps not, but it's not worth grieving over. Torik had said, "Disintegration." Maybe he's even right; the lawyer defending Rovensky also talked about disintegration, but he added: periods of decline are sometimes the most fascinating. Who knows: perhaps not only fascinating but even sublime in their own way? Of course, I'm in the camp that struggles against disintegration; I don't want neighbors; I want all people living on their own islands; but—who knows? One historical truth has already been well demonstrated: one has to pass through disintegration in order to achieve regeneration. That means, decline is like fog before the birth of the sun, or like an early morning dream. Marusya used to say that the most wonderful dreams were those that came in the very early morning. Whose verses are these? "The still imperceptible prophecy of dawn, emerald and cornelian, lilac and azure: thus I dreamed the still unsung words, perhaps, of an unborn poet, a singer of a country not yet fashioned by the Creator, where invisible visions are as silent as music, and where our early morning dreams the moment before awakening provide refuge for a little while." I'm afraid these are my own verses; as I get older, I quote myself more and more often. I'll quote (for the second time) one more thing: "I'm a child of my age—and I love all its blemishes, all its venom."

"Amusing folks . . ." I wander the streets of my city and meet them all again on various corners. The first one I bump into was a lop-eared scatterbrain with bulging eyes: I don't remember his face; a hundred times I've sworn that I don't remember it, but what other kind of eyes could he have, after spending his whole life looking for miracles and seeing them everywhere? An Englishman once wrote some profound words before his death: "Lord, I'm an old man, I've traveled over all the face of Your earth and have found nothing ordinary upon it." Everything's a miracle, every speck of dust, and Marko knew that; that's why his eyes were always bulging. And what could his ears do except stick out, so that all his life he could listen to hear if someone might be calling him—it didn't matter who, Georgia or Russia, from the river or the embankment, drowning in an ice hole or just plain drunk? If someone called to him, that was enough: he had to go.

On the next corner once again stands a good-looking student in a Caucasian fur hat, drunk, "directing traffic." Why is he directing traffic? Just so: it entered his head to do so, a corner turned up where there was no policeman and a host of carriages converging from all sides. If contingencies in his life had transpired in a slightly different manner: if a tribe had turned up in Africa that had buried its black ruler just yesterday; or a gang of smugglers had formed in the city of Odessa seventy years ago; or a party had emerged in the Lithuanian underground, it didn't matter which—he could have, without rhyme or reason, suddenly become their leader in an instant; or even forever, because, if you're born a king's son, sometimes it's difficult to scramble out from under the royal mantle, no matter how fed up you are with it. It's long been known what it means "to be born a king's son": it's a child kissed by a fairy while still in his cradle. On the day of Serezha's birth there was a great commotion in the fairies' palace; they were all pressed into service, every last one; all the good fairies, only the good ones; not one wicked witch was allowed anywhere near him; and each fairy brought a gift that would suffice for an epic hero of heroes for a whole life, a hero of the spirit or the body; but the problem was, there were too many good fairies.

On the third corner, not taking any notice of me, moving fastidiously to one side, walks a cold, blue-eyed beauty wearing the attire of a wealthy, refined kept woman—but I knew that beneath her velvet was a coarse hair shirt, with a belt of barbed wire. If one were to scratch her and get a drop of her blood, one's tongue would be seared by sulfuric acid. All the undiluted passion of the most indomitable race was concentrated in that drop of blood; every fiber of her soul was made of metal; God knows what kind of metal and in which cliffs its deposits lay, but the metal was one hundred percent pure. I saw her for the last time in the Restaurant Vienna, but in fact she lives like a hermit in a small, secluded monastery, tormenting herself in the name of some Christ or other, whose sacrifice has yet to be conceived: Christ-the-abominator; each of His psalms begins with the words, "I curse"; all prayers are supposed to be uttered through clenched teeth. . . . About ten years ago in Paris I met an acquaintance who'd been incarcerated in the Lubyanka prison for some time. She told me that at one time she'd shared a cell with a young or young-looking woman, a brunette with blue eyes and a true Grecian profile—her nose and forehead formed one line. This other prisoner was grieving terribly, not for herself but for her husband, who was in serious trouble. One night, through her tearless sobbing, she whispered into my acquaintance's ear the whole truth about this husband of hers: as a matter of fact, he was in very serious trouble. My friend also had a husband at the time, who'd been arrested even earlier: that night she also wept and whispered. The next morning they summoned the blue-eyed "neighbor" and she never came back to the cell again; soon they released my acquaintance, and as they let her go, they gave her an address where she could reclaim all the belongings and documents left behind by her husband. I asked: "Were the blue-eyed brunette's fingernails bitten off, do you recall?"—but she hadn't noticed.

I don't meet Torik on any corner at all: he's "not one of us," Marusya had said.

I'll have my encounter with Marusya not on the street; we agreed to meet in my Lukaniya. Along the way I'll go past their former house; I won't be bold enough to ring the doorbell and climb the stairs, so I'll merely doff my hat and walk by. The resonant pavement has been covered over with straw so carriage wheels won't rumble and it'll be peaceful all around God's slaughterhouse, so senseless and pointless, and all around their bottomless and endless pain. Up above, on the second floor, the bedroom's furnished in a sweet, innocent *fin-de-siècle* style; two dry eyes stare at the chest of drawers from the pillow; there are five photos standing on the chest, children in short skirts or pants down to their knees; and in each picture, right through the center, sticks a rusty knife.

There's a half moon once again over Lukaniya, it smells of flowers that have finished blooming, one can hear only the music of melodies that have been played nowhere else for quite some time; once again, everything will be as it was on our celibate night together, but this time we'll have to speak with thoughts, not with words. I'll think about what a wonderful word "tenderness" is. Everything that's good on earth, everything is tenderness: the light of the moon, the lapping of the sea, the rustling of branches, the fragrance of flowers, and the sound of music—it's all tenderness. And God, if one can ever manage to reach Him, shake Him, wake Him, and berate Him with one's worst curses about the big mess He's created, and then make one's peace with Him and lay one's head in His lap—most likely, He, too, is tenderness. And the very best and very brightest tenderness is called woman.

It was an amusing city; and laughter itself is also a form of tenderness. By the way, there's probably been no trace left of that Odessa for quite some time now, and there's no reason to regret that I'll never get back there; and, by and large, my story is finished.

Selected Bibliography

Brenner, Lenni. *The Iron Wall: Zionist Revisionism from Jabotinsky to Shamir*. London: Zed Books, 1984.

Herlihy, Patricia. *Odessa: A History, 1794–1914*. Cambridge: Harvard University Press, 1986.

Katz, Shmuel. *Lone Wolf: A Biography of Vladimir (Ze'ev) Jabotinsky*. New York: Barricade Books, 1996.

Nakhimovsky, Alice Stone. *Russian-Jewish Literature and Identity: Jabotinsky, Babel, Grossman, Galich, Roziner, Markish*. Baltimore: Johns Hopkins University Press, 1992.

Safran, Gabriella. *Rewriting the Jew: Assimilation Narratives in the Russian Empire*. Stanford: Stanford University Press, 2000.

Sicher, Efraim. *Jews in Russian Literature after the October Revolution*. Cambridge: Cambridge University Press, 1995.

Stanislawski, Michael. *Zionism and the Fin de Siècle: Cosmopolitanism and Nationalism from Nordau to Jabotinsky*. Berkeley: University of California Press, 2001.

Weinberg, Robert. *The Revolution of 1905 in Odessa: Blood on the Steps*. Bloomington: Indiana University Press, 1993.

Wisse, Ruth R. *The Modern Jewish Canon: A Journey through Literature and Culture*. New York: Free Press, 2000.

Zipperstein, Steven J. *Imagining Russian Jewry: Memory History, Identity*. Seattle: University of Washington Press, 1999.

——. *The Jews of Odessa: A Cultural History, 1794–1881*. Stanford: Stanford University Press, 1985.

CPSIA information can be obtained
at www.ICGtesting.com
Printed in the USA
LVHW092016140720
660693LV00011B/215